SHAW
STORM ENTERPRISES BOOK 1

BJ ALPHA

BJAlpha

Copyright © 2023 by BJ Alpha

All rights reserved.

No part of this book may be reproduced in any form or by any electronic or mechanical means, including information storage and retrieval systems, without written permission from the author, except for the use of brief quotations in a book review.

This book is a work of fiction. Characters, names, places and incidents are products of the authors imagination or used fictitiously.

Any similarity to actual events, locations or persons living or dead is purely coincidental.

Published by BJ Alpha

Edited by Dee Houpt

Proofread by Nay, That Grammar Gal

Photographer RafaGCatala

Model Alejandro Caracuel

Cover Design by Ever After Cover Design

❦ Created with Vellum

To Kate,
Thank you for being so many things rolled into one.
Most importantly thank you for your friendship.

AUTHORS NOTE

WARNING: This book contains triggers. It has sensitive and explicit storylines. Such as:
Violence.
Graphic sexual scenes.
Sexual assault scene.
Strong language.
It is recommended for readers ages eighteen and over.

PROLOGUE

EMILIA

When I slipped Franco, my bodyguard, the sleeping pills half an hour ago, I hadn't expected him to still be standing, watching me with those hawk eyes of his. He stands stoically still, his eyes transfixed on me, making me fidget at his scrutiny.

Picking up my champagne glass, I take another tentative sip and glance around the poker table. As if on cue, I throw my head back on the laugh I've crafted over the last twenty years when the stocky man beside me makes another lame joke about the game being fixed.

Sensing I'm being watched, I glance around, and my eyes latch onto those of a guy leaning against the wall opposite me. He's around thirty, and his bright-blue eyes roam over my body as though he's imagining me naked, and the thought makes me flush in pleasure. He's tall—well, everyone is compared to me. Maybe six foot two? His hair is dark with a slight wave, and it's a little messy too, which I like. The top buttons on his shirt are open, revealing a bronzed chest that makes my mouth water and has my fingers itching to touch.

As we finish our perusal of one another, our eyes draw back to their starting point, and his piercing blue gaze seeps into mine, making my heart stutter. Something passes between us—maybe an acknowledgment of our mutual attraction for one another—but whatever he's thinking makes his lips lift at the corner, gifting me with a sexy smirk. I dart my eyes away as warmth floods me from the inside out, forcing me to take another sip of my champagne to disguise how much I'm attracted to this man.

I turn my head to find Franco looking a little dazed. He braces himself with one hand on the wall, and I decide now is the time to make my move. My heart rate kicks up a notch as I put my carefully orchestrated plan into action.

Two of my brother's men rush toward him as I slip away from the table. My pulse races as I push through the crowded room, away from Franco and the ties that bind me to my future.

If I'm going to take this next step, it will be on my terms, not some dumb Mafia agreement. I will have one night of freedom before I have to spend a lifetime being a slave to the organization. Worst of all, a slave to him. A man I have no attraction to, whatsoever, all for the sake of a business deal.

SHAW

The woman rushes from the table.

When her gaze traveled over my body, my entire being lit up, with flames simmering my veins and forcing all the blood to rush to my cock.

I'm standing in a Las Vegas casino with a raging hard-on, all from a woman simply looking at me. I've never had this reaction before, not even from my ex, Lizzie.

I stared at her. Licking my lips, roaming my gaze over her delicious body, taking in every fucking incredible inch of her. As my gaze slowly traveled up her curves and landed on her delectable tits, her nipples peaked as though realizing how much I craved her. Her blood-red lips parted when my eyes met hers once again, and her eyes were so dark they'd pass as black, and for some unknown reason, I want to see them up close, just to be sure. She's a brunette—also unlike my ex—with thick waves flowing over her shoulders.

As she rushes from the table, I wonder if it had something to do with the short fat man ogling at her tits each time she laughed.

My dick weeps a little at the thought of her tits bouncing while she rides me. I scrub a hand through my hair. *Fuck me, I have it bad.* I need to get laid and satiate this damn drought I'm in, thanks to Lizzie.

Pushing off the wall, I go in search of my little damsel in distress to see if I can appease my cock.

Striding toward the doors on a mission, there's a flash of her red dress near the exit to the casino. She glances over her shoulder, as though checking for someone, and the thought makes my eyebrows furrow, but I don't allow myself to think on it. My legs quicken, determined not to lose her. She's about to push through the doors when I reach out and snag her wrist. She jumps at the contact and stumbles in shock. When she turns her head over her shoulders and our eyes connect, I finally see onyx. They're onyx, not the least bit brown. Beautiful. Unusual. Unique.

We stand there for a minute, staring at one another, and when someone pushes into me, I'm forced against her. My grip on her wrist tightens, and my free hand snakes out to grasp onto her hip to hold us in place.

My cock presses against her, and her eyes widen at the realization, making my lips lift into a cocky grin. I'm about to tell her she can take it for a ride, but an alarm pierces the air, cutting into the sexual haze growing between us.

Fuck, I need to feel more of her. To have her body pressed against mine as I slide inside her. My cock twitches with the thought. *Yeah, I need her right fucking now.*

Her face falls and her eyes startle, and I wonder if the sudden crowds rushing toward us are causing her discomfort. I lean down to speak in her ear. "You wanna get out of here?"

Relief mars her face, and her tense shoulders relax.

I can't help but smile at her. "Yes. Please." She bites into her bottom lip, and I have the sudden urge to tug it from between her teeth and draw it into my mouth with a sharp nip. *Jesus, I need her.*

Instead, I opt for giving her a sharp, confident nod.

"Let's go."

EMI

I can't believe I'm doing this. This isn't me; I don't do things like this. Never. I try to act unfazed by the intoxicating scent of pure masculinity waving off this man. My eyes roam over his broad shoulders, and the magnetic pull takes me to his bright-blue eyes once again.

Pulling my shoulders back, I swallow down the nerves. I'm Emilia Varros, a Mafia princess. I can do this.

His eyebrows narrow a little as though sensing a change in me. Relief hits me when the elevator pings. "This is us. You sure you want to do this, Red?" His mouth breaks into a breathtaking smile that puts me at ease.

I need to do it. I want to do it. For my own sanity, I need this last sliver of control.

Throwing my head back on a playful chuckle, I can't help but laugh at his nickname for me, and I quite like the anonymity it brings with it too. "Sure thing, Blue." I grin back at him, making him choke on a handsome laugh.

I've been brought up around men my entire life and

love nothing more than playful banter when the time allows it.

He takes my hand in his, and I'm shocked at how natural it feels, how his large palm engulfs mine, and how secure I feel with him. Yet with no security around at all.

Odd.

Blue strides toward his room like a man on a mission, and I guess he is. He's on a mission to do me, and I'm about to let him.

We step inside a room and the lights flicker on. I'm not surprised to find the room resembles a penthouse suite. I know because I've stayed in so many, sometimes for weeks on end, other times, months.

The door clicks shut, and I'm surprised to find I have no nerves; I'd already resigned myself to the fact I would lose my virginity tonight. At least this way it's to someone I'm attracted to.

Blue pushes me up against the door, and his large hands grasp my hips as he grinds his solid cock against me. My hands weave around his neck and into his hair, and even in my heels, I have to step on tiptoes. He seems to understand my struggle because he lifts me against the door and my legs wrap around his middle, making my dress scrunch up toward my waist. I drag his head down to mine as his firm hands grip my ass, massaging my cheeks roughly. I whimper at the sensation, and he growls in response. His dominance and control over my compliant body makes me submit with satisfaction. Clearly, he knows what he's doing, so I try not to consider how many women he must have had in this same position.

My lips find his and his tongue darts into my open mouth, making me moan at the sensation of having his solid cock wedged between us and his tongue thrashing against mine, fighting me for possession.

Our kiss is reckless and feverish, soaking my panties like never before. He pulls away from the door and carries me with ease across the room. Our lips never disconnect as we enter another room. It isn't until he lowers me onto a bed that I realize we're in a master bedroom.

"Mmm." I moan against his tongue, and my hands slide into his hair, making him grunt in response when I tug on the strands.

He pulls back to stare down at me, our chests rising in unison. His pupils are blown with lust, but the blue surrounding them is still visible. He searches my face before his gaze trails down. "Fuck, you're beautiful."

His lips part as though in awe, and his wondrous expression makes my heart stutter. "I need you," I mutter.

He snaps into action. His hands fumble to unbutton his shirt, so I lean forward and take over for him as he reaches behind me and pulls down my zipper, allowing my dress to catch at my waist.

A rush of embarrassment creeps over me. No man has ever seen me naked before, no matter how much I've been willing. I swallow, fighting the nerves to look him in the eyes, but as if sensing my hesitance, he reaches for my chin and lifts it, forcing my gaze to lock on his. "You're so fucking beautiful. I'm going to spend all night showing you just how beautiful you are." He tucks a loose curl of hair behind my ear. "All night fucking this hot little body of yours." His hand trails down my arm, causing me to break out in a thousand goose bumps. Then, without warning, he palms my tits, pushing them together while his thumbs breeze over my nipples. He caresses them, squeezing and stroking over the bare flesh. My nipples pucker under his touch.

"Oh god, that feels good." My head drops back when he tweaks them, and he takes my moan as encouragement.

"Fuck yes. Tell me what you like, Red," he pants.

My inexperience makes me second-guess myself, but determined to pursue the sole purpose of tonight, I shove the thoughts to one side and embrace my one night of freedom. "Y-your lips." His lips find my neck while he pushes me down onto the mattress.

"Mmm, such a good girl." I groan in delight at his praise as his soft, wet tongue trails down the column of my neck, over my chest, and circles my nipples, forcing them to peak with arousal.

I can't help but rise off the bed and thrust my hips up into him; I'm so turned on right now. I need him.

He tugs my dress and panties down as he lowers himself to the floor. I lie there, open and exposed. My cheeks heat under his scrutiny.

"Fuck me. You're all wet, pink, and shiny for me, Red. Edible." He inhales my scent, and the action has me squirming, making me uncomfortable under his watchful eyes and also turned on.

I lift my head to meet his and can't help but dart my tongue out over my lips. The words tumble from me before I realize what I'm saying. "Taste me." *Who the hell am I right now?*

He growls and grips my thighs, lowers his head, and breathes me in again before flattening his tongue and trailing it from my hole all the way up to my clit, lapping at my arousal.

I clasp the bed sheets with each flick of his tongue. "Oh

god, Blue." My hand finds his hair, and he moans against me as I hold his head in place, the vibrations of his satisfaction encouraging my need for him. I thrust my hips into his face, grinding against his jaw wantonly. The slurping noises and sucking of my clit is like nothing I've ever experienced. It's incredible. My body is alive below him, aching for his touch. For more. "Please," I beg, unsure what I'm begging for.

He uses one of his hands to undo his belt and fumbles with unbuttoning his pants. The thought that he's touching his cock while licking me makes me clench. I'm so turned on, I'm no longer myself. My inner sex goddess has taken over.

"Oh god. More." I lift to his mouth, pushing myself aggressively against his tongue.

He pulls back just enough to speak. "You taste so fucking good, Red. I want you to come on my tongue like a good girl. Let me taste all of you. Fuck, I'll savor your taste."

When he sucks my clit hard, I erupt, his words helping to send me over the edge. My legs clench around him, and my grip tightens in his hair. "Oh. Oh, Jesus. Yesssss."

SHAW

I sit back on my heels and revel in watching her come down from her orgasm. *Fuck me, she's gorgeous.* Her whole body is pure perfection, with not an ounce of Botox nor plastic in sight. Those natural curves are rare in my world, and those tits . . . I could come from touching them.

She's a vision. And she's all mine, if only for tonight.

My boxers are already drenched from the sounds escaping her blood-red lips. I thought I was going to come in them like a teenage boy.

I quickly kick off my shoes and socks and work my pants and boxers down, taking great delight in her eyes widening as I pump my cock, forcing pre-cum to escape the tip. "I'm going to fuck your little pussy now, Red, and you're going to take every inch of my thick cock."

She nods eagerly, and when her tongue darts out across those pouty lips, I have to stop my fist from moving before I embarrass myself. She surprises me further by reaching out and swiping the pre-cum from the tip of my cock, making me groan in ecstasy when she brings it to her mouth, and sucking it off while we remain entranced in a sexual haze.

All control in me snaps and I swoop down to my pants and pull a condom from my wallet. Our eyes lock as I rip it open and roll the latex down my cock.

Red scoots her ass up the bed until her head is on the pillows, then she spreads her legs, exposing her slick hole. I position myself between her legs and watch in awe as I drag my cock up and down her wetness. Her thighs clamp around me, and I revel in the fact that my girl is still sensitive. *Fuck, her pussy is going to be so damn good.*

A gentle moan escapes her lips, and I have a sudden need to taste them, to swallow her whimpers as I stretch her wide.

Leaning down, I take her lips with mine, loving the fact she can taste her cum on my tongue. Her fingers thread through the ends of my hair, and I groan into her mouth as my cock lines up with her hole. I push in slowly, determined to make this last, determined for this night to be ingrained in our minds for a lifetime.

I might only have this one night with my little red, but it'll be one to remember for an eternity.

Pushing my cock into her pussy, I relish in the tightness. She's really fucking tight. So fucking tight I'm struggling to get in. I pull back from her lips to study her face for discomfort, but I'm yanked back down to her lips and a moan vibrates from her mouth.

Jesus, she likes it. I push harder, struggling not to clench my jaw while her tongue battles with mine. She arches into me, encouraging me further until I hit something I've only ever heard about. Her innocence.

I pull my mouth from hers and stare into her dark eyes.

"Please. I want you," she begs, need dripping from her delectable mouth.

Her words send a wave of uncontrollable possession running through me. This stunning woman is begging me to take her virginity. Begging me to fuck her where no one else has been before. "Please. I need your cock to fill me." She pushes her body upward.

"Jesus Christ," I mumble into her mouth as our lips crash together and our kiss becomes hungry.

I'm consumed with being the only man inside her, the only one able to make her feel good. I draw my cock back, and without a second thought, I drive forward hard, breaking through her barrier. Making her mine.

Air rushes from her lips and her fingers tighten in my hair. I ignore her obvious discomfort and repeat the same motion, thrusting hard inside her tight channel, determined to own this part of her. Stretching her tight little pussy with my cock, making her mine.

A whimper escapes her, and I swallow it down, thrusting harder and harder, determined to make her remember me—the man that took her virginity. I need to mark her, make sure she never forgets.

I pull back from our kiss and work my mouth over her neck. "Fuck, you're incredible, baby girl." *Slam.* "Fucking incredible." *Slam.* "Giving me your tight little cunt." *Slam.* She moans at my words, and it spurs me on. "Fuck, my cock is so hard." *Slam.* "I. Fucking. Own. You!" *Slam.* "This cunt is mine."

Moving my hand to rub over her clit, I suckle her nipple into my mouth and graze my teeth over the tip. I swear to Christ she has the best tits I've ever seen, and yet I have an urge to mark them.

She whimpers around me, and her pussy clenches even tighter as I swell. "Fuck. Fuck. Fuck." I slam inside her faster, knowing I'm about to fill her.

"Ahhh, holy shiiit," she screams, her mouth falls open and I come, with my mouth latched over the flesh of her tit, sucking against it hard enough to leave a mark. My eyes squeeze closed as my orgasm is ripped from me so hard I feel like I'm being stunned, falling into oblivion.

Her pussy holds me inside, even with my cock satiated.

I rise onto my elbows and stare at her. Emotion clogs my throat and I can't understand why. Sure, I've had one-night stands before and never felt a damn thing. Maybe it's because she's given me her virginity and that's something completely new to me?

"Are you okay?" I ask, searching her face for discomfort.

Her lips tip up into a playful smile. "That was . . . hot."

My shoulders relax on her words and relief rolls through me. I slowly withdraw, yet keep my eyes latched onto hers. She winces as I pull out. I move to sit back on my heels, about to dispose of the condom, but when I catch sight of the blood between her thighs and her plump pussy lips coated in a mixture of her arousal and redness, my cock twitches at the thought of causing it. Owning it. I only wish my cum was mixed with it too.

"Fuck." My fingers swoop to her pussy, and I coat her clit with the juices. Red thrusts into my touch, and my cock hardens, eager to get in on the action.

"Fuck. You're bleeding for me, Red." I lick my lips, my eyes transfixed on her pussy.

"Yes. For you." She pushes her tits together, and I

about lose it. I rip the condom from my cock and jack my length over her pussy. "Please."

"Jesus." I use my thumb to circle her clit while two of my fingers find her hole. I shove them in while tugging my cock rapidly. Fuck, I want to see my cum mixed in with hers.

I've never had unprotected sex before, but knowing she's never had sex with anyone but me makes me insane to experience it with her. Only her.

"Are you on birth control?" My eyes snap to hers.

She shakes her head and disappointment curdles inside me so strong I want to smash the fucking room. "Fuck!" I press harder on her clit as she thrusts her hips into me as though she's as eager for me as I am her.

"You want my cock?" My firm voice pierces through her whimpers. "Tell me you want my fucking cock!"

"I want it," she pants. "I want your cock."

"Fuck. Yes, you do. You're a needy little girl." I move quickly, thrusting inside her warm, wet heat with my bare cock. The feeling like no other. My body is alight with need for her, the need to fill her warm cunt with my load.

"Fuck. I wanna come so bad. I want to come inside you so bad, Red." I bury my head into her neck, nipping at her flesh as I slam into her and grind my hips again and again.

"Yes. Yes, please." Her walls spasm around me, tugging me in tighter and tighter.

"Fuck!" I pull out as I shoot cum over her bare pussy. I lean up on one arm to watch as I jack my cock over her clit, rubbing my cum over her pussy lips and down to her hole with my thick tip.

Our breathing settles, and I stare down at the mess we've created. An urge to leave my mark on her further makes me drag my finger through our combined juices and paint her stomach with the pink essence and my name, *Shaw*.

I drop down beside her and tug her onto my heaving chest where sweat coats my skin, and my body relaxes as she settles her hand over my thumping heart. My heart swells with the comfort between us as my arm bands around her, protecting her.

I take her hand in mine, bringing it to my lips. "That was amazing. You're beautiful, Red. Perfect."

Red turns her head to face me, and she nibbles on her bottom lip. "You're not too bad yourself, Blue."

I chuckle at her nickname for me, loving her playful demeanor.

A sudden need to correct her and be honest with who I am overcomes me. Something I never give away when having a one-night stand. I simply forgo my name, or like my friend Tate, I give a fake name. I clear my throat. "Actually, my real name is . . ."

"Shhh." She places her fingers over my lips to stop me from speaking and shakes her head. "I like Blue."

I quirk my eyebrow at her. "You do, huh?"

"Yes." She bites into that lip again, and I groan, her dark eyes shining with acknowledgment.

"I've a feeling my balls will never be blue around you." I smirk at my lame joke.

She scoffs. "Maybe we could work them so well we bruise them." She works her hand down my body, waiting for a reaction from me before palming my balls and rolling them in her hand. Her nails graze my sac, and I suck in a sharp breath. "Fuck yes. We should try that."

Red giggles in response and throws her leg over me so

she's straddling me. Staring down at me with those dark orbs of hers, I know that tomorrow not only will I get Red's real name but I'm also getting her number, because one night with her will never be enough. Something tells me forever could never be enough.

ONE

SHAW

Five months later ...

I throw my pen down on my desk, unable to concentrate on the figures in front of me. I need a new PA and fast. The last one was actually good at her job, but Tate fucked her so hard she broke her hip. Literally broke her hip, and now we have to pay her medical leave and look for another PA.

Owen is constantly telling him to keep his cock out of office pussy, but the dumbfuck never listens. We should rename this company Pussy Enterprises due to him fucking employees. Half of the employees have either been fucked by him or plan on being fucked by him. I wonder if I could get a gay male PA? That would solve a few problems. I tap on my lip, deep in thought.

I'm snapped from my thoughts when my phone rings on my desk and am reminded I have actual work to do instead of daydreaming.

Truth be told, I can't get my head on straight, not since the night with her . . . Red.

When I woke the next morning, she was gone. Who the fuck does that? Who leaves without a goodbye? Okay, what woman does that? Normally I have to push them out the door with a fake name and number, but the only thing Red left behind was her blood on my sheets. A sign of her innocence. My cock swells, like every time I think of her. No amount of sex or jacking off appeases me, because simply, nothing compares to her.

I lift the phone to my ear, and as I do, my door slams open, hitting the wall and causing me to drop the phone to the desk and jump out of my chair.

What the ever-loving fuck?

"Sit." A stern voice fills the room as one guy with slicked-back hair and a dark suit strides toward me with a gun pointed at me. *Holy fucking shit.*

His black eyes are cold and wild, his muscles coiled tight, and his temple pulsates as he tilts his head from side to side, studying me. He looks deranged, and I can only hope security is on their way up here.

Two other men flank him, then a third shorter, much older man follows, and last but not least, two men close the door and block my only exit. I swallow past the lump in my throat.

My body freezes and my heart races in my chest as I wonder what the hell is happening.

"Shaw Grant?" the Mafia-looking dude—the leader—asks, still pointing his gun at my face.

I swallow thickly, unsure whether to admit that's me. The two younger men pull out chairs from my conference table and drag them over toward my desk, allowing the older gentleman to sit down first. They're getting comfortable, so maybe I'm not about to get my head blown off?

My mind races with what could possibly be happening. Has a business deal gone wrong? Are these old enemies of Owen?

"Shaw Grant?" he snipes out, asking again, his voice deadly in warning.

My mouth suddenly feels dry, so I clear my throat. "Yeah, that's me," I admit, raising my chin in defiance. Fuck these pricks for intruding on my space.

My fingers fumble to find the security button under my desk, realizing I might actually need backup. I'm very fucking relieved Owen insisted on us having them installed in the first place, silently thanking him for his persistence.

"What the hell is happening?" I demand, the pissed-off edge in my voice clear.

The dude that looks like something out of a Mafia movie sits down opposite me. His dark eyes drill into mine. He steeples his hands on my desk, and I clamp my fists at my sides, pissed at his arrogance but also aware I'm dangerously outnumbered.

I take in his tattooed hands, the chunky gold rings on his fingers, and shudder at the thought that this man's hands have no doubt killed someone. It's clear he's dangerous. Darkness rolls off him in waves. His deep, black eyes bore into mine, seeping with vengeance.

"Do you know who I am?" His voice is laced in danger; I swear I can smell death oozing from him. I scan his face and then over toward the other guys, who are staring at me with clenched jaws and grinding their teeth. *Nope, not a fucking clue.*

"Not a fucking clue."

His eyes flare in rage, and he tilts his head to the side as though trying to see into my soul. *Jesus, this guy is intense.*

"You should. I'm Luca Varros, and you fucked my sister."

My eyebrows shoot up in shock. *I did?* My mind wanders to who it could be. When Lizzie and I last broke up, I slept with a few people. All one-night stands. All meant nothing. But her.

My heart races because it's obvious this dude is pissed; I allegedly fucked his sister.

"And you've caused me a lot of problems, Shaw." His voice has an unhinged warning behind it.

I swallow past the lump in my throat. "Why's that?"

"My sister was due to marry an associate." I stare at him as his dark eyes appear to get even darker. "She's now classed as soiled goods."

I jolt at his words because who the fuck calls their sister that?

My pulse races. "What's that got to do with me?" I feign confidence.

He leans forward across the table, his face a foot from mine. "Because you're the one that defiled her." Each word slices through me with a warning of vengeance.

I reel back as his words hit me in the chest. "Defiled?" There's only one girl I defiled. *Holy shit, Red, what the hell have we done?*

The door opens, and I rise to my feet at Red being shoved through the door. "Sit!" the asshole barks back at me.

I've no choice but to lower my ass back into the chair as

some dickhead manhandles her into the room, shoving her into the chair beside the older man. My body vibrates with a need to protect her, but hopelessness swallows it up.

Tears streak her face, and her lip quivers as she turns to the older guy. "Papi." He holds his hand up to silence her, not so much as turning in her direction. Red clamps her lips shut, then turns her tormented eyes toward mine.

Emotion swims between us, and my heart races at the desperation etched on her face. *Fuck, she's beautiful.* My heart skips a beat just from looking at her.

The door opens again, and I'm relieved it's Owen pushing past the two guard dogs minding the door.

The slick leader jumps from his chair, but when his eyes settle on Owen, his shoulders relax. "Luca?"

The guy, Luca, smirks back at Owen.

Owen glances over his head at me before his gaze turns venomous. "What the fuck did you do?" His panicked and firm words make me stiffen.

"Your business partner, Shaw Grant, fucked my sister," Luca spits out.

"And now he will pay the consequences," the older guy chimes in with a nod.

"You dumb prick." Owen glares in my direction.

"Papi, please. Not like this." Red shakes her head, and a feeling of dread settles over me. I glance from one man to the other, now taking in the guns tucked in their pants and the bulge of weapons behind their jackets. I swear my life flashes before my eyes. Yet all I see is her.

"You dumb fucking idiot," Owen snipes out in my direction again, making me clench my jaw in annoyance because who the fuck thinks to ask if their one-night stand is part of what appears to be a Mafia family?

"He defiled my sister and knocked her up, and now he will marry her or lose his life."

Words get thrown about but I hear none because "knocked her up" is playing on repeat in my mind.

My eyes search hers before landing on her clasped hands sitting in her lap with a small bump on display. *How the hell did I miss that?* My heart pounds against my chest, forcing my throat to constrict with panic.

"I'm sorry," she utters the words, but I can't digest them.

"The wedding is next Saturday." That snaps me out of my head, and I spring from my chair, forcing the other two men to their feet, drawing weapons in my direction.

Luca turns to face me with the maniacal look in his eyes; he wouldn't think twice about putting a hole between my eyes.

"I can't get fucking married," I spit out, enraged at the suggestion, my body shaking with panic.

His voice is low, calm, and collected, but still, the danger seeps from him, leaving me no choice. "You can and you will."

I shake my head and almost want to laugh at how ludicrous this all is.

"Luca. Are you sure there isn't a misunderstanding? Are you sure the baby is his?" Owen all but whispers as though trying not to insult him.

Luca flicks his fingers toward one of his lackeys, who pulls papers from a file and places them on the desk in front of me.

"It's his." He nods toward the paper, so I pick it up and scrutinize the sheet. They pulled security images of us leaving the casino together, along with images of us in the elevator, corridor, and bursting into the hotel bedroom.

Another image shows Red leaving my hotel room, and a pang of regret fills me at the reminder of my disappointment that morning.

The way I fucked her that night so recklessly, knowing she wasn't on birth control, has now come back to bite me in the ass.

I pinch my fingers over the bridge of my nose and make a last-ditch effort to stop the madness right now.

"I can't marry her. I have a fucking girlfriend." I don't miss the sharp intake of breath to leave Red's lip, but I choose to ignore it, refusing to acknowledge her.

"Get rid of her or we will." Luca shrugs, making my teeth grind with a need to hurt him, a need to lash out.

"But I'm warning you, if you bring shame on my family and cheat on my sister, your cock will be the first thing to go. I'll feed it to you slowly, forcing you to taste every fucking sliver." My stomach rolls and I grimace at the thought. "It's only because she begged me not to hurt you that I chose to keep you alive. Now, the choice is yours. A meeting will take place this Saturday. Details will be sent over. Emi, come." Luca snaps his fingers, and Red jumps up from her chair and follows without a backward glance as they leave the room, taking my whole life with them.

TWO

SHAW

"They said it was okay you came, right?" My leg bounces in the footwell of Owen's SUV.

"Yes. Chill the fuck out." Owen side-eyes me while keeping one hand on the steering wheel. "Did you tell Lizzie yet?"

I grimace at the thought of telling my on-again-off-again girlfriend I got another woman pregnant and, not just that, I'm about to marry her.

It appears Red, whose real name I believe to be Emilia, is part of the Varros family. One of the five Mafia families living in New Jersey and the surrounding areas. Luca is a Capo, so not even the leader of their organization, but holy fuck, the dude is intense and deadly, according to Owen. He went on a killing spree to wipe out the entire bloodline of an opposing Mafia family.

Owen explained I fucked up majorly when I screwed

Emilia and if I want to stay alive, I have no choice but to end things with Lizzie and do exactly as Luca says.

I can't even get my head around the fact that Emilia is pregnant and I'm going to be a dad. It's not something I considered, not anytime soon anyway. Lizzie has been after an engagement ring for as long as I can remember, and our relationship has been a constant battle because I refuse to take the next step. Hence the reason I haven't told her I'm about to do just that, with a stranger no less.

"And you're sure there's no way out of it?" I ask for the hundredth time.

Owen glares at me and not the road, causing me to swallow with nervousness. "No. Not unless you want your body parts floating in the Hudson."

I know he's not joking. I know what the Mafia is capable of.

I scrub a hand over my head but sit forward as the SUV comes to a halt. Owen winds down his window at a security post, and I watch in awe as we are waved on by men with machine guns strapped to their chests. Fucking machine guns.

A wave of panic rushes through me. "Jesus."

Owen's jaw tightens as he sends me a warning glare. "Exactly."

EMI

I stare at the meal in front of me, unable to take another bite, and push the vegetables around with my fork.

A loud thump on the table makes the cutlery clatter. "Fucking eat!" Luca seethes.

I turn to face him and his narrowed eyes, but as my lips part to speak, I'm saved by Shaw.

"Don't fucking shout at her like that." My eyes bug out at his defense for me.

"Jesus," Owen mumbles, dropping his head and shaking it, as though he's annoyed with him for questioning Luca.

When I listened to Luca discuss Owen, I overheard that he runs the security side of the company owned by Shaw and his friends. I can't help but wonder if our impending marriage is part of an elaborate business plan of Luca's or out of some loyalty to Owen, who he's done previous business with.

Owen is taller than Shaw, with broad shoulders, and

handsome. His blond hair is cropped, and his bronze skin is littered with tattoos.

Luca coolly dabs his napkin at the corner of his lips and ignores Shaw's outburst. His voice is much calmer this time. "Emilia. Eat your meal, the baby will need feeding."

My stomach flips thinking about the baby needing food I'm struggling to stomach, so I pick up a green bean and place it in my mouth with a tight smile toward Luca.

"Good girl," Shaw praises from beside me, making memories of our night together come flooding back. I can't help the whimper that slips out on his praising words.

"Did you finish with this woman of yours?" Luca asks, not in the least bit subtle or caring. I can't help but flinch at the thought of Shaw with another woman. Jealousy and hurt swim in my stomach.

Shaw clears his throat and averts his gaze. "Not yet."

Emotion clogs my throat at the thought of sitting around a dinner table, pregnant by another woman's partner. I squeeze my eyes closed as a wave of sickness rises in my stomach.

"May I be excused?"

Luca scans my face. "Not yet. Eat." He points his fork toward my plate.

"Luca, what are your plans for Shaw and Emilia?" Owen asks, breaking the building tension.

Luca takes a slow, calculated sip of his wine and then motions for the waiter to refill the glass.

"They can take one of my properties, and Shaw can continue with his business." This seems to appease Owen because he relaxes back in his chair with a nod of agreement. His broad body is impressive, but truth be told, I'm used to seeing hot Mafia men all the time, yet the only man my body reacts to is the one sitting next to me.

"I have my own house," Shaw snaps back. "I don't need you to provide for me." He glares at Luca with hate, and I want to tell him to stop.

Luca sits forward in his chair, bracing his elbows on the table. "I'm aware of everything you do and don't have, *Shaw*." Venom rolls off his tongue at Shaw's name. "What you don't have is the correct security for my sister and nephew, my properties do. You'll take one of mine and you will be happy about it."

"Nephew?" Shaw glances toward me, swallowing thickly, with a hint of hurt in his eyes.

My heart races to reassure him. I shake my head. "We don't know that."

Luca throws himself back in his chair. "With all the fucking trouble it's causing, it better be a boy."

I roll my eyes, knowing my brother well enough to know he's joking right now.

"The baby will take our surname, of course," he tacks on.

Shaw jolts, his eyebrows shoot up. "I'm sorry, what?" he splutters.

"You should be sorry; Grant is a pathetic surname. No family member of mine will have it." Luca lifts a shoulder.

"Grant means big," Shaw quips back, scrunching up his nose.

"Big dumbass." Owen grins, earning a glare from Shaw.

I stifle a laugh, which Shaw doesn't miss, and he bends his head to whisper in my ear, "Big everything else, right, Red?"

"Varros is a stronger name. A Mafia name," Luca announces proudly, making me want to roll my eyes, but I know better than to do it.

"The baby isn't yours," Shaw argues in disgust, making me wince.

"And I can take it away from you. So, you'll accept the name and be happy about it." Luca's nostrils flare and his black eyes narrow, and the grip on his cutlery tightens as he seethes with rage at being questioned.

Shaw takes a gulp of his wine before slamming his glass down on the table so hard I'm surprised it doesn't shatter. "Thank you very fucking much!"

Owen pinches the bridge of his nose.

Luca turns his attention toward me. "Emilia, go to your room."

I scan around the table, reluctant to leave Shaw with my unpredictable brother. I know him well enough to know when to push him and when not to. Shaw has no clue how the Mafia world works, and it makes me nervous. Not just that, but I worry our baby will not have a father if he doesn't step carefully and comply.

I push my chair away from the table, unsure whether to say goodbye to Shaw or not. As I rise from my chair, I can't help but whisper advice that has been on the tip of my tongue all night. "Don't push him." Shaw's eyes meet mine in a silent acknowledgment, and as I turn and walk out the door, I only hope he can heed my advice.

THREE

SHAW

Hearing Luca bark orders at Emilia makes me grind my teeth so hard I'm surprised I have any molars left.

Before we left the SUV, Owen gave me strict instructions to keep on the right side of Luca. The Mafia Capo is unpredictable at best, and I've no choice but to let him bulldoze into my life and take over.

Owen has reassured me that a lot of the Mafia members can lead separate lives from their wives outside of the organization. I'm not okay with cheating, but if Emilia and I agree to being with other people because we don't want to be with one another, then that's something we can work toward on a discreet level, way in the fucking future. Truthfully, the thought of Emi with another man sends me feral.

And besides, the last thing I need to do is risk my cock and balls. Even the thought makes me wince.

Emilia sat stoically still during the dinner, her back ramrod straight. I couldn't help but keep glancing at her small bump. Knowing there's an actual baby in there makes me want to hold her, protect her, and press kisses over her delicate neck before marking her as mine once again. Preferably covered in my cum.

When Luca called her out for eating, my first thought was to take her in my arms and feed her myself, but I'm pretty sure Luca would flip his shit over that move, so instead, I spoke up in her defense. Mafia or not, nobody is speaking to the mother of my child like that.

"Does Emilia have an eating disorder?" I throw out as soon as she leaves the room.

Luca rears back with a jolt. "Of course fucking not!"

"Then why wasn't she eating?"

"Maybe she wasn't hungry?" Owen suggests with a shrug of his shoulder.

Luca takes a tentative sip of his wine. Every move he makes is calculated, but I'm not even sure he's aware of it.

"She was nervous. She doesn't eat when she's nervous." His voice is low, as though in thought.

"Nervous," I repeat like an idiot. Annoyance rumbles inside me. "Why the hell would she be nervous?"

"She's met the baby's father for the third time today. Am I right? She's completely unaware if her child was conceived from a cheating prick or someone simply wishing to empty his load. She's nervous and ashamed, as she should be." He sits back with his smug lips in a tight smile.

My teeth grind. "I'm not a fucking cheat!" I spit back at him. "For your information, we broke up. We only recently got back together."

Luca watches me closely, as though looking for the truth behind my words. "Mm. Perhaps tell your girlfriend that you got another woman pregnant."

A wave of sickness rushes over me because that's what she is. My girlfriend. Guilt floods me when I think about the situation I'm in.

When me and Lizzie agreed to try again, I already knew it wasn't a good idea, but I can't bear to see her break down like she does. The guys say she has me wrapped around her little finger, but seeing my mother distraught during my childhood makes seeing other women hurting difficult for me. We might not have a loving relationship, but she gets the materialistic aspects of our relationship, and I get the sex. Even if it doesn't come close to my experience with Red, it's been better than having to find a one-night stand every time I need to fulfill my fantasies.

"I'll end it. Tonight." I tack on the latter to appease him. Knowing the sooner I get the inevitable over with, the better.

Owen sits straighter. "What can we expect, Luca? What do you want from Shaw?"

Luca leans forward, his dark eyes drilling into mine. "The wedding takes place a week from today. A small ceremony of signing the official forms."

My attention is piqued because surely Emilia wants an actual wedding, right? "She doesn't want a big wedding?"

Luca scoffs. "She could have had the wedding of her dreams if she'd done as she was supposed to and kept her legs and mouth shut."

My fists pump in frustration hearing him speak about her like that.

"Ravlek, the man she was meant to marry, is pissed. She was a business deal." Bile creeps up my throat at the thought of Emilia being a business deal. *Over my dead fucking body.*

"You'll pay me the twenty-five million he was paying, at the very least for the inconvenience."

My eyes narrow on him. *Twenty-five fucking million?*

Of course, he goes on. "He's to respect my sister. I won't accept cheating," he reiterates.

I open my mouth, but he holds up his hand to stop my words from spilling. "She will have her own security details, as will the child. You will attend functions when I say." Luca sits back in his chair. "Apart from that, I'll allow you to lead your own life."

"Allow." I roll the word over my tongue, fury bubbling in my veins. *Just who the hell does he think he is? Taking over my life, making demands on me, and ruining my plans.*

Luca lifts his cell from the table and presses a button. "Maxim, call a doctor. I want someone that specializes in eating disorders to check on Emi." He works his jaw from side to side. "No, now." He ends the call, then raises his eyes to meet mine.

"You will not hurt my family, Shaw. Do you understand me?"

Blood pumps through my veins, and I swallow hard with the intensity behind his words, the underwritten danger coating each and every syllable.

My throat is dry as I nod in response. "Of course."

EMI

I pace my bedroom for the hundredth time, biting on my fingernails, but the turning of my door handle has me spinning on my heels at my door opening.

Shaw slips into the room, but not before looking over his shoulder as though he's being followed.

I take in his white shirt stretching over his firm shoulders. His styled hair appears a little messy, as though he's been rubbing his hands through it, and my fingers itch to do just that.

"I wanted to make sure that you're okay." He breathes out with concern twinkling in his blue eyes.

His gaze travels over the oversized t-shirt I'm wearing, and I nibble my lip when they stop on the swell of my stomach.

I couldn't wait to change out of the dinner dress I was in, and my feet ache, thanks to those damn heels.

"Thank you, I'm fine."

There's an odd atmosphere between us, where neither of us says a single thing. I mean, where do we start?

"The Mafia, Red?" he chokes out, still disbelieving the situation I've landed us in. His hands rest on his hips, and I wish for nothing more than for him to pull me into his arms like he did the night we were together.

I swallow away the guilt. "I'm sorry. I didn't think that they would find out."

His eyes bulge, and he nods toward my bump. "Really?"

Now it's my turn to become annoyed. "I didn't intend on getting pregnant, *Shaw*," I snipe back, spitting his name like vitriol.

"No, you just used me to pop your cherry before your new husband did, right?"

I roll back on my heels, stunned at his outburst. I've grown up around men, though, so I refuse to back down when I don't need to.

"And you used me to empty your balls. Here's the consequences of our actions." I wave a hand toward my stomach, and his gaze locks there, softening slightly.

Silence fills the room before he breathes out slowly.

"Is the baby okay?" His blue eyes meet mine with concern.

"Do you care?" I can't help but snipe the words out.

His temple pulsates in anger. "Of course I fucking care. It's my baby too. I'm not a monster, Emilia."

"No. You're just a cheat." I cross my arms over my chest and stare back at him with my jaw locking tight. Had I known for one minute he had a girlfriend, I wouldn't have so much as looked at him.

My blood curdles at the thought of being a homewrecker.

His voice becomes low as he moves closer. "I never

cheated. Me and Lizzie have a"—he grimaces—"turbulent relationship." He sighs. "I'm ending it tonight. I realize it's not fair on either of you."

This shocks me. In the Mafia world, if a man wants a mistress, he will have one, and the wife sure as hell has no say in it.

My shoulders deflate with guilt at affecting their relationship. "I'm sorry." And I mean it. I never intended to turn our lives upside down like this.

He stares up at the ceiling and takes a deep breath before focusing back on me. "It's fine. We just need to take one day at a time, right?"

I nod in agreement, hoping above all hope that he's right.

The silence stretches between us, and I hate it, so I offer him an olive branch. "It's Emi. Not Emilia."

"Emi," he repeats with his lips tipping up into a smile that lights up his whole face.

"Nice to meet you, Emi. I'm Shaw." He holds out his hand, and I slide mine into it, my whole body coming alive under his tender touch.

My body betrays me and flushes at the contact just as my bump does a little wiggle.

The three of us.

One day at a time.

FOUR

SHAW

"Where the hell have you been?" Lizzie spits out as soon as the apartment door clicks shut. I swallow hard, trying to fight the urge not to tell her to fuck off, but knowing I'm about to hurt her stops me from arguing with her further.

"I asked you a question, Shaw. I called the office; they said you left this afternoon. Have you been with those men again?" I grind my jaw at her reference to my friends. My best friends who are like brothers to me. She knows they don't approve of her, so she's constantly trying to drive a wedge between us, hating any time I spend with them and not her, causing a constant bone of contention in our relationship, or lack of. She stands from the couch and walks toward me, so I move into the kitchen area and pour myself a scotch. "Shaw!" she shouts, forcing me to spin and face her.

I down the drink and swipe my hand over my mouth, slamming the glass on the counter as I steel myself.

Here goes. "I've got some bad news."

Her blue eyes search my face, and her hand moves to her mouth in shock. "Oh god, have you lost the business?"

"No."

Her eyes bulge further. "The holiday rentals?"

Annoyance bubbles inside me at her concern about the materialistic aspects of our life, a common occurrence in our relationship. "Well, what is it? Spit it out." Her patience is wearing thin, as always.

I clear my throat. "I'm ending things between us."

Lizzie swishes her blonde hair over her shoulder with a confident, mocking laugh. "Really, Shaw, this again?"

"Permanently," I add, hoping she realizes the severity of the situation.

"Mm." She muses while moving toward me. Her long talons find my shirt buttons and she pops them open. I grip her wrist to stop her.

"Lizzie, this is serious." I grit my teeth at her refusal to accept my words.

"I know and so are we." She bites into her plump lip playfully. In the past, I would've been aching to feel it being worked out over my cock, but now all I want to do is push her away from me.

"I got another girl pregnant." She stills and sucks in a sharp breath that causes pity to lance through me. "I'm sorry."

She steps back, stunned, her eyes wide. "Sorry?"

I drag a hand over my head. "We were broken up. I hadn't slept with anyone for months." She stares back at me in silence, so I continue on. "I am sorry. Really fucking sorry, Liz." I stare into her blue eyes, hoping she can see the honesty in mine.

Her lip curls up at the side menacingly, and her eyes narrow with a scowl. "Can she get rid of it?"

My heart sinks on her words. *Is she for real?* "No," I snap back.

"Is she too far gone?"

In all honesty, I don't know the cutoff point for those procedures. But Emi has a bump, and besides, there's no way I'd even consider getting rid of my own flesh and blood. The thought alone sickens and angers me, causing my body to lock up with tension.

"She won't be getting rid of the baby," I say with confidence. *Over my dead fucking body.*

"But if you could, would you?" Her words sear into me. She's not getting this. There's no other option, even if I was prepared to consider any other way.

"Lizzie, she's pregnant and I'm marrying her."

Her pupils dilate as I stand still and wait for a tirade of curse words, the overload of emotions to dispel from her.

Instead, the sharp slap against my cheek stuns me. My hand moves to my face, shocked at her outburst. She's always been volatile, but this is the first time she's physically lashed out.

"I hate you, Shaw Grant. You and your little bastard."

She turns, grabbing her purse from the counter, and storms out of the apartment, slamming the door shut behind her.

My shoulders relax at her exit, almost relieved that it went better than expected. Angry Lizzie I can handle.

Emotional Lizzie, not so much.

My phone pings from my back pocket, and I pull it out

to find a message from Tate.

> Tate: Please tell me you get a bachelor's party.

I scoff at the message and pour myself another drink. Of course he'd find joy in my misery.

> Me: Not a chance. Her brother will have my balls in a jar.

> Owen: Fuck in a jar, he'll have them rammed down your throat.

I grimace at his analogy, knowing it's probably the truth.

> Owen: That's after he's made you deep-throat your own cock.

I cringe, knowing Owen won't be exaggerating.

> Mase: When is the wedding?

> Me: Saturday.

> Mase: Do we have to attend?

Jeez, thanks for the support, dipshit.

> Me: I don't think you're invited.

> Reed: This better not affect business, Shaw.

I roll my eyes at the serious prick. My life is going down the shitter and all he is bothered with is the company. He has the most money out of all of us. If the business went bust, he'd be fine.

> Tate: Is she hot?

I smile at just how hot she is. Beautiful doesn't do her justice.

> Me: Yes. Very.

> Tate: Bonus. Do you get to fuck on your wedding night?

I drag a hand over my jaw. Good fucking question, and my cock likes the thought too, as it swells in my pants thinking about her and her tight pussy.

> Mase: He broke up with Lizzie.

Guilt floods me for letting my mind wander to Emi so quickly.

> Tate: Whoops.

> Mase: T don't be a dick head.

> Owen: It was for the best.

> Tate: Did she try to suck you off?

I choke on a laugh with how well Tate knows Lizzie. Perhaps a little too well, but I push that thought aside.

> Me: She hit me.

> Reed: Ouch.

> Tate: Bitch.

> Owen: He knocked someone up and he's getting married. Everything she wants from him.

Guilt racks through me because Owen is right. I might not have wanted that, but Lizzie sure as hell did. She pushed it on me constantly.

I sigh at the burden of not only hurting Lizzie but the weight of knowing I can't fuck this up. I need to make this work for Emi, and the baby too.

> Me: I'll see you guys in the office tomorrow.

I switch my phone to silent and pour another drink. In one week's time, I will be a married man. Throwing myself down on the couch, I open the encrypted folder on my phone with the images I took when Emi was sleeping.

Her luscious tits peek out above the bedsheet, her lips slightly parted, and I wonder, not for the first time, how those lips would feel wrapped around my shaft. Would I choke her with my length? Make her gag?

My cock jumps in my pants, reminding me it's there. Thickening with visions of Emi.

I wonder if she's given a blow job before? Surely at twenty she's had some experience. Although, maybe her brother has been so strict with her that she's had none. I touch my fingers to my lips. *Was I her first kiss too?* The thought of someone else touching her makes my blood boil.

An overwhelming need to possess her overcomes me, something I've not experienced before.

My cock swells, and I unbuckle my belt and open my pants, lifting my heavy, aching cock out of my boxers. I position it beside my phone so I can see her face as I thrust into my hand.

I hold myself tighter, imagining her soft lips wrapped around my cock. "Fuck, baby girl. Take your first cock in your mouth." I jerk my hips forward, fucking my hand to the motion of fucking her mouth.

My cock drips. "That's it, be a good girl and take it." I imagine her arching her back how she did when I made her come, how her lips part and her tongue darts out. Imagining her licking my slit and then shooting my load over her open mouth, watching in awe as my cum drips down her chin and onto her delectable tits.

My orgasm is torn from me as I thrust hard, tightening my grip on my cock and forcing the cum from the tip. "Jesus." Warm cum shoots out, and I pant as I come down from the intensity, both my hand and phone now covered in warm cum. I try to swipe it from the phone screen but instead swipe to another photo, the one of the bedsheets the day she left.

Smeared with her blood and my cum.

The day we made the baby she now carries.

A mixture of rage at my life being turned upside down and arousal at the thought of Red pregnant with my baby boils inside me.

A dangerous blend of anger and promise fills my veins.

But also, a fierce determination to protect Emi and the baby at whatever cost overwhelms them all.

FIVE

EMI

"You look beautiful." I spin on my heel to face my brother's dark eyes mirroring my own. His eyes give him a deadly and serious intensity, but that shatters the instant his lips tip up at the sides, and I can't help but smile back at him as I place another diamond earring in my ear.

"I look fat."

His eyebrows furrow. "The doctor assured me you don't have an eating disorder." His tone turns serious.

I choke on a chuckle. "Luca. I don't have an eating disorder. I'm pregnant."

"I realize," he deadpans, turning up his lip.

I sigh, exhausted from apologizing and drained from worrying. "I know it's not ideal."

He holds his hand up to stop me from talking. "It's not. But it's dealt with now. This Shaw will make a good husband." He waves his hand out toward the bedroom door, making a flutter of nerves race through me at the thought of Shaw becoming my husband.

"He'll take care of you."

My stomach flips at his comment, and I twist my hands in front of me. "How can you be so sure?"

It's his turn to scoff this time. "Because I'll make sure his death is a slow and painful one if not."

I roll my eyes and face the mirror again, trailing my eyes over the lace wedding dress that flows down my body with the long lace veil matching. My makeup is natural, and my waves have been emphasized.

"I'm proud of you." His comment surprises me as he stands behind me and places his palm on my shoulder in a reassuring gesture. This is as much affection as I'll ever likely receive from Luca, so I take it while I can.

I shift my eyes away from his, guilt swimming in mine. "I doubt that."

"We all make mistakes, Emi." His eyes dart away from the mirror, and I wonder if he's referring to the bloodbath he started when our sister was murdered by an opposing family.

I open my mouth to reassure him, but as usual, anything to do with feelings Luca shuts down. He pulls away and straightens his jacket. "Come. Your husband-to-be will be waiting." He holds out his hand for me, and I place my palm in his, prepared to marry a man I don't know, all for the sake of my family.

In blood we're bound.

In trust we live.

SHAW

My leg bounces, and my thoughts flit back to her walking down the aisle, the swell of her stomach encased in a loose lace dress clearly meant to disguise her pregnancy.

Her grandfather, who she refers to as Papi, was a witness, as was Owen. The remaining congregation was security detail, apart from Emi's adopted brother, Maxim.

When the officiant pronounced us husband and wife, I wasn't sure if I was allowed to kiss her or not. Too damn nervous to get my balls fed to me, it took Luca prompting me with what I can only describe as a thinly veiled threat. "*Kiss your fucking bride,*" he gritted through clenched teeth.

Our kiss was short and sweet, more of a peck than anything else. As much as I'd have liked to have deepened the kiss, I wasn't about to lose my cock before using it again.

"You can relax now." Her soft voice is a whisper, yet fills the limousine with a comfort I'm not used to.

I snap my gaze from the window to her. Her beauty hits me square in the chest, and I'm forced to swallow away the lump clogging in my throat. "I'm sorry." I roll my lips. *What the fuck is wrong with me?* "It's a lot," I admit like a sap.

Emi ducks her head. "I know. I get that." She gazes out the window, and I have a sudden need to reassure her too.

"Have you seen the house we're about to move into?" I try to disguise the snipe in my comment.

Emi spins to face me with a smile that would put me on my ass if I wasn't already on it. "No, but knowing my brother, it's ridiculous." She rolls her eyes on a chuckle, and I laugh with her, then she points her finger at me. "But safe." She grins wider, making me throw my head back on a laugh.

I like her sense of humor. A lot. It's not something I'm used to when around women. Either I'm not around them long enough to have a conversation or, like Lizzie, they're serious all the time or talking about shopping and restaurants. Neither of which I give a shit about.

I like the change and am thanking my lucky fucking stars I'm sitting in a car with Emi and not some botoxed bitch who you can't tell if their face is moving or not.

"Honestly, Shaw, once my brother has settled down, we could live separate lives if that's what you prefer. I don't want to ruin your life for you." She sighs. "We just need to present a united front until then."

Dread fills my stomach at the thought of my family living a separate life from me. *Is that what she wants?* "Is that what you want? To live a separate life?"

I watch her, not missing the flush and rise of her chest. "No. I want my child to have two parents that are happy, together." Her black eyes hold mine hostage with sincerity and hope.

My heart races and my Adam's apple bobs in relief. "Me too."

Her shoulders relax and her lips turn up into a gentle smile. "So . . ."

"So, we try and make this work. You, me, and—" I nod toward her bump while trying to tamper down the excitement bubbling inside me.

I might not have wanted a wife and baby, but now that I have them, I intend to make this work and keep them above everything else.

SIX

SHAW

"Jesus fucking Christ. It's ridiculous." I exhale, scanning the foyer that's big enough to be a ballroom.

"I know, right?" Emi agrees with deflated shoulders.

"I mean, I've seen some pretty elaborate homes. Hell, I'm worth a fortune, but seriously, Emi. This is ridiculous." I wave my hand around the entrance, struggling to take in what appears to be gold door frames. I shake my head in disapproval. *How fucking absurd.*

Spinning on my heels to face her, I take her in. She's biting into her bottom lip, and I want to tug it from her mouth and suck it into mine while hearing those needy whimpers rumble inside her that haunt my dreams on replay.

"Are you okay?" She searches my face.

I snap out of my thoughts. "Huh?"

"You're staring at me and zoned out." She flaps her

hand in front of me, emphasizing how crazy I must be acting right now.

How the fuck do I tell her I zoned out imagining sucking on her lips without sounding like a complete weirdo?

"I'm in shock." *At how gorgeous you are and how much I need you.*

Her eyes widen and her shoulders drop. "I'm sorry."

I shake my head. "Stop apologizing. Like you said previously, we are both to blame for our situation." My eyes trail down to her bump, and I long to touch it. To feel our baby inside her. *Does the baby move?*

"Should we take our bags upstairs?" She crooks her thumb toward the gold-spindled staircase, and I scoff at the flamboyance of it.

"Sure." I move to pick up the two bags before she does.

I guess, at some point, I will have to move more of my things over here from the apartment. *Or do I keep the apartment in case something goes wrong?*

Emi follows me as we make our way upstairs. As we approach the landing, the huge bow on a double door gives no room for guessing which one is the master suite.

"The housekeeper probably did it." Emi huffs and shoves past me to rip the bow off the doors and throws them open.

A ginormous bed fills the center of the room. Decorated in soft golds and creams, the room looks expensive, even at first glance. I step inside and place the bags down.

My feet sink into the plush carpet, and if I wasn't so pissed at my current situation, I'm sure I'd be able to appreciate the glamour of it all.

"The bathroom is through there and the walk-in wardrobe over there." Emi points out as she opens each door and pokes her head inside. She unclips her veil and places it on the dresser, then she flicks off her heels with a moan that hits me square in the balls, making them ache with need and my cock swell with hunger.

"Do you mind unzipping my dress for me?" She brushes her hair to one side, exposing the bare flesh of her shoulder and the zipper that starts at the top of her spine and stops at the top of her luscious ass.

I clear my throat and step forward. "Sure."

"I was so relieved to get those shoes off. I dread to think what I'll be like in another few months."

My hand finds her hip to hold her in place as the other finds her zipper. Painstakingly slowly, I drag the zipper down while my fingers graze over the softness of her skin. My veins pump with a need to throw her on the bed and fuck her.

With Emi, I have a primal urge to fuck her senseless, to mark her soft, delicate skin and make it my own. I've never felt so uncontrollable around a woman, and I can't decide whether I like it or not. The reward is like nothing I've had before, yet the punishment is just as bad. It makes me want to punish her for it. For the position we're in.

I grind my teeth as my rock-hard cock rubs against the waistband of my tux pants, and I watch in fascination as her skin breaks out in goose bumps against the mere touch of my fingers.

"We don't have to do anything," I whisper against her ear. I say one thing, but I sure as hell think the other. "Just because we're married, we don't have to—"

"Fuck?" She finishes my sentence and turns to face me.

I scrub a hand through my hair, take a step back, and exhale. "Right. We don't have to fuck." *But I want to, so bad.*

Her hands leave the top of her dress, and in the blink of an eye, it's pooling at her bare feet.

Emi stands there in front of me in her white lace panties and garter belt with her perfect full tits on display and a small bump. Her fingers tremble, proving her innocence.

I suck in a sharp breath because I've never seen anyone so breathtaking in my entire life. Her olive skin gleams under the low lighting, and I lick my lips while imagining trailing my tongue over her silky skin. I work my gaze back up, taking in every blemish, every change since the last time I memorized her body.

Her tits have grown, and I long to hold them, feel the weight, drag my tongue over her peaked nipple before sucking them into my mouth, gently at first, then harder, just to test her limits. My cock drips at the thought. Then my eyes travel toward her flushed chest, up the column of her throat I long to hold in my grasp, and finally land on her beautiful face. Her darkened eyes full of intrigue and lust but vulnerability too. She's nervous, and the thought excites me and makes me want to reassure her. Preferably with my cock deep inside her.

I swallow hard, not wanting to overstep but also desperately wanting her plump lips wrapped around my cock; something we never got around to the last time we were together.

I wonder if I would be her first blow job.

I want to know, I need to know every . . . fucking . . . thing my wife has and hasn't done in her life, and suddenly, the need is more important than breathing itself.

"How many cocks have you tasted?" I take a menacing step toward her. Her eyes narrow on me, and she takes far too long to answer, annoying the hell out of me. "When I ask you a question, I expect you to answer, Emi." Her eyes flare at my commanding tone, and I revel in it. "Now, how many cocks have you sucked?"

She swallows but her eyes remain on mine, as though testing me. I love and loathe her confidence. "I haven't," she admits, crossing her arms.

I take one more step toward her so we're chest to chest. So close her bump is pressed to my thigh, and my fingers twitch to hold her bump.

I tuck a curl behind her ear, then place my hand around her throat. "You've never given a blow job?" I stare into her eyes again, looking for deceit, lack of confidence, anything other than what she's telling me, because she's an insanely beautiful young twenty-year-old woman with zero experience, and in my world, that's hard to believe, yet in hers, I can foresee it.

My cock throbs in its confines, desperate for a taste of her. To paint her lips with my cum, to ruin her body in the best possible way.

"You're going to get a lesson in sucking cock, Red." I lick my lips, embracing the control I have over my untouched princess. "On your knees."

Emi moves to her knees without breaking our stare, like the perfect submissive. Her innocence makes my cock harder, even though I wouldn't have thought it humanly possible.

My chest heaves as my eyes stay transfixed on hers until her tongue darts out to wet her bottom lip, and I move to unbuckle my belt while I have her compliance.

I push my pants past my ass and lower my boxers to below my balls, taking delight when her eyes widen at my heavy, dripping, hard cock. It's big, I know it is. I've seen other guys' in the restrooms, and they wish their cocks were as big as mine. No wonder my girl bled so much when I fucked her. I like that, the thought of only me fucking her.

A sharp realization hits me in the chest, stopping me in my tracks. "Have you fucked anyone else?"

She startles. "No. Of course not, Shaw." Her eyes bug out. "Have you met my brother?"

My cock jumps with a burst of excitement, and my lips curl into a grin. *Jesus, I'm a sick fuck.* Enjoying my wife having only experienced me is a feeling like no other.

Ownership.

I caress her cheek.

Possession.

Using my thumb, I pluck her bottom lip from between her teeth.

Control.

I push my thumb into her mouth. "Suck." And she does, she pulls it between her lips and flicks her tongue over my digit. I'm transfixed at her ability to make my cock drip with pre-cum from her simple touch.

I wrap my free hand around my cock and jerk it back and forth.

"Fuck, that's good." My hips thrust forward, needing to fuck harder.

Before I can lose my load over my hand, I pull my thumb from her mouth with a pop. Then I take my cock in both hands and drag the swollen tip over her delicate lips, sucking in a deep breath when her wet lips graze the thick head, painting them with my pre-cum. *Jesus.*

I move my left hand to behind her head and encourage

her to move forward. "Take me in your mouth, Emi. Like a good girl. Take your first cock in your mouth, baby." My head drops back and my eyes roll when she pushes her face into my groin, making herself choke on my thickness but not stopping.

She wants to prove a point, that she can take what I have. That she can satisfy me, and fuck me, does she do just that. The head of my cock hits the back of her throat, and my hand tangles with force in her hair. I expect her to flinch, to bitch about me being rough like Lizzie always did. I didn't expect for her to moan around my cock as though she loves it and push further forward as though she's just as desperate and hungry for this as me.

"Oh, fuck. Yes. Fuck," I pant out uncontrollably.

My hips jerk when her hand comes up to cup my balls. "Fuck, yes. Jesus, yes. That's it, Red. Don't stop. You know just how I like it, baby. You were made for me."

Emi drags me out of her mouth, leaving saliva trailing down my cock. I take a heavy breath and stare down at her with my jaw lax due to how incredible it feels when she drags her tongue up my shaft, trailing the vein protruding from my cock. "Mm, fuck. So good." I thrust my hips, desperate for some relief.

"Fuck, baby. Wrap your lips around my cock again. Let me come inside that sweet mouth of yours. Let me feed you my cum."

"Mm." She moans in response, making the vibration shoot to my balls before dipping her tongue into my slit, forcing more pre-cum to leak out.

"Fuck. You like that, don't you? You like the taste of me?"

Emi nods at my words, making me feel ten feet tall. "Fuck, I want to fuck your face so bad, Emi."

My grip in her hair tightens, but I restrain myself, afraid of hurting her. I've never done that before, never unleashed the need I've occasionally felt. But nothing, nothing compares to her innocence and beauty being wrapped around me. My eyes latch onto her heavy tits, and I groan, imagining her covered in my cum. *Jesus.* I thrust harder, losing control.

She pops off my cock. "Use me. Please, use me." Her chin is wet with our combined juices, and I relish in it. "I want to feel you. The real you." The look in her eyes, the heaviness of her tits, her begging for me to use her. All of it screams, *fuck me*. The beast inside me rages, and an urge to fuck her like I want to, to fuck her senseless, overwhelms me.

And I do. I grip her hair tighter, and on a snarl, I push her face into my groin, so close I can feel her breathing through her nose as I thrust hard into her mouth. Thrust after thrust I ram into her little mouth while she chokes.

"Fuck. Yes. Fuck." Sweat coats my skin. I don't stop. I hold her head as I surge inside her mouth. "Take that cock. Take that fucking cock, like my own little slut." Her eyes fill with lust at my words, and my balls ache and as I'm about to explode, I have an overwhelming urge to see her covered in me. I yank her head back, her mouth still open as I come. Using my hand to angle my cock at her open lips, her chin, and then finally allowing some cum to spurt onto her chest.

Fuck, it should have hit her tits too.

"Swallow. Taste me." My cock twitches when she stares

back at me and swallows my load, then nibbles at her lip, waiting for me to tell her what to do next.

My chest heaves as I stare at her in awe. I can't believe my luck to have her.

So fucking beautiful and all mine.

Never anyone else's.

My jaw locks tight with the thought. I won't ever let anyone else touch her. She's my wife.

Mine.

SEVEN

EMI

Shaw makes quick work of removing his shirt, throwing it beside the bed with a growl as though angry. He kicks off his bottoms before tugging me to my feet by my arm. His control wavering.

My throat hurts a little but not nearly as much as the throbbing between my legs.

Sure, I've never given a blow job before. But I've sneaked a look at enough of Pornhub and YouTube to know what you have to do.

I might be inexperienced, but I'm not naïve, and staring at Shaw's body makes it easy for me to want to please him. Eager even.

"Get on the bed." I still have his cum on my face and over my chest, so I flit my eyes over the room for something to use.

"Now," he all but barks, making me jump.

I climb onto the bed and sit up on my knees, unsure if

he wants me to lie down or not. He circles the bed as though he's a predator and I'm his prey. I try not to fidget under his scrutiny and try to feign a confidence I most definitely do not feel right now. Not with a protruding stomach and tits so heavy they sag.

"I want to taste every fucking inch of you, Emi. Every inch." His gravelly voice sends a shudder down my spine, causing my nipples to pebble. His eyes zero in on them, and he licks his lips.

Shaw climbs onto the bed beside me and rests his head on the pillow. "Climb up, baby. You're going to ride my face. I'm going to lick you ass to slit, and you're going to fill my mouth with your sweet taste."

I gasp, flush, and throb all in one. My body trembles ever so slightly, but Shaw doesn't miss it. His face softens, and he holds out his palm. "Come on, baby, let me show you how it's done."

I place my hand in his, and he heaves me over his chest, forcing a giggle to rumble from me. I swipe at him playfully.

Shaw stares up at me from below, his eyes eating me up as they roam over my tits. "Good girl. Fuck, such a good girl saving the taste of your cunt for me." He breathes me in, and I whimper at his words, and when he pries my thighs apart, I let them drop on either side of his head. He snaps each side of my panties and throws the fabric to the floor.

Shaw grips onto my ass cheeks, then drags me over his open mouth. I jump when his tongue finds my asshole and can't help but moan at the weirdly amazing intrusion. He holds me still and pushes his tongue into my hole. "Oh, shit, Shaw." I grip the headboard behind him with both hands.

"Mm." He moans into my ass, and I can't find it in me to be disgusted. My body lights up at the foreign feeling and arousal drips from me. "Oh," I whimper.

Then he drags his tongue out of my hole, licks his lips, and places kisses on each of my inner thighs before dragging me over his mouth all the way up to my clit where he sucks hard.

Shaw drags me back and forth over his face. "Fuck my face, baby. Work your tight little ass over my mouth. Take what you need."

"Oh god." My orgasm builds as he flicks his tongue over my clit and sucks it into his mouth. I grind down on his face, pushing hard against his open mouth, forcing him to take me.

I drop my head and our eyes connect. He stares up at me, only just able to see me due to my bump. Our bump.

Something passes between us, and in this moment, I might not be experienced, but I am confident. I am the strong female my brother taught me to be.

So I take what I want and give Shaw something I know he'll enjoy. A show.

I grind against his face one more time. Then I take my hands off the headboard and take hold of my heavy breasts, pushing them together and plucking at my nipples until they stiffen.

Shaw groans below me, and his eyes flare, encouraging me. I drag a finger up into his now almost dry cum and swipe at it. Lifting my finger to my mouth, I suck it in and release a loud moan.

He pants below me, and the vibrations of his groan

rumble my thighs, then he holds me still while his head thrashes from side to side, and he devours me like a man possessed.

My orgasm crashes into me, and I throw my head back with my mouth slackened. "Yes, Shaw. Yes!" My thighs clench around his head as stars explode before my eyes with the greatest orgasm I've ever experienced.

SHAW

I don't give her time to come down from her orgasm before I have her on her back with her legs open. Her bump rests between us, and it's the sexiest thing I've ever seen because I put it there. I put a baby inside her, and I fucking love it.

I move between her legs, rubbing my engorged cock through our juices. Emi looks disheveled, thoroughly fucked, and I delight in it.

My cock aches to fill her, and knowing I can fuck her raw has brought out the animal in me. My thick cock stretches her small hole, and I have to grind my teeth to stop myself from coming.

"Fuck, you're so damn tight." Her lip's part, and I work my eyes down her body to her delectable tits. *Fuck, I need to taste them so bad.*

When she put on a show for me, I swear I nearly came. Never in my life have I come from eating pussy and watching a woman play with her tits. And fuck me, her tits are simply incredible. The best I've ever seen. Her nipples have grown and are darker, and I thank my lucky stars I'm here to witness it all. As if sensing my thoughts, her hands move toward her tits. "Fuck yes, baby, play with them."

I thrust inside her warm, wet pussy and withdraw. "Play with your nipples." Then I repeat the action. "Pull them, baby." *Thrust.* "Present them to me." She holds them out to me, squeezing them as they spill from her hands. "That's it." I clench my teeth, staving off my orgasm.

"Shaw." Her eyes are heavy, and she clenches around me as though she's going to come again, her wet pussy as tight as a vise. "Fuck. You turn me on so damn much." I slam inside her, making her tits bounce as she holds onto them.

"Yes. Oh god, yes." *Slam.*

"Hold your tits, baby. Hold them while I fuck you." *Slam.*

She drags her thumbs over her nipples and moans. My mouth drops open along with the noise escaping her lips. "Fuck." *Slam.* "Fuck, you feel good." *Slam.* "I'm going to come inside you." *Slam.*

I grind my teeth as my balls tighten. "Shit." I move a hand to her pussy and give it an abrupt smack. Emi lifts her head off the pillow on a silent scream that makes my cock erupt. Ropes of cum flood her pussy as my movements stutter with the force.

"Fuck." My head drops forward in the crook of her neck, and my chest heaves from exertion. "Fucking incredible."

EIGHT

EMI

Shaw pulls out and drops down beside me, his chest heaving. I scan his muscular build and bite my lip as I roll to face him.

I never had a vision of a wedding night, not beyond being forced to participate in a sexual encounter with someone I didn't want to marry. So, to have a wedding night with Shaw, someone I'm not only attracted to but also kind of like, makes the day feel somewhat special.

He clears his throat. "Can I touch the baby?" His eyes gleam with uncertainty.

I startle at his words, feeling incredibly guilty that he hasn't felt our baby, hasn't so much as experienced anything regarding our baby yet.

"Of course. You don't have to ask, Shaw. This baby is yours as much as it is mine." His shoulders relax, and he places his large palm on my stomach. The simple touch feels like a blanket of protection and care.

My bump is neatly round and the size of a soccer ball already. "Can you feel the baby move?" he asks.

I smile at the serious expression on his face as his hand gently moves in each direction, trying to feel for movement.

I take his hand and move it to the spot my bump always moves and hold it there. "I usually feel it here." Shaw nods but doesn't look away from our connected hands, and as I'm about to tell him the baby must be sleeping, there's movement.

Shaw jumps. "Fuck, Emi. I felt it." His face breaks into a huge smile that makes me smile back. "Jesus. That's incredible."

"It is," I agree with a smile. Ever since the baby started moving, I've felt an emotion I've only ever heard of: love.

I'm sure I love my brother too, but in the Mafia, respect comes above all else. According to Luca, love has no place in the Mafia.

My heart sinks at the thought of our sister's death. Any bit of love Luca could have felt would have been abolished the moment she died. Of course it just solidified his opinion.

"You've had doctors appointments, right? Everything's going okay?" Shaw snaps me out of my thoughts.

"Yes. Luca insists on the best." I roll my eyes with a smile on my face.

Shaw drops his head against the pillow and places one hand behind his head while tugging me to lie on his chest. I throw my leg over him, and he weaves his free hand around to hold onto my bump. I've never felt so close and so treasured in my entire life, and the thought makes me warm, but a sliver of panic rushes through me at how dependent I'm becoming on him already.

"Tell me about yourself, Emi." He sighs. "Jesus, how fucked up is it that I barely know you. But . . ."

"But?" I question, lifting my head enough to face him.

His eyebrows furrow, as though confused. "I feel close to you."

"Me too," I admit while my heart races at his words.

"Maybe it's the baby." He tilts his head toward my stomach, and my heart plummets. Of course it's the baby. It's the only true connection we actually have, and I need to remember that.

"I'm twenty."

He chuckles. "I know that part."

"Okay, well, I'm almost twenty-one. That's when I was due to get married."

He stiffens below me. "What's he like? The guy you were supposed to marry. Did you love him?"

My heart pounds in my chest. "His name's Ravlek, he's thirty-three and part of the Russian Mafia, equivalent to our Capos. He held out on getting married for me." I hold his eyes.

Shaw stares back at me. "You were more than a deal to him. He liked you." It's a statement not a question.

I nod. "Yeah. I didn't like him back. He's cold and ruthless. A bastard."

Shaw grins to lighten the mood. "He sounds like your brother."

I bite my lip to stifle a laugh before my heart sinks when I think of Luca's pain. "He's hurting. He's always had to be the strong one. Women are allowed to be weak.

Expected to be." I swallow away the guilt when I consider the weight Luca holds. "My sister, Eleanor, was murdered by an opposing Mafia family five years ago." Tears well in my eyes at mentioning her, but I refuse to let them fall.

Shaw freezes. I swallow past the lump in my throat. "When Luca found out, he went wild. He was determined to end the bloodline of the Ricci family altogether."

Shaw's heart is racing below me. "Did he?"

"No. Our Don ordered him to stop, but I'm scared about the damage he's caused. The repercussions it'll bring . . ."

"The security?"

I nod, agreeing with Shaw that my brother's security measures are intense, even for the Mafia.

"I'm sorry. About your sister." His voice is soft and laced in sincerity.

"It's okay." I fidget. "I mean, it's not. But thank you." I swallow back the emotion as I think of not only my sister's death but the deaths following hers. My brother's need for vengeance becoming an obsession that no one could control, not until our Don finally put a stop to it. But it still simmers inside him. I see it and our Don Lorenzo does too, and that terrifies me.

"Our family oath is 'In blood we're bound. In trust we live.' We live by this oath, and Luca sees Eleanor's death as his responsibility. We're bound in blood, and we trust so we live, and none of that helped her, and it haunts him."

The atmosphere is somber, and I hate it.

He tucks a curl behind my ear. "Tell me something good about your family, Emi," he suggests, as though picking up on the change too.

"My Papi. He might be true Mafia through and through, but he has a soft spot for me. Women are weaknesses in the Mafia, but he's never made any attempt to hide how much he cares about me. Not until the day in your office anyway."

"Were you mad at him for not standing up for you?"

"No. He let Luca take control like he should have."

"What about your parents? They're not in the picture?"

I sigh and rest my head back onto his chest. "My parents died when I was younger. My mother died when I was five, and my father was killed in an attack at a restaurant when I was nine. Maxim's parents died that day too, so Papi took custody of him and brought him up as our brother."

Shaw strokes the top of my head, the simple gesture bringing me comfort I didn't know I needed. "Your Papi sounds like a good man, Emi."

"He is." We lie in silence, his fingers threading through my hair. I want to close my eyes and savor the moment, yet I don't want to fall asleep and miss it either.

I raise my head and place my hand on his chest, resting my chin on top of my hand. "How about you?"

"Huh?"

"You have to tell me about you now, Shaw Grant, who works at STORM Enterprises." I grin at him with the little knowledge I have.

He smiles back down, his face lighting up. "Okay. Let's see. I'm Shaw Grant. Thirty-one. I built STORM Enterprises with my four best friends. We named the company after the first letter of each of our names." His tone is light, and he talks like he's in a job interview.

"What do you do there?"

"Lots of things. Mainly the entertainment industry. Advertising, et cetera. We have a security department run by Owen, the guy you already met. He's an ex-Navy SEAL and has great contacts. So, if anyone needs security in the industry, we can provide that service at the same time as the entertainment side."

"I've seen Owen before. He was at a function I went to last year."

Shaw's eyes narrow on me, and his jaw sharpens. "You remember him, huh?" The change in him confuses me.

He flicks his bottom lip between his teeth and takes his hand from behind his head, placing it behind mine. "You're my wife, Emi. You belong to me."

His eyes drill into mine, and my heart jumps at his intensity. "And what about you? Are you mine?"

His Adam's apple bobs. "You know I am." His eyes dart away, and my pulse races at the awareness of him disconnecting from me.

"What about your ex?"

He flits his gaze back toward me. "She's exactly that, Emi. An ex. I'm not a cheat." His eyes bore into mine, the truth radiating from him.

Sickness rolls in my stomach, but I need to know. "Do you love her?"

He stills for a moment, and I have my answer without even needing to hear it. And because I can't bear to see the disappointment in his eyes or feel the guilt any longer, I rest my head back on his chest and close my eyes, ignoring the fact that Shaw fucked me tonight because he needed to get off. Because he had no other option but to fuck the girl he mistakenly knocked up when the one he loves is out of reach.

I close my eyes and imagine it's my wedding night and I just had mad, passionate sex with my husband so good we connected in a way a Mafia marriage would never do.

We didn't just have sex.

We felt something too.

NINE

SHAW

I left her this morning like a coward. When I stared down at her body, I was torn between having feelings toward her and the baby so soon and feeling guilty for breaking Lizzie's heart just last week. The woman I was meant to love but never did. I never should have let our situation drag on for as long as I did.

Yet there was an overwhelming need to spread her parted legs farther and slip between them to fuck away my guilt.

Instead, I tucked my hard cock into my slacks and forced myself to come into work.

My door bursts open with Tate and Owen pushing inside like a pair of school kids. They laugh but then freeze when they see me sitting behind my desk with a solemn expression.

They share a look before looking back at me.

"What the fuck are you doing here?" Tate asks while

throwing himself down on the couch. My office is the biggest and has always been where we have our private meetings. I have amazing views over New Jersey, and instead of a boardroom table, like in Tate's office, I have couches, complete with a basketball hoop, where we throw shitty business documents into the trash.

Owen flops down into the spinning chair he favors. His broad shoulders make his shirt so tight it looks like it's about to rip.

Tate loosens his tie, kicks off his shoes, and unclips his cufflinks. His hair is a tussled mess, which leads me to believe he either just got fucked or he's stressed out of his mind. He's currently grinning at me like an idiot, so I'll go with the former.

"Why are you in my office if you don't expect me to be here?" I quip back.

Owen sighs and rolls his eyes. He's definitely the more straight-to-the-point one out of all of us; he doesn't have the patience for messing around. Good job he doesn't work in one of the offices and have to broker deals, because this business bullshit would make the dude's head explode.

"Your office is more comfortable." Tate smiles back, somehow wider than before. He points at me. "More importantly. What are you doing here?"

I exhale in annoyance. I came to work hoping to get away from questions, hoping to be alone on a Sunday.

"Working. What the fuck does it look like?"

Owen swivels to face me. "Looks to me like you're running from your problems. Aren't you meant to have a honeymoon or something when you get married?"

My heart hammers and regret floods through me.

Shit.

Is that what Emi would have expected? Should I have booked us a honeymoon somewhere?

I shrug. "Nobody said."

"Did you fuck her? Was your wedding night good at least?" Tate smirks at me, and I want to knock his perfect white teeth down his throat for talking about her like that.

"None of your goddamn business," I snipe back and glance down at the papers for the Gold fragrance contract I've recently been working on.

"You could have at least taken the day off to be with her." I snap my head up to face Owen, his expression serious.

I open my mouth to respond, but the office door swinging open saves me from arguing, and in strolls Reed and Mase. Fan-fucking-tastic. I pinch my forehead.

"What are you doing here?" Reed asks as he heads toward the small table I use as extra workspace. He's the only one out of all of us with a stick so far up his ass he cannot unwind. Ever.

He's always immaculately dressed and so well put together. I swear the guy sleeps in a suit too.

"Aren't you meant to be on your honeymoon?" Mase smiles while kicking Tate's feet off the small coffee table.

I pinch the bridge of my nose as I become more annoyed and angrier by the second at their presence.

Tate chuckles. "He's pinching the bridge of his nose."

"Uh oh. Watch out. He's going to explode." Mase raises his eyebrows in jest.

Reed's voice is deep and sharp, leaving no room for joking or argument. *Typical fucking lawyer.* "What the fuck's the problem?"

I sigh. *Is he being serious right now?* I roll my head toward him, his face a mirror of indifference. Yes, he's being serious. "I'm married." I hold up my wedding ring that Luca insisted on me wearing despite my protests, only to be told that if I took the ring off, my cock would follow suit.

Reed's eyes flit toward the ring, and he gives me a firm nod. "I had to break up with Lizzie." Again, he nods. "I fucked my wife." He nods. "I kind of like her." His eyes bug out slightly, then he nods again, unperturbed by my troublesome mind. He's so emotionally stumped; I think he's past intervention of any kind.

"Least you like your wife." Tate shrugs, drawing my attention back to him. "Mase can't stand his."

"Very fucking funny." Mase elbows Tate in the stomach, earning a wince from him.

"It's true," he grumbles while rubbing his stomach.

"So, you fucked your wife and it was good. You like her, and that's a problem, why?" Owen stares at me as though I'm the idiot in this.

"It was better than good." I throw out there.

"'Cause she's pregnant?" Tate's eyebrows narrow in confusion as all our gaze's swivel toward him. "What? I heard pregnancy sex was off the fucking charts."

"Jesus. I don't want to know where you heard that," Reed grumbles.

"Pft. I don't watch pregnancy porn if that's what you think." Tate rolls his eyes at Reed.

My ears prick up. *Is that even a thing?* I mean, my woman is hot as hell pregnant, but before her, I never even considered having sex with a pregnant woman.

"Just get to the point, Shaw. What's wrong?" Reed snaps, making me flinch.

"I feel guilty. I just broke up with Lizzie and now I'm married with a kid on the way. It's a lot," I admit, swallowing back the anxiety creeping in.

"And he likes his wife," Tate tacks on, earning him a glare from us all.

"Lizzie's a venomous bitch. We know it, you know it." Owen lifts a shoulder as though he didn't just call my ex a bitch.

"Agreed," Mase adds.

My shoulders tighten, preparing to defend Lizzie like I always do around them. "Shaw. Don't try and defend her again. You know what she's like. It's why you spent half your so-called time together broken up." Reed lays it out, as always, the voice of reason, even if it is abrupt. "She knew how to pull at your heartstrings and get you to put your hand in your pocket to keep her quiet." He's right, of course.

"It's just everything she wanted, and I couldn't commit." I wince at the pity in my voice.

"Wouldn't. Not couldn't, and there's a reason for that." Owen stares at me, and for the first time since marrying Emi, I actually think he has a point. I chose not to commit for a reason, yet I took my marriage with Emi in stride.

Reed clears his throat. "Can we actually discuss the Gold fragrance contract now?" He throws his arm out toward the file I'm resting on, forcing me back into my work headspace. I gather up the documents and hand them over.

"Fuck, daddy, put your baby batter in me. Fuck me hard, big boy," Tate's phone blurts out as we all turn to face him and the ridiculously loud porn. Mase cranes his neck, and Owen jumps up from his chair. Reed drops his head back to stare at the ceiling while I watch on with a chuckle.

I'm feeling a hell of a lot lighter than I did earlier. Being surrounded by my friends always makes me feel alive. They've been the only constant in my life, and we hold each other up when we need to, even if our methods are not always the expected.

My phone buzzes across my desk, and when I catch sight of the name *Luca*, I feel like every bit of happiness is sucked right out of me.

I'm in literal hell where this man is concerned.

EMI

I rearrange my clothes again.

When I woke this morning to find Shaw gone, I can't say I wasn't surprised, nor will I say I wasn't disappointed.

We might have had good sex. Great sex even, but I will not lie to myself by saying I expect us to live happily ever after.

I stole him from another woman, for Christ's sake. Even though he told me he never cheated, it's obvious he loves her. Something I'm standing in the way of. A wave of sickness rushes through me at the thought of him with her right now.

"Emi. What the fuck are you doing?" I turn toward my brother's deep voice as he scans me up and down.

"Rearranging my clothes. I unpacked this morning."

His eyes search my face in confusion. "You have housekeeping for that. You're pregnant, Emi."

I let out a huff. "I'm pregnant, Luca, not injured. Besides, I want to unpack my own clothes."

"Where's your husband?"

"Shaw?" I ask, shocked he's even here in the first place, let alone wanting to speak to Shaw. If he knows he left me here, he'd be pissed. "He popped out."

His dark eyes scrutinize my face. "Where?"

"I'm not sure, Luca. I'm not his keeper." I grind my teeth in frustration.

He stares at me a moment longer as I stand from the floor. He takes his phone out and presses a number as I watch on. "I want a location on Shaw. Now," he barks into the phone before turning on his heel and walking out of my bedroom.

I glance over toward my nightstand at my phone, wondering if I should contact him and give him a heads-up, but then I realize I don't even have his number.

I don't have my own husband's phone number. I shake my head at the ridiculousness.

I follow Luca and smile when I see my brother, Maxim, at the bottom of the stairs. "Hey, beautiful." I wrap my arms around his neck.

"Are you missing me yet?" I pull back and smile up at him.

"I'm missing your baking, if that counts?" His eyes light up in glee.

Ever since I was a little girl, I've helped out dozens of nannies, cooks, and housekeepers in the kitchen. My family and staff have been the only ones to sample the results though.

"Maxim. Get in here," my brother bellows from my new dining room.

Maxim sighs but grins down at me and nods toward the open door, encouraging me along also.

I have a fantastic relationship with Maxim. While Luca has always been cold and collected, Maxim has always worn his heart on his sleeve. Luca said it makes him weak and vulnerable, but I beg to differ. It doesn't make him any less of a man; at least he's approachable, unlike my brother.

"I want their fucking heads on a platter, and I mean a literal platter. There's no fucking reason shipments should go missing. We're not the O'Connell's, they lose their damn shipments every fucking week. I refuse to accept any excuse. Wipe the fucking warehouse out, for all I care." Luca pauses as though listening to whoever is on the other end of the call. "Fine, then get me new men." He throws his phone across the table, causing it to spin toward us.

When his eyes meet mine, they're so dark I can no longer make out his pupils. "I don't have time for games, Emi. When I come around, I expect your husband here." He stabs his finger down on the table as though he expects Shaw to magically appear.

I clench my teeth together. "We didn't know you were coming, Luca."

"I have places to fucking be." He bangs his fist on the table, making it and me jump.

I rub a hand over my belly. "What did you want?" Luca's eyes follow the movement and soften at my action.

A knock on the door interrupts us, and one of the guards pokes his head inside. "Sir, Mr. Grant is arriving shortly."

"About fucking time," he snipes back, causing me to take a deep breath for whatever is about to come.

TEN

SHAW

I gnoring Luca's call was probably not the best move, but the man is an energy and mood drainer.

However, as I turn into my new driveway and see four blackened SUVs parked outside my ostentatious new home, I'm thinking I made a big mistake in not picking up the phone.

My stomach rolls. *Did something happen to Emi and the baby? Shit, I should have answered.*

I park the car and practically fall over myself getting out the door. I ignore the guy standing on my doorstep with two fucking guns strapped to his chest and stride inside, my blood rushing with panic. "Emi." My voice echoes in the large foyer.

"In here." Her soft voice comes from the dining room, not sounding the least bit hurt.

When I open the door and my eyes land on hers, I finally relax. "Are you okay?" I take her face in the palm of my hand while I scan over her body, looking for any sign of injury, fixing my hand on her stomach as I scan over her again just to be sure. I mean, she said I could touch the baby any time.

A throat clears, and my eyes dart toward Luca sitting in the chair at the head of the table like he owns the place. Annoyance rumbles inside me when I remind myself he does own the place. Maxim stands off to the side like he's there for the show, and even that thought humors me enough to crack a condescending smile.

"You're making me waste time, Shaw." Luca's eyes drill into mine. "My time is valuable."

I stare back at him, refusing to back down from his clear act of trying to intimidate me.

"How so?"

"I called. When I call, you fucking answer."

Anger flows from him, the vein on his temple pulsates, and I wonder what got him so agitated. "What do you want to talk about? I was at work, I'm busy too." I can't help but have a small dig back.

His lip tips up at the side, and I'm unsure if it's in genuine amusement or condescending.

"Emi, leave." He doesn't so much as glance at Emi, and that thought alone pisses me off.

"Can you not speak to her like a dog? Just ask her to leave us alone, politely. Preferably with please tacked on to the end."

I catch sight of Maxim biting into his lip to stifle a grin while Luca glares daggers at me before jolting slightly. If I'd blinked, I'd have missed it. Luca's eyes move to Emi's. "Very well. Emi, would you leave us alone?" Emi moves away from me. "Please," he adds on with a smile, making

Emi appear more nervous than before, and I can't help but wonder what the fuck is going on. Emi nods and scurries out of the room.

"Sit."

I'm about to tell him I don't need a chair, but two of his men walk into the room, and I take a seat because there's no doubt in my mind they'd force me to use one.

Luca leans forward, steepling his fingers in front of him. His voice is low and controlled, then it darkens. "When I call, you answer."

I give him a sharp nod because, to be honest, I've had enough of today already. I've had to deal with shit at work, along with my dickhead best friends all afternoon, so the last thing I want to do is come home and have to deal with an even bigger one here.

"I don't appreciate you leaving my sister at home the day after your wedding. That's not very husbandlike." I stare back at him, unsure of how he wants me to respond, because he doesn't want to hear how I'd much rather partake in husband duties and fuck my wife six ways to next Sunday. Thankfully, he saves me from having to say anything at all.

"I need your company's assistance with a matter."

And there it is. The real reason he's here. My chest tightens with dread and my jaw locks in anger. I had a bad feeling about this whole setup, and he's confirming my suspicions.

"I need to borrow some of your security."

My eyebrows shoot up because that's not what I was expecting him to say. As my temper simmers down, and before I can think straight once again, I'm able to get words out without wanting to berate him completely. "We don't deal with illegal activities, Luca. I want your business and mine staying separate." I speak the words low but firmly, no matter how much I want to scream them out.

"Your business is my business." His scrutinizing eyes don't leave my face.

My shoulders bunch tight. Refusing to back down, refusing to allow him access to my business. Our business. "Wrong. Emi might be your sister, but that is where our connection ends."

He slams his fist on the table, making me push back in shock at his outburst. "You ruined my little sister, and you think that you can get away with it?" He points his finger at me, spit flying from his mouth with venom in his tone. "You will help me and pay the price for disrespecting my family, Shaw!"

My jaw locks and I take deep breaths, trying to control myself, not wanting to escalate matters further. "I paid the price. More than the money it cost you too." I grit my teeth on every word, resentment pouring from me.

He sits forward, and he looks like he's about ready to slaughter me; his eyes hold a wild fury to them. The atmosphere is so tense between us that Maxim flinches and steps forward, but Luca holds his hand up to stop him in his tracks.

"You think you're better than us? Deserve better than Emi, is that it?"

I slink back in my chair. "Quite the opposite. I know she deserves better than me"—I glare back at him—"and better than you, for that matter."

This seems to appease him, because the deranged look

he was wielding only seconds ago has lifted from his calculated face.

"We can agree on that." Luca clears his throat, and his shoulders relax slightly. "I need your security team to act as decoys for me." He appeases me with the small detail, but something tells me that's as much as I will get from him.

I search his face. "Then what, Luca? There's got to be more to it than that."

He chuckles. "There is, but like you said, you don't want to get involved with illegal activities."

"So what you're saying is, you don't want them to do anything apart from becoming decoys for you?"

"What I'm saying is, I'm unwilling to discuss it further with you."

This man is enough to drive anyone to insanity. How the fuck can I agree on something without knowing the facts?

"I'll discuss it with Owen. He's in charge of security, is that right?" Of course Luca knows Owen is head of security. There's no doubt in my mind the man knows everything about me and my company.

"And then we're square. After this, if Owen agrees, we're square. Right?" I stare at him with hope in my voice.

He brushes a finger over his bottom lip. "Mm. We're family now, Shaw. We'll never be square." *Fucking asshole, exactly what I thought. I'll be forever indebted to him.* He smirks at me as though hearing my every thought, and I hate him all the more for it.

Luca leans back in his chair. "In one month, we will hold a party to celebrate your nuptials. You will be there, and you will very much be in love with my sister."

I raise an eyebrow at his statement.

Luca elaborates further but not before grinding his jaw from side to side. "We had to tell people you were madly in love. Therefore, you were willing to risk it all to be together. I, of course, was the accepting older brother and stood by my sister in her choices."

I scoff. "Right. Her choices."

"Exactly that." He taps his finger on the table, then rises from his chair, straightening his suit jacket in the process.

He turns to walk away, then stops in his tracks, as though remembering something, and I lift my head in curiosity, only to find him pointing a gun with a silencer attached to the end. I feel the sharp pain before I can register what he did. My left hand draws up to meet the searing agony of my damp shoulder. "That's for disrespecting me in my own home."

"Motherfucker!" I bellow as he slams the door shut behind him.

I hate Luca Varros.

But I hate Emilia more.

ELEVEN

EMI

I pace the room back and forth, listening out for anything untoward. Luca was angsty tonight, and when Shaw disrespected him, I wanted to throw myself in front of him and beg Luca not to make him pay.

I made quick work of changing out of my summer dress and throwing on a bathrobe for comfort.

The bedroom door flies open with a bang, and my eyes draw in Shaw and his blood-stained shirt. I flinch at the realization that Luca shot him.

Before Shaw can close the door, I'm across the room and trying to inspect his wound. "Oh my god, Shaw. I'm so sorry, Luca was a little angsty tonight."

Shaw shrugs me off and pushes past me, storming to the bathroom. "Fucking angsty? The man is a fucking psychopath!" I follow him into the bathroom and try to ignore his pissed-off attitude, reminding myself he's not from our world.

I lean against the door frame, trying to stop myself from reaching out to help.

He rips his shirt off with a fierce growl. His toned body is dripping blood, and I can't help but feel the pulsating between my thighs at the sight of the perfect v leading into his pants.

Since having sex, it's all I've been craving.

"You disrespected him, Shaw. You need to learn to rein it in, for both our sakes."

His narrowed eyes lock with mine in the mirror as he holds a hand towel to his shoulder. "Rein it fucking in?" he grits out and then follows it up with a hiss. "Your brother shot me for having an opinion, Emi. With a fucking gun!" He booms, making the muscles in his neck protrude.

I roll my eyes, used to men screaming and shouting to get their point across.

"Don't roll your goddamn eyes at me, Emi."

"You're being an ass," I bite back, then clamp my lips shut, knowing I overstepped.

His jaw tics and his face darkens. His blue eyes are focused on me, making me swallow at his scrutinizing stare. "Call me an ass one more fucking time and see what happens," he grits back, edging for a fight.

My pulse quickens and my heart races. I bite my lip, torn between making matters worse and wanting to calm him down. Yet I find myself willing to push the boundaries further to find out what he could do to me. The tension is thick between us, his bullet wound forgotten. He glares at me daringly.

I stare straight back at him and raise my chin. "You're an ass."

Fire flares in his eyes as he snaps out of our stare-off and lunges toward me, making me back into the bedroom.

Shaw spins me around, and before I know what is happening, he has my wrists behind my back and the belt from my robe bound around them.

"Sh-Shaw?"

"Shut the fuck up and take your goddamn punishment." I struggle to contemplate what's happening as he pushes me over the bed with my face pushed into the mattress and my ass up in the air.

"Have you any fucking idea how hard it is to sit there and not have a damn opinion where your brother is concerned, Emi?" I want to scoff and ask him if he's joking.

"Have you?"

I don't reply. Like the good Mafia princess, I don't respond.

Out of the corner of my eye, I watch him snag my hairbrush from the dresser. Cold air hits my ass cheeks when he raises my robe, making me tense with uncertainty.

His hand rips through the air and a sharp, hard smack hits my ass, causing me to wince and bite into my bottom lip. I whimper into the mattress from the sting left behind by the hairbrush.

"Then I have to put up with your shit when all I want is silence."

Smack.

The pain sears into my flesh.

Smack.

But this time, I surprise myself when I whimper into the sheets, the sound no longer coming from a place of discomfort. It comes from somewhere else; it comes from arousal at his dominance.

"Some fucking understanding."

My heart seizes in my chest at his words, and I make a mental note to be there for him. Be the wife he needs me to be.

Smack.

My lips part and I moan against the sheets as my clit throbs on each punishing smack, my ass now burning with heat.

After another brutal smack, he stops, and I turn my head at an awkward angle to see his chest heaving. His eyes are locked onto my ass, completely transfixed.

"Fuck. Why the hell does this turn me on so damn much?" he mumbles as though shocked, then drops the brush to the floor.

I can't help the word as it tumbles from my mouth on a plea. "Please."

His gaze flicks to mine, and I swear he can see the longing behind my eyes.

"Jesus," he groans and moves forward, placing his large palms on the globes of my reddened ass. I hiss when he massages the burning heat of my cheeks, but I groan into the sheets when his hands become rougher and his hips jerk against me, letting me feel how hard he is. *God, how I wish he was naked right now.* "Shaw, please."

Shaw jolts, seemingly with a realization, and takes a step back. He removes his hands from my ass and shoots me a smug smirk before trailing a finger down the crack of my ass, then he dips his finger into my dripping pussy.

"Fuck, you're soaked. You like being punished, don't you?" He shoves two fingers inside me. "Fucking take it.

My innocent Mafia princess can be a needy slut for me, can't you?" I moan at his words. He pulls them out and then plunges them inside again harder. "Fuck. That's it, drip on my fingers, dirty little slut." His words are my undoing, the filthy way he talks making me clench in anticipation.

A low whimper escapes my throat when he withdraws them altogether. His belt clangs, and he fumbles with his pants and boxers. His hard angry cock stands tall, dripping at the end. I long to touch it, taste it, and trail my tongue over the ridge of his swollen vein protruding alongside it.

"You want my cock, don't you?" I nod into the sheets.

"Beg me to fill you." He jerks his cock roughly. "Fucking beg, Emi," he chokes out with desperation.

"Please. Please, I want your cock."

His lust-filled eyes lock onto mine, and a menacing smile takes over his face. "Not a fucking chance."

He scoops the hairbrush up by the head and pushes the handle inside me, making me jolt and my body tighten at the intrusion. "Fuck yourself on the brush, Emi. That's the only fucking thing you're getting." He bends over me to whisper in my ear, gripping my hair, causing a sharp pinch to my scalp. "Fuck yourself on it. Show me how much you want my cock."

I'm so desperate to come, so needy, I'd do anything right now. Groaning, I push back against the brush.

"That's it. Take it in your tight cunt." His voice is choked and full of need. My pussy clenches around the handle, and my eyes flutter closed as I try and imagine fucking him. The feel of him inside me, only him.

His heavy cock is grinding against my ass as I push

back and forth against him, encouraging the handle deeper inside me.

"So fucking innocent and all mine to corrupt." He moans at me as pleasure shoots through my body, my orgasm about to hit.

"Oh. Oh god." I tighten. "I'm—" He withdraws the brush, stopping my orgasm before it reaches. My eyes shoot open to see him staring down at me, standing above me fisting his cock aggressively. Sweat and blood dripping down his body, he bites into his bottom lip, his hooded eyes fixed on my ass.

I've never seen a man look so psychotically gorgeous as he does in this moment. He comes undone and ropes of hot cum splash my ass and back, making me whimper at the loss of my orgasm.

He's punishing me by not allowing me to come.

And I want to throat-punch him for it.

SHAW

My cum lands on her perfect reddened globes, and the feeling of euphoria is incredible. The need to control her is something I've never experienced before. Maybe it's because I have such little control in the situation I find myself in, so this allows me to assert my power in some way.

Over her.

Whatever the reason, I can admit to myself that Emi is an addiction. She has the ability to leave me craving more, even after I've had the high.

My vision blurs and I'm lightheaded.

"Shaw? Shaw, are you okay?" *I don't feel okay.* I want to tell her but stumble as I try to stay focused. My head swirls and my body feels light. "Maybe you should sit down. I think you need a doctor." I can hear her move around me when my ass touches the bed, but then as I float away, I feel nothing.

All I see are her black orbs as I drift into a deep sleep.

All I see is her.

My eyes flutter open, and I'm unsure where I am. I groan when I try to move, a shooting pain searing through my shoulder. "Jesus. Fuck." My hand goes toward it as I sit up and take in the room.

Light seeps through the blinds, making me realize it's a new day. I wince when thoughts of the previous day run through my mind: Luca and the gunshot. I touch my bandage before wondering how the hell it became bandaged. "You passed out, so I called the on-site doctor." My eyes snap toward my wife's, and I suck in a sharp breath as I take her in. She's lying beside me with her head on the pillow, watching me with such tenderness it makes my heart race. Her plump lips make my cock jerk, and I groan with the need to feel them wrapped around my shaft once again.

She nibbles on her lip as though reading my mind, so I shake the thoughts from my head and go over what she said. She had the doctor check me over.

"You have an on-site doctor?"

Emi rolls her eyes. "Of course I do. Especially after you suggested I have issues with food." She looks at me with raised eyebrows as though chastising me, but then her lips tip up into the most beautiful smile that causes the air to be stolen from my lungs.

"The doctor took the bullet out and treated the wound. You should be fine soon enough."

She talks as though I wasn't just shot by a madman, as though I hadn't nearly died from blood loss.

But when she flinches, any thought of the pain in my

shoulder is replaced with concern for her. "What's wrong?"

Her hand moves below the sheet. "Nothing, the baby kicked. Little bump is always active first thing in the morning, it makes me need to pee," she grumbles as she throws the sheet off herself and climbs out of bed. The flimsy camisole top and lacy thong make my cock stand to attention, but it's her bump that gets me really hard. *I put that there.* A feeling of possession takes over me. No matter what, I'll always share this connection with Emi, and I sure as hell never want it to leave. I want all of her. To possess her like she possesses me. The toilet flushes, and the tap switches on and off, then the bathroom door opens and her eyes find mine. She stands still in the doorway as though unsure of what to do next.

I take control of that situation too. "Come here, Red. Let me wish you and our little one good morning." I tilt my head toward the bed, so she clambers on, looking so small and lost on top of the huge bed that it makes me chuckle.

She chews on her bottom lip and her cheeks pinken, and the part of myself that loves her innocence wishes I could keep her like this forever. But the bigger part of me —the part that craves her—wants to corrupt her and mold her into everything I never knew I wanted.

"Show me my baby, Emi."

She swallows and her neck flushes as she lifts the bottom of her camisole, exposing her neat, round little bump. My heart skips a beat at the beauty of it, our baby growing inside there. Something I never contemplated having, but since the moment I found out about the baby,

I've been all in. The fact that the mother of my child is Emi is a bonus on top of a beautiful gift.

I bend forward, ignoring the sting of pain when I lower my head but keep eye contact with my girl as I place a gentle kiss on the swell of her stomach.

My balls tighten, reminding me of the overwhelming need to come. Another kiss leaves my lips as I caress her bump, and when I feel movement beneath my hand, my eyes widen in shock. "Hey, little one, can you hear me in there?" I whisper against her stomach. The ripple against my palm makes me emotional at how utterly amazing Emi's body is for carrying our little one.

I pull away slightly but leave my palm on her stomach, and instead, I rest my head on her lap. Emi's fingers find my hair and, in a soothing way I've never felt before, her fingers work through my strands almost lovingly.

All the tension and stress fades away with my wife and baby by my side. The comfort it brings is like a blanket of security I never want to leave.

"I want you to do this every day." My voice has a guttural edge to it. "I want you to show me the baby every day and let me be a part of this."

Emi's fingers tighten in my hair. "I want that too." Her voice is clogged with emotion, and I want nothing more than to take away any unease she feels, so I sit up and take her chin in the palm of my hand.

"Tell me what you need, Emi." I expect her to tell me she needs me by her side, or she needs me to find peace with her brother.

"I need you to kiss me," she pants out the words as my eyes search hers, full of vulnerability, which I hate. She needs to be reassured and confident in our relationship, no matter how forced upon us it may be.

My lips find hers tenderly. I push my tongue through her parted lips, groaning when her tongue mixes with mine. My fingers tangle in her hair as I hold her in place with one hand and my other palm resting on our baby. Our kiss deepens, our tongues becoming thirstier for one another, thrashing about in search of the same crazy high. My cock twitches hungrily but this kiss is every . . . fucking . . . thing and far more important.

She whimpers against me, the sensation so consuming it's like no other kisses ever existed. Like this one kiss is everything. I pull back, panting, to stare into her darkened orbs. Our chests heave in sync.

I stroke my thumb over her swollen lip.

A thought occurs to me, causing my heart to soar and my cock to swell. "Was I your first kiss, Emi?"

She pulls back and her eyes search my face.

She shakes her head, and I narrow my eyes in confusion. "N-n-n-no."

It's like a dagger to my heart. She might as well have shot me with her brother's fucking gun; she couldn't have hurt me any more than she has right now.

The hurt is soon replaced with anger. I drop my hand from her stomach and tug off the sheets with a grunt.

"Sh-Shaw? Are you okay?"

I spin on my heel and glare at her. *Is she fucking serious?* Of course I'm not okay. I shake away the hurt on her face and tug on the clothes left out on the armchair: a loose t-shirt and joggers. Then I swing open the walk-in closet doors and find all my belongings inside.

Anger boils inside me. *When the hell did these arrive?*

And who the hell packed them up and put them here in the first place? How did they get access to my apartment?

"Where the fuck did my clothes come from, Emi?" I bark back toward the bedroom as I move around the room to find my sneakers.

"Luca sent them over." I hear her move off the bed but ignore her presence.

How dare he? How dare he control every aspect of my life?

"Of course he fucking sent them over. Controlling bastard," I grumble as I step into each sneaker.

"Do you need help with anything?" I can feel her presence in the doorway but again choose to ignore her, unwilling to discuss the feeling bubbling inside me right now.

"I'm not a fucking invalid! Just because your deranged brother took a cheap shot at me does not make me weak, Emi," I snipe the words in her direction as I tug on a hoodie, fighting the urge to wince in pain as I do.

"I don't think you're weak, Shaw."

I scoff and shake my head, refusing to acknowledge her, and push past her and make my way downstairs into the obscene foyer. My eyes wildly search around for my car keys.

"Sir, may I help you with anything?" An older man in a butler suit approaches me, making my eyes bug out at how absurd this is.

"Who the fuck are you?"

He disregards my ignorance. "Henry, sir. Would you like assistance with anything?"

This is meant to be my home, yet I'm the stranger in it, and I hate it. I want my life back.

I choke on annoyance and grind my teeth. "I want my fucking car keys."

"Would sir like a driver to take him somewhere?"

I roll back on my feet in shock. *Is this motherfucker deaf?* "I said I want my fucking car keys," I grind out, my voice deadly.

The butler doesn't bat an eye at my appalling attitude. His mouth moves, but it's not his voice I hear.

"Your keys are on the dresser, Shaw." My eyes snap up toward Emi standing at the top of the stairs covered in a robe, and she points toward the glass dresser near the entrance.

I nod and ignore her look of hurt as I scoop up my keys and storm through the door, slamming it for effect on the way out.

I hate them all right now.

TWELVE

SHAW

"So, let me get this straight. You're pissed that your wife has kissed another man, before you got married?" Mase asks, tipping his beer bottle in my direction. His voice is laced with disdain.

I grunt out a "Yes" and take another swig of my beer, ignoring his disgusted tone.

When I left the house, I called my STORM buddies to come to my rescue. We're now at Tate's apartment going over my drama. The guys are amused as hell at my outburst, which just pisses me off even more.

"Jesus. Fuck, you have it bad." My eyes dart toward Tate in question. "It's a fucking kiss, man. Before she married you. Jesus, Mase has to put up with his wife fucking another man." He shrugs nonchalantly like the bastard he is, taking no regard for anyone else's feelings, but I noticed the flinch Mase gave when Tate called out his wife's indiscretions.

"Leave fucking Tara out of this, you dumb shit." Owen kicks Tate's feet off the coffee table.

Tate's lips tighten on a wince as he opens his mouth. "Sorry, man."

Mase brushes a hand through his hair. "All good. She fucked up. Takes some getting over."

"Or under," Reed dryly adds.

"You guys doing okay?" I ask, knowing I'm not the only one with problems. Tara might not be our number one fan, but Mase is married to her, so the least we can do is try and be supportive of his choice to stay with her.

He lifts a shoulder on a shrug and takes another swig of his beer. "Kinda."

"You guys fucking again?" Tate asks, making me want to hit him in the balls.

Mase stares at the wall. "Nope."

"Jesus. How long has it been now?" Reed gasps.

"Sixteen months, four weeks, and three days."

Tate snorts. "You keep track?"

Mase turns his head to face him. "Yeah, I do."

I shake my head, gobsmacked at my friend's dedication to his wife. When he married her just out of high school, we all told him he was a lovestruck idiot. He spent the first year blissfully happy and the next god-knows-how-many years miserable as sin. Each time he raises the idea of a divorce, Tara throws herself into the marriage once again. It's a shame Mase can't see beyond being a faithful and reliable husband to someone who clearly doesn't deserve it.

This happens when you have abandonment issues like we all do. In one way or another, we've each been dealt a shit card starting out in life, and if it wasn't for Tate's adoptive parents, none of us would have a semblance of what a normal family life could be like.

Maybe this is why I feel so attached to Emi and the baby. My worst nightmare would be for my child to grow up without a family, without the support network of what two loving parents can bring.

I clench my jaw. There's no way I'll allow that to happen to my child. No way at all.

"You should get this app." Reed tilts his phone toward Mase as Tate leans in with intrigue. "It's called Indulgence. So you basically pick the perfect woman for you, and they send her over."

I smile against my drink when Mase turns his nose up in disgust, the action making Owen throw his head back on a loud chuckle.

"Seriously, Shaw. If it was a kiss, I don't know what you're so pissed about. We all know you've done more than kiss. I'm sure she knows it too, am I right? She has to deal with your past and yet you only have to contend with a kiss," Mase says while leaning forward on his elbows.

I mull his words over and sigh, knowing I'm being unreasonable but still annoyed I'm not her first kiss. "I want all her firsts." I can't help but pout like a child.

Owen bursts out laughing. "Have you heard yourself? You snagged a Mafia princess who was untouched. I'm pretty sure you've had her firsts. It was a fucking kiss, it probably meant nothing. Do you remember all your kisses?" He raises an eyebrow at me, but I've no choice but to shake my head at such a dumb question. "There you go, then." He grins as though proud of his analogy.

"You can't change it. And let's face it, your woman is a hidden gem. How many of us get to sample untouched goods at our age unless we go for jailbait? And who the fuck wants to do that?" Owen chuckles with a shake of his head, and I don't miss the flinch from Tate and how his face pales. We were all convinced Tate had a fling with a much younger girl years ago, but he swears nothing happened between them. None of us missed the longing behind his eyes though.

I sit back and zone out their banter as I consider what my best friends have surmised for me. Maybe she was so young she kissed someone during a game or something? Or a kiss was stolen from her, maybe that was it? After all, her brother had her on such a tight lockdown I'm pretty damn sure he'd have known if she had kissed anyone.

A feeling of regret courses through me when I think back to the hurt on Emi's face as I stormed out of the house.

I jump to my feet with a new determination.

"Where are you going?" Tate asks, throwing another chip in his mouth.

"Home." I cringe as I call that monstrosity my home, but as an image of a pregnant Emi flashes before my eyes, I know that's what it is.

Because wherever she and my baby are, that's home.

EMI

I stir the sauce again, my mind wandering to Shaw and his outburst. The moment I mentioned he wasn't my first kiss, he withdrew. *Surely he can't be jealous?*

I mean, the man had a girlfriend until I came in and destroyed his relationship with my little truth bomb. If anyone has reason to be jealous, it should be me. After all, I feel like I'm competing with someone he actually loves.

"Something smells good." I startle at Shaw's appearance behind me, so far in my head I hadn't even realized he'd entered the house, let alone the room.

My hand stills on the wooden spoon, and I turn to face him. His blue eyes shimmer and his lip curls into a smile, making my knees weak. His outburst is seemingly forgotten.

"It's spaghetti carbonara."

"Sounds good. Should I set the table?" He tilts his head toward the small breakfast table overlooking the grounds, but his eyes never leave mine. *God, he's gorgeous.* Heat travels up my neck as I stand here swooning over my husband.

The intensity of his stare makes me squirm as my panties grow moist, and I clear my throat before swallowing hard. "That would be great, thank you." He smirks back at me, as if knowing my thoughts before turning and opening numerous cupboards, no doubt in search of tableware. I lean back against the counter with a smile on my face when he huffs and puffs in frustration.

"You're not going to help me, are you?" He lifts his head over a cupboard door.

"Nope. I think you got this." I grin back at him and turn to stir the sauce.

His loud grumblings about the kitchen being too big and not being able to find a damn thing because of all the "useless appliances that jackass bought" makes me bite my lip to stifle a giggle.

"You cook really well, Emi. I'm impressed." He dabs the napkin on the side of his mouth after clearing his plate. "That might just be my favorite meal. You did good, Red."

I blush at his praise. A hint of pride travels through me at his words.

"Who taught you to cook?"

I shrug. "The chefs, the nannies, housekeepers."

"Not some Italian grandmother, then?" He smiles back at me, no doubt hearing about the Italian heritage of the women passing down their skills in the kitchen.

"No. Just the staff." I move the last of my spaghetti around my plate. My mood is a little solemn at the lack of family relationships I have. Even when my sister was alive, we didn't have much of a relationship. It's something I've longed for. Another reason I could never regret this baby. I get to love something, and they'll love me back. Unconditionally.

I spent most of my life living at my Papi's house while Eleanor went to boarding school and stayed with Luca when she was home. It was like we were two families.

"I never had much of a family either." My eyes snap up to meet Shaw's, and his admission makes my heart thump in my chest. So loud I wonder if he can hear it.

His eyebrows furrow a little as though deep in thought. "My mother left when I was a child, she suffered from bipolar. She used to have emotional outbursts, and my father didn't know how to deal with her, so he dumped me in boarding school and my mother in a mental health facility."

I reach for his hand across the table, desperate to touch him, reassure him. "I'm sorry, Shaw. That's awful."

He swallows with emotion. "She committed suicide when I was seven." I try to hide the gasp slipping my lips, but Shaw recognizes it and strokes his thumb over mine, reassuring me when it should be the other way around.

"How old were you, when you went to boarding school?"

"Five."

I practically whimper thinking about a little Shaw being abandoned in school.

"I met Reed there. He was two years older than me, but he looked out for me. Even though he doesn't show much emotion, the guy was a rock for me."

My heart hurts for Shaw, and Reed too. To be so young

and forgotten about. There's no way I'd put my child in a boarding school. My hand finds my stomach protectively.

"I agree." Shaw stares at me intensely.

I hadn't realized I'd said the words out loud.

"You're lucky to have friends like them, Shaw." I glance away as emotion creeps in, a part of me pleased for him and a tiny part jealous at their relationship. I have no one.

"I know." His hand turns over in mine, and when he laces our fingers together, I feel like my chest is being crushed with love. Which is just ridiculous.

Do I really crave affection so badly that this simple gesture is making me look into things that are not there? Shaw is here for the baby, and I need to remember that.

"Emi, about earlier." His voice is soft and coaxing, and I open my eyes, not even aware I'd closed them.

"I was wrong to be mad at you. I'm sorry."

I suck in a sharp breath of air, because his eyes speak a thousand truths, and I could swim in the depths of his deep-blue eyes.

"It's okay," I force past the lump in my throat.

Shaw shakes his head. "It's not, baby. I . . . I seem to get pretty fucking jealous about you." He exhales heavily and drags his hand through his hair. "I've never been like that before, and I don't know how to control it."

That gets my attention as hope floods my veins, especially considering he's in love with his ex. "Never?"

He stares down at our joined hands. "Never." His gaze comes back up to meet mine. "Who was he?"

My heart thumps as I contemplate answering him, knowing the damage it could cause. I bite my lip. But I decide to be truthful with him. Knowing how open he's being with me, he deserves the same treatment.

"He was one of the soldiers."

Shaw nods. His jaw tics. "Did you do anything else?" He grinds his teeth.

I shake my head. "No. I swear we didn't."

"So he never touched you, I mean?"

He wouldn't have dared. As much as I craved him, we knew we couldn't cross that line. "No."

"So I'm the only man to have my fingers in your pussy?" He licks his bottom lip, and I swear I can feel it between my legs as my clit throbs. The heat from his gaze burns holes through me, making my heart hammer against my chest with need.

My breathing escalates and flush travels up my neck. "You are," I reply breathlessly, the air between us crackling.

"Good girl." His lip tips up at the side. "Go upstairs, Emi. I want you naked on our bed on all fours. I'll put the dishes away and join you in a few minutes. I'm going to fuck every thought of that piece of shit out of your head. Do you understand me?"

His dominating words make me clench my thighs together.

I can barely whimper a reply. "Yes."

"Good girl."

I push back from my seat, his words replaying in my mind.

If only he knew every thought is consumed with him, and I'm pretty sure my heart is too.

THIRTEEN

SHAW

I open the bedroom door and the sight before me is almost enough to bring me to my knees. My girl, my innocent Mafia princess, my wife, is completely bare and exposed to me.

She faces the headboard with her ass on full display. That perfect little virgin asshole staring at me for the taking.

I unbutton my shirt and kick off my shoes and socks. I tell myself to slow down, but I can't help the rush of excitement pumping through my veins and flowing to my cock, causing it to leak as I push down my pants and boxers.

I grip my cock, giving it a few quick pumps to offer myself relief, but it's no use, not when my girl waits for me, practically begging to be filled.

Moving behind her, she flinches when my fingers drag through her pussy and over her sensitive nub. "You're ready for me already, Red." It's not a question, more of a statement due to her neediness.

"Yes," she breathes out.

I pump two fingers inside her, making her hands ball into fists. Her juices saturate my hand, and I revel in it. I did that, I made her so wet that her cunt drips with need.

"Fuck, Emi. You turn me feral. I've never wanted to control someone so damn much." I can't help but pump into her harder, earning a little gasp from her lips. "I want to fuck you so rough, but I don't want to hurt you. I don't want to hurt the baby," I admit.

"I want you to fuck me rough. I want to experience that too." Her voice is breathy and full of need, but her words make me still my movements. "You won't hurt the baby, I promise."

Emi turns her head to the side, and our gazes collide. My chest heaves with anticipation. *Does she mean that? Does she even realize what that would mean?*

"That's what I want, Shaw. I want to feel you when I walk. I want you to command me and give me everything that you need. I want to be your everything." My nostrils flare with possession at her words because I'm pretty damn sure she's already my everything.

My cock drips pre-cum, excited by her words.

I've always enjoyed sex, but I've always held back. Worried I might go too far and scare a partner, or worse, hurt them.

And what if I hurt her or the baby?

"The baby?" I mumble.

"You can't hurt the baby, Shaw. I promise."

"You'll tell me if I hurt you?"

"Of course."

I trail a finger down her spine, loving the shiver that takes over her body from my simple touch.

My palms caress her ass cheeks, still red from the spanking. Again, something else I hadn't done before Emi. My hand twitches as I raise it and smack her ass, making her jolt with the force.

"Your lips are mine, Emi." I raise my hand and spank her hard. "Mine."

I repeat the action again. "Yours," she pants, making my balls draw up with need.

I grip her hips and tug her body down the bed so her pussy hole is level with my cock. Then I lean over her back, take hold of her hair, and wrap it around my fist, tugging her head back as I thrust inside her with brutal force.

"Oh god," she screams as her spine arches into my chest. "More." *Fuck.* I clench my jaw as my balls attempt to draw up.

I smack her ass again. "That's it, baby, beg me." *Smack.* "You only beg for me." *Smack.*

I ride her hard, slamming inside her without restraint. One hand holds her hip while the other pulls ruthlessly on her hair.

"Please, Shaw. Harder." *Slam.*

"Such a good girl. Taking my cock how I want." *Slam.* "Getting fucked hard by your man." *Slam.* "Such a tight little pussy for me to fuck." *Slam* "To fill with my cum." *Slam.* "Putting a baby inside you." Her pussy clenches, and I can't hold it in any longer. "That's it, take my cum. Milk me, Red." *Slam.*

She screams with need as my cock pulsates deep inside her, my hips still thrusting, determined to fill her to the hilt.

Her arms give way, making her chest fall onto the mattress, but I still have a hold of her hip so I keep her bump from hitting the bed too.

My footing wavers with the force of my orgasm, but I grip her tighter to steady myself, my head falling back as my eyes flutter closed. "Fuck. So good."

When I pull my cock from her swollen pussy, my cum leaks out of her. The thought annoys me, so I drag my fingers through it and push it back inside her hole. I gently release her hip, and a feeling of pride racks through me when I see the handprint on her hip. My hand.

Emi pants and rolls onto her back, closing her legs in the process. I grind my teeth in annoyance.

"Emi. Open your fucking legs and let me see my cum."

Her head darts up from the mattress, her dark eyes meeting mine. If her face wasn't already red, I'm sure it would be now. I nod at her encouragingly. She opens her legs, allowing me to see the cum trailing down her pussy and around her ass. *Fuck, that's hot.* I lick my lips as I gaze over her bare pussy, our baby bump, her heavy tits, and finally up to her beautiful face.

EMI

Shaw moves from the bed, and I'm intrigued as he maneuvers the freestanding mirror toward the edge of the bed.

His cock is still hard, and the look in his eyes when he turns around tells me he isn't finished with me yet.

He moves the pillows, climbs on the bed beside me, and rests his back against them.

"Come and rest on my chest, baby." I practically melt at his gentle voice. I don't know which one turns me on more, his deep dominant voice or his gentle caring one. Each is a caress to my heart and my pussy.

I do as he asks and climb over his leg, sitting my ass down so his hardened cock is flush against my back. My head rests beneath his chin, and when he wraps his arms around me to place his palms on our baby, I feel like my heart will combust with a love I can't possibly be feeling.

"Do you want to find out the sex?" He breathes into my ear.

I bite my lip. "Do you?"

"I asked first, Red." He smiles against me.

"The men decide that, Shaw." I almost flinch at my monotone words.

Shaw chuckles behind me. "Of course they do." I can practically see his eyes rolling when he says that. "But what do you want?"

My breath stutters. Never have I been asked what I want. In my world, it doesn't matter what the woman wants. What we should want is to please our man, and what they say goes, our opinions be damned.

"I'd love a surprise." I hold my breath and wait for him to decide the outcome.

"Then that's what we'll do. We'll wait. Gotta keep Mommy happy. Haven't we, little one?" He strokes over my tummy and all restraint melts away, his loving touch meaning everything and so, so much more. More than I ever dreamed was possible.

"Now, open your legs nice and wide."

I do as he says without question. So willingly it's borderline pathetic how he can control me with such simple commands.

Shaw's hand trails down to my pussy while his other hand moves upward to my tit, palming it in his large grip, squeezing and tweaking my nipple to the point of pain. But the pain eases and gives way to pleasure when he strokes over my clit. Moving his fingers in circles, I lift my hips toward them as encouragement. My pulse races and soft mewls leave my lips.

"That's it, good girl," he coos on a heavy breath. He whispers through my hair, "I like my sticky cum dripping out of your pussy, Emi. Leaking everywhere. It tells me what a good girl you've been, letting me fuck a baby into you."

I gasp wantonly with need. My head drops back on his chest. His words make my clit throb with desperation and my pussy muscles clench, eager for him to fill me.

"Please, Shaw."

"Mm, you're greedy for my cock, aren't you, baby? Your first cock and now you need it all the time." He swoops his head down and tugs on the skin on my neck, sucking it hard between his teeth. "Fuck, I'm obsessed with you." He chuckles almost in disbelief, then he rams two fingers inside me, making me arch my back.

His cock is sticky and hard behind me, and I want to beg him to fill me, but when he removes his fingers, my body sags in disappointment.

He trails them down my pussy to my ass. "My cum has leaked all down here, baby, can you see?" He nods toward the mirror, and I gasp at forgetting it was there, so consumed with the sexual tension growing between us.

I take in my splayed legs, my pussy dripping his cum, his fingers stroking over me, and his hand playing with my breast. My stomach bulge is obvious, my hair is a sweaty mess, my cheeks are flushed, and my chest heaves. I look needy, even to my own eyes.

Shaw's firm shoulders look strained, as though he's fighting to keep control. His sharp jaw is angled toward me, but his eyes flit down at my pussy and back up at the mirror, then settle back on my face before dropping a tender kiss on top of my head.

His fingers circle my asshole, and I clench with apprehension. "It's okay, Red. Let me stretch your ass for my cock."

I suck in a deep breath at his words, and my fingernails dig into his thighs, causing Shaw to chuckle lowly at my response. "I'll do my best to make you feel good, I promise." He nips at my ear.

Shaw's fingers are drenched in his cum, and he uses it as lube as he slowly presses one finger into my tight muscle. "Play with your clit while I finger-fuck your ass, Red."

My hand moves down toward my clit, hoping to take the edge off his finger easing in and out of my ass. As soon as my body relaxes at my touch, I watch through the mirror as he adds another finger, stretching my ass. My heels dig into the mattress, and our eyes connect in the mirror. "So hot, Emi. So fucking hot, baby." His chest heaves as he peppers kisses down the column of my neck, nipping occasionally before working back up.

"Oh god. It's good, Shaw. So good."

"Mm. So fucking good. Rub your clit hard. Really fucking hard while I fuck your ass," he grits the words out, making my hand move frantically. Shaw's fingers work inside me, a combination of pumping and scissoring while I press harder against my clit. "Fuck, that's it. Faster, baby." He pushes up into me, his hard cock wet on my spine making me moan in desperation.

"Tell me you want my cock in your ass, Emi." He pumps harder and groans with a rise of his hips. "Tell me you want me to fill it with cum."

My head falls back onto his chest, no longer looking through the mirror but staring directly up at him. "Please, fill me, Shaw."

As soon as the words leave my lips, Shaw pushes me

up, forcing me to drop onto my hands and knees. He kneels behind me. "Keep fucking your hand, otherwise this will hurt more." His eyes hold mine hostage in the mirror, wild and eager with an edge of dark behind them. His sharp jaw is clenched, tight, showing all restraint has been banished. My pussy drips with the intensity of his stare.

I rub frantic circles over my stimulated clit. "Slap your pussy, Emi. I want to hear you get off while you slap yourself before I fill your ass."

I do as he commands, hitting my pussy hard. "Oh god." I do it again. Something, before now, I've never considered doing.

"Fuck. That's it, Red. Slap your little clit for me."

I press down harder this time on impact, and my whole body shakes and my mouth falls open.

"Fuck," he grunts as the head of his thick cock pushes past my tight barrier and my body tenses. The burning behind the action makes me hit myself again.

Shaw grips my hip tighter. "That's it. Fucking take my cock in your virgin ass." He pushes farther inside, his words dark and gritty. "Let me break this ass in like I did my girl's pussy."

His filthy words cause me to moan.

"My little Mafia princess taking her first cock in her ass." He pushes harder, forcing my mouth to fall open. I drop my head, unable to take the overloading sensations.

Shaw wraps his hand in my hair before tugging my head back and forcing our eyes to clash in the mirror. "Fucking watch me fuck you." His eyes bore into mine. "Watch your ass take all of me." His frenzied gaze locks on to mine. He looks completely consumed by me, and the thought fills me with encouragement. I push back into him, causing his lips to part on a groan.

I allow him to fuck me hard, to use my ass how he pleases because I relish in making him unravel, making him crazed thinking about me belonging to him.

"Please. Fuck me hard, Shaw." His spine bolts straight before he slams his hips back and forth, his thick cock driving into my ass, making me wince. My hand works harder, faster. "Oh shit, Shaw. Shaw, I'm . . ." My orgasm hits me hard.

"Fuuuuck." *Slam.* "This is my ass." *Slam.* "Mine." *Slam.* "You're fucking mine!" he roars and swells inside me, his hard cock pumping thick cum into my ass, and I clench around him, milking him dry.

"Yours. I'm yours . . ." I'm exhausted, and I know every word I spilled is the truth.

I'll always be his.

I just hope he'll always be mine too.

FOURTEEN

SHAW

I pepper kisses down Emi's neck before tugging the sheet down to her waist. Her pregnant stomach is on display for me, and my palm finds it. Bending, I whisper, "Good morning, little one." Emi's fingers find my hair, and I smile into her bump at how much I love it. I'm pretty convinced I love them, but guilt tugs at my heartstrings, so I pull back.

I tower above her, and her face is laced in disappointment. I hate it, and annoyance takes over my good mood.

"You're ready for work already?"

I'm not used to being questioned in the morning, and I don't fucking like it. I like to suit myself. Something else I've had to quickly get used to without the option of choosing to do so, all because of Luca Varros. I grind my teeth at him entering my thoughts once again.

"Normal people have jobs, Emi. We can't all live off our

families." She flinches at my harsh words, and I hate myself instantly for it.

"You're right, Shaw. But some of us were born with choices and some of us weren't." She sits up in bed, allowing her heavy tits to hang bare and her palm to find her bump. *I wonder if the baby is kicking.*

Again, anger bubbles inside me when my cock jumps, appreciating her body exposed to mine for the taking. Even my cock doesn't listen when I'm pissed anymore. It's almost like I have no control around my little Mafia princess, and what control I do have is only domination during sex.

I stare back at her glaring eyes, hers as enraged as my own.

My cock leaks at the thought of putting her back in her place, gaining control over the situation.

I slowly unbuckle my belt and tug my shirt from my pants, then I lower the zipper, never taking my eyes from hers.

Emi stares back at me with a combination of arousal and hate. And I fucking love it because I'm about to show her what real hate is.

"Hurry the fuck up and sit on the end of the bed and suck my cock. I can't go to work with a hard cock when I'm not allowed to fuck anyone else." It's an asshole thing to say, but I can't seem to help it.

Her jaw tics, and if looks could kill, I'd be ten feet under by now, but she moves to the end of the bed, making my cock leak in delight.

I pull it from my boxers eagerly. My fist pumping it is a poor substitute now that Emi is in my life. I tighten my hold and grind my teeth at how dependent I'm becoming on her.

I thread my fingers through her hair with one hand and hold out my cock with the other. "Open." Her lips part only slightly, and I chuckle at her attitude. "Kiss it." I push her head forward to help with her decision, and when her wet tongue laps at my pre-cum, I feel like my knees are going to give way. A guttural groan escapes me from deep within, a groan of ownership and possessiveness combined.

"Fuck, Emi. Again." I push into her mouth, and she moans as my pre-cum hits her tongue. I may think I control Emilia, but she's the one that controls me. Every part of me.

My hands tremble with need, and when her tongue travels along the underside of my cock, I surge forward without preamble. Her teeth scrape along my cock, and it only adds to my unraveling. "Fuck, take my cock how I like it. Make it nice and wet, Red." I pull back when she chokes on my cock before surging forward, ignoring her whimpers. Again and again, I pump into her mouth. Our eyes hold one another's hostage as she works my cock perfectly, and my free hand trails over the softness of her cheek and tightens in her hair when my balls draw up. Fuck, I'm going to come already.

I pull out, making the decision not to let her swallow me down, deciding to punish her instead.

I tug her head back; her mouth is still open, gasping for breath, as I jack my cock over her neck. My eyes latch onto her perfect tits, and I aim my cock over them and her throat. The force of the cum exiting the tip makes me lose my footing, but I right myself and watch in rapture at the beautiful sight of my girl covered in my white cum over her heaving, flushed chest and dripping down to her tits.

I step back to admire her beauty, but Emi jumps to her feet with anger radiating from her. My princess is pissed.

"Shaw, what the fuck!" Her eyes bug out, making me chuckle.

"You were bad. Only good girls get to feed on my cum." I smirk with a shrug as I tuck my shirt back into my pants.

When I move my gaze back to hers, I swallow away the guilt at how I'm treating her. Instead, I offer a lifeline—I hold out my hand to her. Emi hesitates before her body sags, and she reluctantly gives in, slipping her soft hand into mine. I pull her toward me, my lips finding hers without thinking. I can taste my cum on her, not something I've done before. If anything, I've avoided it, but I like the thought of me inside all of her holes, full of my cum. I smile into the kiss at the thought.

She pulls back to stare into my eyes. Those black orbs of hers sparkle, and I find myself getting lost in them, not wanting to pull away when I really should be leaving. The baby kicks and my heart skips a beat, but not even that can break the pull between us right now. I feel, for the first time in my life, this is where I'm meant to be. Even with all the crazy shit she has going on with her family.

This right here is my family.

This is my home.

I bring her fingers to my lips and kiss them.

"I'll try and not be late, then we could watch a movie or something?"

Her lips tip up into a serene smile, and my heart swells with pride at knowing I put it there. I vow to make her smile like that every fucking day if this is how good it feels.

"That sounds great." I bend down and kiss her once again while bump gives another kick, making me chuckle.

Maybe I should figure something out for the three of us.

Something special.

SHAW

I throw my pen across my desk in anger. While loosening my tie, I try to massage the tension building in my forehead with my fingers.

"Look, I don't really give a fuck how we figure the advertisement out, but we need to nail it. That presentation we just saw was shit, and with Flawless being the leading company in the market for the fragrance industry, we need to not look like idiots." I sigh.

Mase sits forward on the couch. "What about the new interns? We need a fresh approach, and with the shit these kids know about social media and trends, they're the ones we should be asking. We need to utilize them."

"They don't have the fucking experience. All they have is the papers they walk in here with, that's why they're interning with us. To get the damn experience," Tate snaps, equally as frustrated at our marketing department presentation as me.

"You need to give them a shot. Some of those kids worked on some big projects," Mase counters.

"We don't have time to wheedle out possible ideas. We need fucking results." Tate sighs, then cracks his neck in frustration. The dude is beyond disappointed.

Mase turns toward Tate. "Look, let's just have a select few sit in on the next brainstorm. It's not going to hurt." He shrugs. "If we come away with nothing, so be it. But, Tate, anything is worth a shot right now. The only thing we can agree on is that presentation was shit!" He points at the door.

Tate runs a hand through his hair. "Fine."

My office door opens and in strolls Reed with his briefcase in hand. I give him a chin lift. "You good?"

He smiles from ear to ear, which is rare for the miserable bastard. I glance at Mase and Tate, both with equally shocked expressions. "I am very good." He sits down in the swivel chair Owen normally occupies, making all of us look at him like he's losing the plot. For Reed to be in such a good mood is almost unheard of.

"Fucking share, then, dick." Tate throws what was an important set of notes from the meeting, screwed up into a ball, at Reed's head.

I lean back in my chair, taking in the camaraderie.

"I just had a meeting with George Fanzio." We all sit forward in our seats because this is a big fucking deal. George Fanzio is a billionaire property mogul. "He wants me to complete a sale on a plot of land and then he's selling us the land at a reduced fee. It's perfect for an entertainment venue."

"Wait. Back the fuck up, why would he sell it us cheaper?" I stare at him with furrowed brows.

Reed's grin widens, if that is even possible. "Because he knows how ruthless I am."

"Fuck." Mase sighs dramatically, causing us all to laugh. "What the hell have you got to do?"

Reed smirks, and even I can acknowledge how sinister it looks. "He needs me to shut down a community project and clear a few houses."

"Clear a few fucking houses?" Mase grumbles through a clenched jaw. His eyebrows shoot up and his nostrils flare.

"This could be bad publicity, Reed," I argue back.

Reed holds his hand up. "I have a plan. Don't worry. We'll be the heroes, the good Samaritans." He smiles a toothy, knowing grin, reassuring us he knows exactly what the hell he's doing.

"What the fuck ever. I have a wife to get home to. Just don't rock the boat, we've created an empire here. People get angsty when you want to touch their properties."

I push back in my chair but don't miss the furrow of his eyebrows. "It isn't their property to begin with, they pay rent."

Mase snorts. "And that is the exact reason why we should be worried." He points at Reed, whose face is contorted in confusion.

"How's the wife going, anyway?" Tate wiggles his eyebrows as I tidy around my desk. "Is it true what they say, happy wife, happy life?"

I choke on a sardonic laugh. "She's great."

"Great?" Reed responds, wide-eyed in disbelief.

And it's true, she is great. If it wasn't for her brother, things would be better than great.

When I lift my head from the stack of paperwork for tomorrow, I'm greeted by all three of my friends staring at me. "What?"

Mase shrugs. "You seem . . . happy."

"I heard that pregnant women are horny all the time. Is that true?" Tate throws in, breaking the very moment I was going to tell them I am happy.

My temper rockets and the veins protrude in my head. *Is he for fucking real?* "I'm not discussing our sex life with you!"

"Never stopped you from discussing Lizzie." His cocky smile widens, and he wiggles his eyebrows.

"*She* wasn't my fucking wife."

Tate holds his hands up in surrender.

My phone vibrates on the desk, and I pick it up. All anger is erased when I see confirmation for my surprise for Emi and bump. I pocket my phone and ignore my friends' jibes on the way out of the door, only lifting my hand to give them all the finger.

FIFTEEN

EMI

It's been almost a week of me and Shaw getting along. The morning he came all over me, something changed between us, leading us to make more of an effort with one another.

Shaw wakes in the morning and has a chat to bump before we either have sex or I give him a blow job. Then he goes to work while I hang around the house. In the afternoon, I message him, asking him what meal he fancies for dinner, and he always replies the same.

> Shaw: Something Italian and food.

He makes me smile every damn time at giving me the freedom to choose our meals. A simple act I never envisaged having control over but loving it, nevertheless.

I'm plating the vegetables when his scent invades me. I

love how I can still smell his aftershave on him even though he's been at work all day.

He palms my stomach. "Did you miss me?" Shaw poses the same question every day, and I'm never really sure if it's aimed at me or bump.

I always reply with the same answer. "We both did."

He smiles against my hair. "Good girl." And I melt against him.

He turns and opens multiple cupboards, looking for the same tableware we use every evening. I bite my bottom lip to stifle a laugh at his inability to grasp where everything is by now.

Shaw pops his head over the top of the cupboard door. "Keep giggling and I'll be spanking that ass." He grins back at me, making my heart yearn for every part of him, including his spanking.

I dish the rest of our meal and set it onto the table, then wait for Shaw to cut into the lasagna before I start on mine.

"I have a surprise for you tomorrow." Shaw stares at me with a smile on his handsome face and hope in his eyes, but I freeze.

My throat goes dry. "I don't think I've ever had a surprise before. Not the good kind anyway." My eyes dart away when I consider all the surprises I have received. I inwardly shudder thinking about the bloodshed and violence brought to our doorstep in every form of a surprise. I close my eyes at the pain of losing my parents, my sister, and a multitude of extended family members on my brother's quest for vengeance.

A soft hand grazes my cheek, and my eyes flare open to clash with Shaw's concerned ones; he's moved from his chair and sits kneeling on the floor before me. "What's the matter, baby?" He sits back on his heels and watches me, waiting for my response.

My throat clogs. "I don't like surprises," I rush out.

Shaw's face softens and he nods in understanding—when in reality, I doubt he can understand.

"Okay. No surprises." His lips tighten into an appeasing smile. "Shall I tell you and bump?" He places his palm on my stomach, making my muscles relax at his touch.

I nod. "Please."

"Good girl." He places a kiss on my forehead.

"Well, you're going to come to my office tomorrow afternoon so I can show you around." Excitement hums through me at the thought of Shaw letting me into his life beyond our arrangement. His smile widens, and I liken it to childlike, making me smile just as happily back at him. "Then we're taking this little one for one of those 3D scans. You know, where we can see bump's face. I did some research, and it looks incredible." Emotion wells inside me, threatening to spill over, something not okay to do in the Mafia world.

Tears well in my eyes at his thoughtfulness, something he's looked into not just for bump but for me too. His hand moves from my stomach, and I instantly feel the loss, only for him to replace it with gentle fingers grazing over a lone tear falling down my cheek.

"Are these good tears?"

I choke on a laugh. "Yes."

"Good girl." He smirks back at me, and wetness pools between my legs. "Fuck, you're beautiful."

His head dips down to my stomach and presses a soft

kiss to my bump. I suck in a sharp breath as my fingers tangle in his hair.

A thought hits me. "Did you ask Luca if it was okay for me to go?"

Shaw's head reels back, and stunned, he stares at me. Then his eyebrows furrow in confusion.

I elaborate. "I have to get permission to go somewhere different, Shaw. The guards need to be aware of any changes and make sure the premises are secure."

His jaw tightens and the veins on his forehead protrude, anger taking over his features.

"You're safe with me," he snaps back and stands with his hands on his hips, his chest heaving. "You're my fucking wife!" His loud voice makes me jolt, but at the same time, my heart races with pleasure at his possessiveness.

"If I want to take my wife out, I'll fucking do it." He picks a glass up from the countertop and launches it at the wall. The shattering launches me to my feet, and I don't think twice before I have his face in the palms of my hands.

"Fuck. He even gets to decide when you leave the house. This is so fucked up," he seethes, pacing the kitchen like an animal prowling. "He doesn't fucking own you. You're *my* goddamn wife." He stabs his finger to his chest.

"I'm yours," I reassure him.

His gaze locks with mine, and heat boils between us. "Mine," he mutters with a deep growl that heats my body with need.

He stalks toward me then. His hand shoots out and he wraps it around the back of my hair, tugging my head hard enough that I wince from the pain.

His other hand fumbles with his belt while I help him push down his boxers to release his wet cock. I wrap my hand around him and pump him, and he hisses through his teeth, allowing me to fist his cock. "So fucking good." His chest rises, but this time, it's in need instead of anger, and the thought I can turn his mood around so quickly fills me with pride. "Keep pumping, baby. Pump harder." He moans through open lips. "So fucking good. Such a good girl. You belong to me, Emi. You both do. You're fucking mine." He bends down and takes my mouth in his, nipping enough at my lip to cause a sting of pain before he sucks it into his mouth. His hips move against me, making my pussy throb with need.

"Don't stop, Red. Don't fucking stop." My hand works faster, harder. "I'm going to come all over your hand. Fuck yes, I am." Shaw's head drops back, and he lets out a long, deep groan. "Fuckkk." His thick, warm cum hits my hand and wrist.

Shaw brings his head forward as though it causes him effort to do so. "Fuck, that was good." He grins at me.

I release his cock, and he maneuvers himself back into his boxers and pants as I lean over the counter for the paper towel to wipe up his cum.

His chest heaves as he watches me from the opposite end of the counter, his hands gripping the sides. "I won't be dictated to by your brother, Emi. If I want to take my family out, I won't ask for permission, and it's fucked up that you think that's even acceptable."

I wipe the excess cum from my arm, amazed at how far it travels. Shaw ignores the fact I'm cleaning his cum from me and continues on with his tirade. "Do you ever leave the house without permission at all?" His voice grows louder at my lack of response.

"No," I simply say because that's the truth. I always run things past Luca or Maxim.

Shaw's face contorts with anger again, and I cringe thinking about him losing his temper when I've just calmed him down. "And don't think you can jack my cock every time we have a disagreement and I'll give in. That's not how this shit works." He clenches his jaw and glares down at me with something bordering on hate, and I despise that he associates his feelings with me that way.

Emotion clogs my throat, and I have to clear it before speaking. "The last time someone left the house without guards, my sister's remains were found. She'd been strangled and raped, Shaw. My brother's overprotective for a reason. He doesn't want to see me and my baby as a product of the Mafia world, he wants us kept safe."

Shaw's body sags and his face softens, but I turn to ignore him, pissed I had to bring Eleanor into the conversation again. I head toward the stairs, leaving Shaw in the kitchen.

He needs to understand there's a reason for the security. It's not done as a possessive action; it's done as an act of protectiveness and ultimately, love.

SHAW

My rage at Luca's control over my family dissipated in a matter of seconds when Emi explained the reasoning behind his overprotective behavior.

I can't imagine losing a loved one in such circumstances, and when Emi indicated that could happen to her and the baby, a deep-seated sickness spread from the pit of my stomach into my bones. The fact that she referred to bump as her baby pissed me off beyond belief, but she was hurting at my childish reaction, so I'll give her that jibe for now.

I reach for the whiskey and pour myself a glass, tossing it back in one go. I ignore the heat of it and pick up my cell phone to call the one man I cannot fucking stand: Luca Varros.

He answers within seconds. "Is Emi okay?" I brush my hand over my heart at the concern in his voice. The guy genuinely cares for his family, and I need to be more understanding of their circumstances.

"She's fine."

"The baby?" Again, guilt pricks me in the chest.

"Fine. They're both fine."

"Then what the fuck do you want? You can't back out of this; I'll fucking kill you myself if you try." I almost chuckle at his taunt and the fact that he thinks I would be so weak as to give up on Emi and our baby.

I clear my throat and try to remain diplomatic, but I don't intend on asking his permission either.

"Emi is coming to my office tomorrow and then I'm taking her for a baby scan; she mentioned you may need to add additional security." I drag a hand through my hair at his silence.

Anxiety creeps in, and it feels like minutes tick by before he utters a word.

"You have an on-site doctor," he clips back, void of any emotion.

I clench my teeth, trying to remain calm. Keeping my voice low and controlled, I reply with ease, "You're right but this scan is a 3D one. We'll be able to see the baby's features, it's really clear compared to any other scan Emi has had, and it'll be my first experience of one too. I want it to be special for her."

Silence fills the air. So much so I pull the phone from my ear to make sure we haven't been disconnected.

Until I hear him exhale. "You organized this?"

"Yes. I thought it would be nice for Emi." My tone is snippier, and I kick myself for not remaining as calm as I'd hoped.

"I'll need the locations and times. She'll have extra guards."

Again, I remind myself this is for her and the baby's safety. "Of course."

Luca ends the call, leaving me dumbstruck. *Who ends a call without a goodbye?*

I scratch my head in frustration. *That was a definite yes, though, right?*

My feet move toward the bedroom with a newfound purpose, *my wife*. I smile as I take the stairs two at a time, excited at the prospect of giving her the good news.

When I open the bedroom door, I feel like the air is being sucked from my lungs. I lean against the doorframe to take her in.

Jesus, she's gorgeous.

Emi lies with her hair splayed across the pillow, and the white camisole she's wearing lifts above her protruding belly, making my cock jump at the thought of me putting a baby in her. My eyes travel up, over her enlarged nipples and bulging tits, to her beautiful face.

"Ours." My voice is gruff and full of longing.

She sits up in bed to look at me, and my heart races. The atmosphere between us becomes sexual.

"What?"

"Downstairs, you said my baby. The baby is ours." She tilts her head to the side and swallows deeply.

"I did, you're right." She takes a deep breath, our eyes locked. "I'm sorry."

"Say the baby is ours."

Her cheeks pinken. "Ours. Luca wants to keep our baby safe."

I push off the doorframe and walk toward the bed.

"And so do I, my little Mafia princess." I lean over the bed and place my hands on her ankles. "Let me make my outburst up to you." I drag her down the bed, and she licks her lips.

"Let me show you how much you're mine. You both are."

Emi's smile weakens my resolve and makes my heart swell.

"I'll never let anyone hurt you, Red. Never." I trail my hands up her legs. "Never," I vow with certainty.

SIXTEEN

SHAW

I've been bubbling with excitement all day at the thought of having Emi and the baby here in my office. I check my watch again. Jesus, why does time stand still when you want it to move quicker, yet when you wish time would slow down, it rushes away from you.

My mind drifts back to last night when I held her in my arms. I peppered kisses over the top of her head, even when she was sleeping, determined to keep her safe forever. I've never felt such protectiveness over a woman in my entire life.

Maybe it's because she's pregnant with my child? I laugh at my own idiocy, it's more than that. It has been since the first moment I saw her. A pull, a magnetized strength like no other, drawing us together.

I'm thinking this is what love is. Someone you think about constantly, care for, your emotions unraveled to the point you can't control yourself. Devoted.

The office door opens, and my ass leaves my chair, only for it to find it again pretty damn quick when Tate walks through, looking completely disheveled.

"What the hell happened to you?"

His tie is loose, his eyes heavy, and his hair is a mess—basically, he looks like he hasn't slept at all. He's normally so well put together, but judging by the dark bags under his eyes, I was right, he hasn't slept.

"Nothing." He drops down onto the couch with spread legs, staring at the carpet.

"Did you hit someone with your car?"

His eyes snap up to mine with a glare that tells me he thinks I'm crazy. "No, dipshit, I didn't hit someone with my car."

I lean back in my chair and chuckle, letting him know I'm joking.

I tap my finger against my lip, enjoying the opportunity to ridicule him when it's normally him that's the playful one. "Let me guess, you have an STD?"

His lip curls up in disgust and he scrunches his nose up. "No, dude, you know I get regular checks. Besides, I always wrap it up, you know that."

"Apart from that one time," I counter with a raised eyebrow.

When Tate had too much to drink one night, and we were discussing our sexual conquests, he was the only one that admitted he purposely didn't wear a condom with one girl because he was so turned on he needed to see his cum dripping out of her.

The memory of Emi gets me hard when an image of my cum escaping her this morning flashes in my mind. At the time, I didn't get it, but now? Now I understand. It's primal and possessive.

My gaze snaps to Tate's, and his face is whiter than before.

"Shit, did you knock her up or something?" My heart races. *Surely, he hasn't got a girl pregnant too?*

Tate continues to stare back at me, then he jolts. "No. She was on birth control. I told you that."

I sigh in annoyance. "What the hell is wrong with you, then?"

He opens his mouth to respond, but a knock at the door interrupts him. "Come in," I shout. My eyes turn to the door, and the air is pulled from my lungs because she's here. She steps into the office, and I rise from my chair to greet her. My heart races like a lovestruck teenager as I take her in. She wears her hair up in a messy bun, a t-shirt covers her bump but it strains against it, leggings fit her sculptured legs, and her face is clear of makeup, exposing the little freckles beside her nose. A shiny substance is on her lips, and I have an overwhelming urge to taste it.

I pull her toward me and back her against the wall, my arms resting above her head as I cage her in.

"You don't need to knock, Red. You're family. Family doesn't knock."

I can see her chest rising beneath her top, heat spreading over her chest. I dip my head and take her lips in mine; her body relaxes against me, and her small bump pushes against my stomach. I slip my tongue into her mouth, and she whimpers, making my cock stand to attention.

Emi wraps her arms around my neck and draws me in

impossibly closer. Our tongues clash, and when she digs her nails into the base of my neck, I growl into the kiss.

A throat clears behind me, making me jump and causing Emi to gasp.

I turn to see Tate standing near my desk with a shit-eating grin on his face. "This must be Emi, right?"

I tug Emi in front of me, trying to disguise my raging hard-on. My hand finds her bump, and Tate doesn't miss the action. His lips tip up at the sides as his eyes roam over her body. I want to punch him in the balls, so my grip tightens on Emi.

"Emi, this is Tate, my business partner," I grunt the words out.

"Try best friend, asshole." Tate grins.

Before I know what's happening, she pulls away from me and walks over to Tate, holding her hand out to greet him. "Nice to meet you, Tate. I've heard so much about you guys."

Tate shakes her hand with a genuine smile.

"It's so good to finally meet you, I've heard so much about you all. We'd love it if you could all join us for dinner one night, right, Shaw?" She turns back to me with a genuine, enthusiastic smile, and I stand there dumbfounded. Me and Lizzie were off and on for years, and she couldn't bear my friends' company for the shortest of times, let alone a dinner date.

"That sounds amazing, thank you, Emi. I'll get the guys together to schedule a date." He winks at me, and I narrow my eyes. "Well, I guess I best go back to doing some work. I'll catch up with you guys soon." He walks past Emi but stops at me, lowering his voice. "Fuck, man. Your cock looks painful." His eyes travel down my body, and I ball my palms into fists, ready to lash out. Tate gives me a knowing chuckle.

"Shaw? I'm a little early, right?"

My eyes snap back to Emi leaning against my desk while Tate leaves the office, the door clicking shut behind him.

"Yes." My pulse races with need as I stare at her, those black orbs of hers drawing me in further.

"I've always wanted to have sex in an office." Her eyes flick around the office space, but my eyes are fixed solely on her, filled with lust as I stride toward her with purpose, my adrenaline skyrocketing.

"This is going to be real quick, baby. Real fucking quick, my cock is leaking for you so bad."

I spin her around and tug her leggings down to her thighs, shocked to discover she isn't wearing any panties. "What the fuck, Emi?" I move one hand to her dripping pussy while the other unbuckles my belt and tugs my thick cock from my boxers.

My eyes close at my touch, desperation edging at the tip of my cock. "You're a naughty girl, not wearing panties, Red." I drag my cock over the crack of her ass and down to her pussy hole, so wet for the taking. "So fucking naughty." I push inside her, and as soon as her warm, wet heat encompasses me, I have to bite the inside of my mouth to stop myself from coming.

"Please," she begs, pushing back against me.

I shake my head, ignoring the fact that she can't see. "I can't. Just . . . just gimme a minute, otherwise I'll come already."

I grip her hips, holding her still as she tries once again

to push back on me, encouraging me to move. "Please, Shaw. I'm nearly there already."

Fuck. My girl is needy today. I pull back. "This what you want?" I slam inside her, earning a sharp gasp. "You want my cock to fill your pussy?" She moans on my words, and I grind my hips into her, her tight hole sucking me in to the point of no return. "You're desperate for my cock, aren't you?"

Emi moans as I hit her G-spot. "Yes and your cum." She clenches around me, and holy shit, my balls draw up tight hearing that and the feeling of her walls locking me in tight.

I drop my head to the crook of her neck and bite into her skin hard to stop myself from roaring her name.

"Oh fuck, Shawww," she screeches through her orgasm, sending my cock into overdrive as my cum floods her tight hole. Ropes upon ropes of cum spurt from my cock as I come, the force of my orgasm blurring my vision.

EMI

Shaw pulls out of me, and his cum drips down my thighs, making me regret only wearing leggings.

I turn, panicked. "Shaw, I have to go to the obstetrician like this." He bends and pulls my leggings up, making me cringe at the feeling of his excess cum on my legs sticking against the material.

Shaw chuckles, making me swipe playfully at him. "It's not funny, you ass. What if they want to examine me internally?"

He freezes and his eyes connect with mine, possessiveness riddled in them as his jaw tightens. "Why the fuck would they want to examine you internally?" He crosses his arms over his chest as his eyes drill into mine.

I sigh and rearrange my messy bun at his caveman attitude. Shaw doesn't care for the Mafia lifestyle, but he sure as hell mimics it in his actions.

"I don't know why. But sometimes it's what they do." I shrug.

He moves forward, bringing us flush together. "Has

someone else been in your pussy, Emi? My pussy?" His hand tightens on my hip.

I'm breathless at the intensity around us, his stare drilling into me. "No. They haven't," I mumble. "I'm just saying, they might."

His hand moves to my ass and dips below the waistband, traveling past my asshole and around my pussy, and he pumps two fingers inside me before withdrawing them. I stand there in shock, his eyes laser-focused on mine as he holds his two fingers up. They're covered in cum, mine and his. Our juices run down his fingers.

Fire burns behind his eyes. "Lick them clean." The command in his tone leaves for no objection, and the deepness in his voice makes me clench my thighs with need.

I move my lips toward his fingers, and as my tongue connects with our essence, he closes his eyes on a low groan before flaring them open when I suck both his fingers into my mouth. "Good girl," he grunts. "Suck our cum from my fingers." I suck harder, loving the gravelly groan coming from the back of his throat.

"Only I get to touch your cunt. You hear me?"

I trail my tongue over the remnants of our cum. "Yes," I reply breathlessly.

The door swings open with a bang, and our heads turn in the direction.

A woman stands in the doorway. She has straight platinum hair past her shoulders, plump lips, and a narrow waist. Wearing high red stilettos and a fitted red dress, she looks a combination of businesswoman and elite. My eyes travel back up toward her face, and it's then I take in the streak marks of mascara on her cheeks and her reddened eyes.

Shaw jolts and pulls away from me, rushing toward her, leaving a gaping hole when I realize who she is.

"Lizzie. Jesus, are you okay?" The panic and concern in his voice is evident, and my heart constricts at hearing it.

His arms wrap around her as she cries into his shoulder, making me flinch at the tenderness between them.

My heart plummets at the sight before me, feeling like an outsider, wrapping my arms around myself for security when a lump clogs my throat at watching my husband comfort another woman.

Only to realize I am the other woman. I swallow away the bitterness in my mouth.

"What happened, Liz." His soft voice coos over her as his hands travel up and down her back, and I hate it. I hate it so damn much that he's touching her with such care. Such love.

Tears well in my eyes at how much love they have for one another. Me being the mistake he made while on a break from his long-term relationship. I squeeze my eyes closed at the sting of pain lancing through my heart and stirring as sickness in my stomach.

"Shaw. Pl-please. You need to give us another chance. Please. I'll do anything."

Shaw's Adam's apple bobs at her words, emotion clogging his throat too.

"Please. We can make it work," she begs again, her eyes imploring his.

I wince at the desperation in her tone, and my heart races with panic at wondering how he will react. Internally, I'm begging him not to.

Where will this leave me and bump and ultimately, Shaw. There's far too much at stake.

I step forward to interject. "Shaw?"

His sharp eyes snap toward mine. His jaw tics in annoyance, making me take a step back at the cruel glare behind them.

"Emi." He drags a hand through his hair and exhales loudly. "Just give us a fucking minute, would you?" His voice booms, making me and Lizzie jump, but as I hold onto the desk in shock at his reaction, she clings onto him.

I stare back at him and open my mouth to apologize.

"Just go, will you?" His voice is low, and he averts his gaze, hurting me in the process. He can't even look at me.

My pulse races, laced in sadness as I rush toward his office door. I don't miss the thank you that Lizzie sniffles into his chest as the door clicks shut behind me.

I take a deep breath and walk to the waiting area, taking a seat on one of the couches with anxiety coursing through my veins, making me bite on my fingernails and bounce my leg as I unravel in despair.

Minutes tick by but I can't bring myself to knock on the door.

"Can I help you?" A lady stares down at me with a polite smile. I think she's one of the receptionists.

"I . . . I." I cringe at my inability to form a sentence. Before taking a deep breath, straightening my spine, I start again, only this time as the Mafia princess who doesn't show emotion.

"I'm waiting for Shaw, thank you."

She glances toward Shaw's office, then back at me before bending down and lowering her voice. "Between you and me. He's in there with his girlfriend, so he'll probably be in there a while, if you catch my drift?" She gives me a sultry wink before walking away. A wave of sickness rolls through me, and I squeeze my eyes closed at the hurt in my chest.

My throat feels dry at the thought of his staff not being aware that he's now married.

To me.

And yet I'm the one sitting outside his office while he does god-knows-what with his ex beyond the door. Disappointment and dread fill my stomach. I'm the other woman, the one that gets used for them to pump and dump inside.

Bump takes this moment to kick, and I feel the force right in my gut, making me suck in a sharp breath. It's like a reminder of what I'm doing here. A reminder of who I am.

Snapping my eyes open with renewed vigor, I check my watch. Staring back at the door, I realize we need to be leaving to get there in time for the scan.

I tell myself to not let the anxiety creep in. The horrible ache inside my chest is burning and spreading like a wildfire through my entire body, burning away any semblance of a relationship we were developing behind the office door.

A throat clears beside me. "Miss. I'm sorry to interrupt you, but if you want to make the scheduled appointment, we need to be leaving now." One of my additional security men points out delicately, as if sensing my unease.

I glance at my watch again, disappointed that another fifteen minutes has gone by and they're still in there. The receptionist's words come back to me. *"He'll probably be in there a while."* Followed by Shaw's words, *"You don't have to knock, family doesn't knock."* Lizzie didn't knock, and the realization sends a feeling of sadness through me. I hug myself for comfort.

Is this what it's going to be like? Him, her, me, and the baby. Like all the other Mafia families, I guess. I was hoping for so much more.

I bite my lip to stifle the threat of my emotion spilling over.

"Should I see if Mr. Varros is available?" my security suggests, making my heart swell with hope that I don't have to approach the door.

"Please." I stand and brush down invisible lint to steel myself.

He knocks on the door.

"For Christ's sake. Fuck off!" Shaw roars, making me flinch.

The security guard sneers in the door's direction before turning back toward me, quickly masking any initial reaction. "Would you like to wait, Miss?"

I contemplate his question, then consider what Luca would suggest. He'd expect me to be the strong Mafia woman I've been trained to become.

I pull my shoulders back with purpose. "Absolutely not. Let's go." I stride toward the doors with a confidence I don't feel, with disappointment ebbing at my already sensitive heart. With his cum deposited deep inside me and remnants on my legs, I remind myself I was never meant to be his wife.

Maybe it's better I realize this now, before I fall in too deep.

If I haven't already.

SEVENTEEN

SHAW

As soon as the office door clicks shut, Lizzie pulls away from me.

My mind can't seem to accept the hurt behind Emi's eyes when I shouted at her. My gaze burns holes into the door, unsure of whether to make a move toward her or sort my shit out here first.

But hearing Lizzie cry about our broken relationship while my wife and baby were in the room and my fingers still wet from our juices put me on fucking edge, and she took the brunt of it. *Shit, I fucked up big time. She didn't deserve that.* I exhale loudly.

"Do you even care? Shaw! I asked you a question, do you even care?" She stamps her foot, bringing my attention back to her.

"What?"

"I said, do you even care?"

I take in her disheveled appearance, quite the contrast

to her normally being so well put together. She's clearly hurting, so I take a deep breath and try and sympathize with the situation I've put us in. "Of course I care. I don't like seeing you so upset, Liz, you know that. But I don't have a choice in the matter." I swallow away the guilt at my words. Even if I had a choice, I wouldn't choose anything differently.

Emi is beautiful and strong. Resilient and carefree, she matches my sexual energy, and she's going to be as much an amazing mom as she is a wife.

"Don't have a choice," she mumbles. Her chest rises higher and higher. "I don't have a choice in how I feel about you!" She practically screams, making me walk to her in shock.

"Will you keep your fucking voice down?" My voice is low, deadly.

Her lower lip trembles, and she shakes uncontrollably. In the past, I would have backed down easily. But now I'm left with no choice, I'm finally seeing the real her.

For the first time since knowing her, I struggle to find compassion for her as my gaze trails over her body. She's everything Emi is not, and for the first time in my life, I can't believe I've allowed myself to become controlled by her manipulative behavior. Just what the hell was I thinking? Superficial, self-centered, money-oriented, and manipulative.

Emi is none of those things; all she cares about is her family.

Lizzie holds her stomach, rocking back and forth on her high heels before dropping to the floor, her performance Oscar-worthy. I pinch the bridge of my nose and stare up toward the ceiling as though searching for some divine inspiration.

"Get up off the floor, Liz," I grit out, trying to disguise my anger, knowing it only sends her further over the edge.

"I . . . I can't. It hurts too much." She snivels. "My love for you. It hurts too much, Shaw."

I roll my eyes at her words. She's lacking the tugging of the hair this time, but I wonder if it's about to come when her talons meet with her head. The last time she pulled at her hair, her extensions came out and I had to pay some overpriced hair stylist to fix her. She shakes profusely. *Oh shit, here we go.*

"I love you so much." She crawls toward me, and I have to fight the urge not to kick her away from my feet. Each drone of her voice is like nails on a chalkboard, making me cringe.

"You're my worllld." She pulls her body up, using my pant legs to stabilize herself. "And you don't even care."

"Lizzie. Our so-called relationship has been a train wreck and you know it. It should have been over a long time ago."

"I wanted more, and you wouldn't give it to me," she spits at me when she's eye level with me.

"You're right. I didn't want that."

"But you can have it with her." She throws her hand out toward the door. "Some one-night stand that got knocked up." I grind my teeth at how she talks about Emi. "You wouldn't even have sex with me without a condom, Shaw!"

I tamper down my comeback, trying to keep her calm, not wanting all my office to hear about what is sure to be the start of her exploiting herself sexually. "With good reason." We both had numerous partners outside of when we were together.

I know how Lizzie works; I can read her like a damn book, and we've played this game far too long for me not to recognize every move she makes. It's a shame I've been too weak to put a stop to it before now. The regular sex and someone on my arm at events that could swoon the birds from the trees became an easy convenience. Until things would come to an abrupt explosion of emotions.

She reaches toward my cock, but I grasp her wrist to stop her. Biting my cheek, I keep my voice low as I spit the words out. "I'm a married man, Liz. Get that through your thick fucking skull. My cock belongs to my wife and my wife only." I throw her wrist away, making her glare back at me in malice.

You'd think I'd been clear enough, but when she steps back with a smile tugging at her plump lips, I know she's only getting started.

I knock back another whiskey and slam the glass down on the table while holding my hand up for another.

Tate drops down opposite me, scanning my face. "How'd it go?"

"Brutal. Absolutely. Fucking. Brutal."

His jaw drops open as the waitress places my drink on the table. "Bring me the bottle," I clip in her direction.

"What the hell happened?"

"She crawled on all fucking fours, then tried to seduce me. When I called security, she refused to put her dress back on. Instead, she took her fucking bra off, man. In front of the security." I clench my jaw at the shame, and my head pounds with tension, but I ignore it. I take another swig of my drink and continue on with the story. "Her tits were hanging out. She wrapped the bra around her hand and started waving it around like a damn flag. Telling the whole floor how I refused to let her get bigger tit implants."

Tate stares at me in shock. His face would be comical if I wasn't so pissed.

"She was insane. Out of control. One of the worst and most embarrassing situations of my entire life."

"No fucking way!" Tate gasps, horrified.

I take another drink. "Way." I nod, just as fucking mortified. At least he didn't have to watch his ex get hauled out of the building with her panties around her ankles and her stringy hair between her fingers making her resemble an even more deranged Cruella de Vil.

"God, I hope the baby is okay. She seemed so fucking normal." His gaze is despondent as he searches for the right words. "So nice." He grimaces with a shudder. "That shit can have a real impact on babies mentally too." He sighs as I struggle to understand what he means. "You're gonna have to get the baby checked out. You need to take the kid to a specialist as soon as it's born, Shaw," Tate tacks on with concern as I stare at him dumbfounded.

"What the fuck are you talking about?" I quip back, wondering if my friend has indeed lost the damn plot like my ex. *I mean, Jesus, am I the only sane one here?*

"Huh?"

"Why would the baby have problems?" I grit out, annoyed he even implied it in the first place.

Tate moves closer and lowers his voice. "You just

admitted your wife crawled across the fucking floor, Shaw, and exposed herself to everyone. That's not normal."

I jolt in shock at his words. He really is a dumbshit. "No. I didn't." I shake my head. "I was explaining how brutal it was when Lizzie came into the office and I tried to let her down. *Again*."

Tate rears back, wide-eyed. "Oh. Well, I was asking how the scan went."

My mind plays catch up on his words before panic courses through me. "Oh shit." I stumble to stand. "I fucked up." I turn around in a circle like an idiot. "Oh shit, I fucked up real bad."

"Why, what did you do?" Tate watches me wide-eyed.

"I . . ." I turn again on the spot, as though the answer is going to jump out at me. "I forgot about the fucking scan." My chest heaves with disappointment. "I forgot about Emi. Shit." I tug at my hair, wondering how the hell the day could have started off so incredible, only to end so fucked up.

I grab my jacket and make my way toward the door.

"Jesus, Shaw. Even I'm not so dumb as to forget my own baby's scan."

I spin to face my idiot friend. "You don't even have a baby, dipshit."

"Not yet!" He grins from ear to ear and wiggles his eyebrows in jest. I exhale and head out the door, hoping all the progress I've made with Emi doesn't come crashing down on me.

I rub at the pain in my chest at the thought of losing her and the baby, and I refuse to accept it.

They're it for me.

They both are.

EIGHTEEN

EMI

I roll over in bed as the light streams through the windows, making me blink in uncertainty at the shadow on the chair.

Moving to sit up, I rub the sleep from my eyes and focus more, realizing it's Shaw.

"I'm sorry." His tone is full of sympathy, but I choose to ignore it. A good Mafia wife bites her tongue, after all.

Instead, I throw the sheet off me and head toward the bathroom. Just as I begin to pee, Shaw walks in, and I gasp in shock. "Shaw, I'm peeing."

He waves his hand. "Yeah. I don't mind. I need you to know how sorry I am." I take in the dark circles below his eyes and his messy hair, his shirt untucked and the sincerity in his voice.

I move my hand to tug off the toilet tissue, but Shaw is already there with a piece for me. *What the hell?* He thrusts it into my hand when I don't make a move for it.

I discreetly wipe and then flush the toilet. Washing my hands, I take a deep breath. "It's fine."

I clench my eyes shut when his palms wrap around my bump and his soft breath grazes my neck as he places a gentle kiss there.

"It's not fine and I'm sorry, Red."

I flinch at his contact, making him draw back as my eyes flare open. They lock with his through the mirror, and the intensity of his stare sends a shiver down my spine. "I'm sorry, baby. Really fucking sorry."

I nod at his words and dry my hands on the hand towel.

"I'll call in to work today. I'm sure they can get another scan for us."

I grind my jaw. He's made no attempt to explain what the holdup was and why the hell his so-called ex-girlfriend was in his office for so long, nor any attempt to explain what actually happened between them. I'll be damned if I let him think he can fix this by throwing money at another scan.

"It's fine. I was happy with the scan I had yesterday." I lift my chin.

He freezes and his chest heaves, but I ignore him and push past him, heading toward the bedroom.

"You went without me?" Accusation in his voice makes my pulse race with anger. He follows me, mouth agape as I get dressed, anger bubbling to the surface once again.

"I knocked on your door and you told me to fuck off." I shrug at my white lie.

Shaw's mouth drops open before he clamps it shut again, seemingly lost for words. He spins on his heel, walks back into the bathroom, and slams the door shut behind him. I jump at a loud thud.

I ignore the outburst and instead throw myself into doing something constructive. Seeing the baby yesterday made me truly excited, and today is going to be a great day. I refuse to let Shaw Grant and his ex affect me and my baby.

SHAW

I sent text after text asking where she'd gone. I was even tempted to call her brother but refrained from doing so, knowing he would probably shoot me in the head— or worse, my balls—for hurting his sister.

When Emi told me she went for our baby's scan, I felt like I'd been kicked in the gut. Not only was that something I wanted to witness, but it was something meant to be special between the two of us and bump. The thought of her seeing bump's face for the first time without me sends a searing pain shooting through my chest and disappointment curdling inside my stomach.

I fucked up. Big time. And I need to make it right.

When I heard the knock on the door, Emi never entered my mind. All I could think about was stopping my crazy ass ex from losing her shit and causing a scene even further. Look where that got me. Now my wife thinks I don't want her.

Sure, she hasn't said as much, but I can see the look of hurt and the insecurity behind her eyes, and I hate it. She deserves to be treasured, respected, and loved. I did none of those things yesterday, and I hate myself for it.

I'm determined to make it up to her. I stir the sauce as I try to follow her handwriting for the spaghetti carbonara recipe, becoming more and more frustrated with not knowing where she is.

I glance at the table, proud of myself for following Google's instructions on "how to impress your wife." Pink rose petals cover the table and the candles flicker, giving it a romantic vibe.

The front door opens and I rush to greet her, only to see our guards bringing in bags upon bags of items. She went on a shopping spree. Lizzie always did that when she was pissed too.

"Could you place them in the nursery, please?" Her soft voice makes my heart race as she speaks to the guards. Then she turns to face me and stops.

She went baby shopping without me?

I glance toward the bags but have to look away. This is something we should have done together too. I'm already failing at being a father, just like I am at being a husband.

My heart hammers in my chest, hoping she doesn't hate me. My fingers twitch to pull her toward me as her dark eyes stare at me in question. "I made dinner."

Her eyes search mine, and her lips part.

Fuck, I want to ram my tongue down her throat right now. My dick likes the idea too, as it jumps in my joggers. Emi's eyes connect with my cock, and I actually cringe, imagining she thinks I went to this effort just to have sex.

"I made dinner," I repeat, hoping she realizes this pull between us isn't just about sex.

"Thank you." I search her eyes for insincerity but struggle to find any. My shoulders relax.

"It's about ready." I motion to the kitchen door, and she gives me a swift nod, stopping to take off her coat and shoes and then following me into the kitchen.

The moment she gasps, I turn to face her. Her hand is covering her mouth, and I can't help but remove it, entwining our fingers as I do.

"I'm sorry," I repeat for what feels like the hundredth time, but at the same time, it doesn't quite seem enough.

"Did you do all this?" She scans over the room before coming back to my face, making my lips turn into a proud smile.

"I did. And I cooked dinner." I tilt my head toward the stove.

Emi giggles. "You said that already."

I drop my forehead against hers and breathe her in. But the incessant beeping breaks our moment, causing my eyes to snap over at the hob at the sauce boiling over. "Go sit your ass down and I'll bring it over." I tap her ass as I move past her.

Everything feels right with Emi by my side.

EMI

"What exactly is it?" I take another small nibble and then blow on it, pretending it's too hot rather than far too salty.

"It's spaghetti carbonara. It was the first meal you ever cooked for me, so I figured it would be the first meal I ever cooked for you too, that way it's significant to us." My heart melts at his thoughtful words.

I clear my throat. "It's delicious." I beam at him.

Shaw chuckles. "Red, you're scrunching your nose up as you smile." He pushes his full plate away from him. "It tastes fucking awful. I can't cook." He pouts, making me laugh.

"I'll teach you, Shaw."

His hand moves toward mine and he entwines our fingers. "I really am sorry, Emi."

I swallow away the emotion, determined not to let him see how hurt I am. "Okay. Let's just start again."

He rears back as though I've slapped him. "I don't want to start a-fucking-gain."

My pulse races. *Did I misread his intentions?*

"I want us to work, Emi. We're not starting from the beginning; I should have been there for you and bump, I fucked up. That's on me, it won't happen again." He shakes his head as his chest heaves. Clearly, he's enraged with himself. "I want you to rely on me, and I'm sorry you weren't able to."

His words whirl in my mind, but he's not once mentioned Lizzie and what happened between them. He's given me no explanation at all.

Maybe I need to ignore it and recognize he's sorry for missing the scan. Maybe I don't have any right to be annoyed at their situation at all.

Afterall, in the Mafia I would have no control whatsoever over my husband.

I take a deep breath, determined to get my point across. "Shaw, I refuse to come second to another woman."

Shaw reels back in shock. "Is that what you think?"

My eyes narrow on his. "You chose another woman over me yesterday. Over us." I place my hand on bump. "You hurt me, Shaw. You said you wanted this to work between us, but at the first sign of difficulty, you push me away."

He swallows thickly and nods. "I can see how you think that. But that's not how it was, I swear it."

"I might not have a choice but to stay married to you, Shaw. But I won't allow you to treat me poorly. If you want to live a separate life—"

He holds his hand up. "I don't want a separate fucking life. I want you and my baby." He drags a hand through his hair, his chest rising in panic. His fingers tighten on my hand. "I need you both in my life, Emi. Please, tell me you need that too." His eyes implore mine, making my heart skip a beat at his sincerity. I might not be well-versed in relationships, but I swear love seeps from his eyes, causing my pulse to race with hope.

I gift him with a nod. "Okay."

His eyes light up in hope. "Yeah?" His shoulders relax.

"Yes." I smile back at him, determined to make this work.

"Can I make it right by taking you to bed and fucking you senseless?" His eyes sparkle with mirth.

I splutter on my water, and Shaw throws his head back with laughter, and I can't help but join in. It's what we need after the past couple of days. Shaw making a mess of dinner has quite literally turned things around, and I appreciate the gesture and him being so romantic.

"Go take a bath or something. I'll tidy up here." He gestures toward the mess on the counter.

"You could leave it for Marla?" I bite my lip, hoping he'll join me in the bath.

Shaw stares at me. "Who the hell is Marla?"

"Our housekeeper. How did you not know that?"

He drags a hand through his hair. "Honestly—" He exhales heavily. "I just rush off to work and then can't wait to get back to you." My heart quickens. "I don't like it when the house is full of staff. I like it just being us," he admits, struggling to maintain eye contact. I squeeze our joined fingers for reassurance.

His eyes move over my face, and I lick my suddenly dry lips, making his gaze fixate on them. Now the room feels smaller, and my heart rate quickens. I squeeze my thighs together at the urge to feel him between my legs, pounding into me.

"Red, go take a bath. I'll be up shortly."

I push away from the table, already feeling the loss of his touch, but the heat from his searing gaze urges me forward.

NINETEEN

SHAW

I've never cleaned a kitchen so goddamn quick in my entire life. I practically run up the stairs, my raging hard-on painful against the waistband of my joggers, making it difficult to put one leg in front of the other.

I take a deep breath as I open the bedroom door and step inside, but I'm stunned to the spot at the sight laid out before me.

Jesus, she takes my breath away.

Her hair is splayed out on the pillow, her cami top has risen above bump, her cute little sleep shorts rest on her hips, and her ass cheeks hang from the back. She lies on her side but rolls over when she realizes I'm watching her.

I take a step toward the bed, and without me asking, she slips her shorts down her legs. Our eyes remain locked as I push my joggers down, allowing my solid cock to spring free. I ignore the ache in my balls and watch in rapture as she lifts her top over her head, allowing her heavy tits to bounce freely. The room is filled with a sexual energy so great I feel like my body is vibrating on the spot with need.

I crawl onto the bed and her legs open, accepting me like I belong there. I growl at the thought. I pepper gentle kisses up her legs all the way up toward her pussy where she gasps when my lips meet her fold. I kiss her there too, and her hand brushes into my hair as I flick my tongue over her slickness.

She whimpers under my touch, and she arches into my face as I make out with her clit, using my lips and tongue to give her the tenderness she deserves. "Shaw . . ." My mouth clamps over her swollen bud before flicking it with my tongue over and over again.

Her spine straightens and her legs tighten, but our eyes remain locked as she comes silently around my mouth, letting me drink in her pleasure.

I place a gentle kiss on her pussy, then work up and over bump, dotting loving pecks over her swollen belly.

Her hand remains on my head as I trail up toward her tits, the sight of them making my cock spurt with need. I close my eyes at the overwhelming sensation, determined not to come already. Conscious of our severed gaze, I snap my eyes back open with a renewed vigor, to show her how much she means to me.

Sucking her nipple into my mouth, I use my free hand to squeeze the other, delighting in her soft moans of pleasure. I nibble at her peak, and her hand tightening in my hair forces a chuckle from me to vibrate against her flesh. "Mm, so fucking beautiful, Red." She blushes even more, the action reminding me of her nickname. "Beautiful, Red," I repeat as I suckle her other nipple into my mouth.

When they've received equal attention and I feel her on edge again, I trail my kisses up her heated chest, over the column of her throat, nipping at the flesh there, leaving small marks in my wake, then on to her waiting lips.

I rest on my elbows, conscious of the bump between us. Staring down into her darkened pools, I hope she can see what she means to me. The love I feel for them both but struggle to convey into words. I swallow past the lump in my throat and jolt when her hand touches my cock, placing me against her needy hole.

"You're going to have my baby, Red." She nods back at me, her eyes still holding mine. "We're going to be a family." Tears fill her eyes, and I lean down to place a tender kiss on her forehead as I push inside her.

Air rushes from her lips as my hard cock pushes into her clenched channel. Already wet and tight from her orgasm, she molds around my cock. "You're made for me, Red." Her eyes glisten, causing my heart to constrict and my movements to falter, but as I draw my hips out and push back inside her, we stay connected. As our lips find one another's and our tongues thrash with need, we stay connected.

When our groans and the gentle slapping of our skin fill the room, we stay connected.

"You're it for me, Red. You and bump." Pleasure shoots through my body as hers tightens around me.

My balls draw up, and when she utters the words I need to hear, I allow myself to come with her.

"I'm falling for you, Blue."

EMI

The love seeping from his eyes was almost too much to bear, but part of me can't help but wonder if it compares to how he feels about Lizzie. Am I second best? Is it love? He never uttered those very words, after all.

But I feel something deep down. I just wish he'd talk to me about it.

We lie in silence, his hand stroking over my spine as I listen to the rhythmic thud of his heart.

"I allowed her to control me with her emotional behavior." His admission makes me freeze. "She scared me with how she would act." I tilt my head to face him, and he squeezes his eyes closed, as though struggling with his words. His Adam's apple slides up and down his throat slowly. "My mom was emotionally charged too. I always used to try and calm her down. Lizzie would be the same. I don't know when she realized this was how she could control me, but today I learned it was just that, Red. Control. She manipulated me, knowing I hate seeing women cry." My heart skips a beat, hurt lancing through my heart at how she's treated him.

How incredibly tentative he is with my needs too. "I'd never use my emotions to control you. I swear it, Shaw."

His eyes shoot open, and his heart hammers against me. "I know," he whispers the truth passing between us. A connection.

"I really wanted to be at the scan." He licks his lips. "I know I let you down. I won't do that again. I swear it."

My lips clash with his, and I moan into his mouth when his tongue thrashes against mine.

He pulls back. "Can you believe I need to pee?" He chuckles. "I don't want to move from here, Red." I squeeze against him tighter. He leans down and kisses the top of my head as I slink to the side, allowing him to slide out of bed.

I hear him in the bathroom and bite my lip at the thought of how to please him further . . .

TWENTY

SHAW

I wash my hands, butt naked, as my cock bobs against my stomach while I stare into my reflection.

I almost told her I loved her. Fucking almost.

The last time I uttered those words, it was to my mom before my father had her committed. I lost the only woman I ever loved, never to see her again. I can't let that happen to Emi. So I push the thought aside and swing open the bathroom door.

I stop in my tracks. Emi lies on the bed, bared to me, with her legs parted and one hand stroking over her glistening pussy while the other caresses her heavy tit, palming and squeezing it. My cock spurts, and I have to stroke it to give myself some relief at the dull ache becoming more and more painful, begging for a release.

I move forward. "Fuck. Keep doing that, baby. Keep yourself nice and wet for me." I step closer to the bed. Our arousal permeates the air, and my mouth waters to taste her sweet pussy with my cum inside. I promise myself I'll never fuck up so bad again.

"Please," she pants. Her hair is damp and sticking to her face, and she bites her lip, making me want to suck it into my mouth.

She's had the sweet side of me, the side I've only ever allowed and wanted with her. But now I get to control her with the filthy dominance we both desperately need. The thought excites me. How far would she be willing to let me go?

"Does my girl need something?" I stroke myself a few times, allowing the pleasure to flow through me, my eyes heavy with need. My balls are already drawn up and ready for action. "Fuck, Red, you make me want to come already, being such a good girl playing with your pussy for me. Getting it all nice and ready for me to slip inside that warm, wet cunt again." She moans at my words, and it spurs me on, enjoying it just as much as her. "Getting your pussy ready for a good fucking, for me to unload inside." I fist myself harder. "For me to fill with my warm cum again. Greedy little slut, aren't you?"

She whimpers.

"Shaw, I need your cock to fill me." She thrusts her hips up high. "To stretch me." Jesus, do I want to stretch her. Nice and wide for our baby.

I climb onto the bed, between her legs, and rest back on my heels, the perfect sight before me. Emi's fingers work her clit frantically as her pussy glistens with our combined arousal.

Jesus, that's hot. She pants as she works her hand over her pussy. "Shaw, please."

I have an overwhelming urge to push our boundaries

further, so I lean forward and spit on her pussy, reveling in the gasp that escapes her lips.

"I need you to rub that into your little cunt while I watch you play, Red." I glare down at her fingers mixing my spit with our juices. *Fuck, that's incredible.*

"Oh god, Shaw." I smirk at her, loving the fact that my girl enjoys me being so dirty. Something I've been desperate to delve deeper into. Another testament for how perfect we are for one another.

Her tits heave, drawing my attention back to those glorious nipples begging to be sucked and toyed with.

I pump my cock harder, tighter, as my eyes flick between her ample tits and her fingers working furiously over her pussy while her bump nestles between the two. I lean over her and caress her stomach, in awe that I filled her enough to create such beauty, to have created our baby. I did that. Mine.

My hand bats hers away and I take over, using my thumb to rub circles over her engorged clit. I push two fingers into her gushing hole with ease, so I add a third. She stretches slightly and my cock jumps, leaking pre-cum at the thought of stretching her for our baby.

"Oh god, Shaw," she pants. I glance up at her tweaking her nipples. I add a fourth finger, loving how her pussy adapts to it. My hand almost all the way inside her, her spine arches, making me swallow away the lump of desperation I have to own her inside and out.

"P-play with your clit for me. I need to stretch your cunt for the baby." Her eyes flare with need as her hand moves quickly, her palm covering her pussy as it rotates with the rise of her ass.

"Fuck." I watch in awe as my hand pushes into my girl.

Once fully inside, I ball my palm into a fist. She winces, making me freeze. "You okay, Red?"

"Yes. It hurts a little." She licks her lips. "But don't stop. I like it."

My balls draw up, and I swallow, forcing down my orgasm at the sight and sensation of her pussy sucking me in, clamping around me. I move my fist up and down, drawing it almost all the way out of her pussy before pushing it back in.

"Shaw, I'm . . ." Her body tenses, her pussy spasms.

"Oh fuck!" My cock spits cum from the tip. "Fuck, I want you pregnant forever."

She thrusts her hips up toward me. "Yes. Shit, yes. I want you to fill me with your cum, Shaw. Cover me in it."

Her words fill me with a rush of ecstasy as I lean my cock over her pussy with my fist fully inside. She throws her head back, screaming my name. "Shaawww."

"Fuck yes." I work my hand faster. "Take—" I pant heavily. "My fucking—" I grind my teeth and tighten my grip. "Cum." My eyes fixate on my cum as it hits her clit. "Take it all." I shuffle forward to allow it to hit her tits. The overwhelming urge to mark her again as mine sends me spiraling. "Mine!"

Our bodies fall lax.

"Mine." My tone is gentle and loving as I swirl the tip of my finger through my cum, once again writing my name on her skin. Only this time, it's filled with our baby, and the last time I created it.

EMI

His dominance turns me on so much it's indescribable. The way he spat at my fingers, stretched my pussy wide, and caressed our bump while he came made my orgasm soar.

My chest heaves as I come down from pleasuring myself as I sit up on my elbows to watch him stare at my bump. "Shaw, are you okay?"

His eyes snap up to mine, and my heart skips a beat at the possession behind his stare. "I meant it, you know."

I swallow under his scrutiny. "I want to keep you pregnant." His large palm strokes circles on my stomach, and I desperately need him.

"Shaw—" I lick my lips. "I need you."

His eyes light up with lust and his nostrils flare. "Go get your toy from out of your drawer." My eyes dart to the drawer beside the bed, my cheeks pinkening at the thought of Shaw knowing about it. "Emi"—his voice is firm—"be a good girl and do as I ask."

I scurry off the bed and open the drawer, moving aside my book to grab the bright-pink vibrator.

"Come here, baby. Climb onto my lap." Shaw sits on the edge of the bed, holding one hand out for me while the other strokes his cock. The fact that this man can get hard so quickly must be some kind of record.

I take his hand, and he spins me so my back is against his chest but not close enough to touch. His hard cock pokes into me as he works his fist up and down in the space between us.

"Fuck, Emi. You're going to lean forward, baby, and I'm going to stuff my cock in your ass, okay?"

I nod at his words.

"My cum is dripping from your pussy, and I'm not going to let it go to waste."

I whimper. "Okay." What more can he possibly have in store for us?

"Good girl. I need to use my cum to lube your tight little asshole." Again, I whimper, and Shaw chuckles. "Lean forward, baby." He presses on my spine, encouraging me to lean forward. Two fingers glide around my pussy, then dip inside, and taking our combined wetness, he drags it over my forbidden hole.

When he pushes one finger inside my asshole, I tense a little, and Shaw hisses through his teeth. "Fuck, I love how goddamn tight this is." His warm breath touches my back as he places gentle kisses down my spine while he adds another finger into my ass. "Good girl," he coos. My pussy clenches on his words. "Such a good fucking girl."

He positions the engorged head of his thick cock against my hole. "Switch your toy on, baby. Rub it against your clit." I do as he asks, loving his dominance and the feeling of security when one of his arms bands around my bump to hold us. I buck against the vibration on the toy, my clit tender from the multiple orgasms. But Shaw holds me firmly in place, leaving me no choice but to hold the toy against me. He uses the opportunity to slide the tip of his cock inside my tight hole. "Fuck," he pants. "Such a good girl for taking my thick cock in this tiny hole."

I moan and my head drops forward, but Shaw has other ideas as he inches his cock deeper and wraps my hair around his fist and yanks my head back. "Look in the mirror." His dark voice sends a shiver over my exposed body as he pushes farther inside, making me wince at the burn yet moan at the pleasure. My body is at an intoxicating war with itself. My eyes latch onto his in the mirror, and his fierce gaze matches my own, consumed with one another as though the hunger will never truly be satisfied.

His jaw clenches and his grip tightens as he rams up into me, making me jolt with the force and reminding me to use the vibrator. "Good girl. Push it into your pussy, Emi."

"Oh god," I moan.

"Push it in, Red."

My body floods with scorching heat as I move the toy to my opening and push it inside. "Ram it in, baby." He grunts as he fucks me ruthlessly. "Ram it all the way fucking in."

The room is filled with our groans and the slapping of our bodies.

I shove the vibrator higher, stretching my pussy open. The sensation of feeling completely full and stretched is incredible. "Oh god, Shaw. Don't . . . don't stop. Please don't stop." My fingernails dig into his thigh, no doubt leaving him with scratches.

"Fuck no, I'll never stop. My dirty girl taking two cocks, goddamn. Mine." He leans forward and bites my neck, sending me spiraling toward an orgasm.

"Oh. Oh fuck, Shaw. Jesus."

"Tell me you want my cum in your ass."

"I want it. I want it in my ass."

"Fucking take ittt!" His cock expands, shooting his cum inside me. "Fucking my pregnant wife's tight little ass." His palm finds my bump, and I give in to the raging inferno as my jaw drops open when I come so hard I see blackness and my body drops lax.

I'm vaguely aware of Shaw's chest heaving and the beat of his heart against my back as he maneuvers me, the gentle kiss to my head as he places me in bed, and the tender words to bump, "You mean the world to me," as he tugs the sheets around us.

I only wish his words were meant for me too.

TWENTY-ONE

SHAW

I glance around the waiting area again. My eyes lock onto a couple with a small child; they smile down at him lovingly, and it makes my heart constrict with an empty feeling of never having that love as a child. Emi squeezes my hand, making my eyes dart toward hers. Sympathy and understanding ooze from them, forcing an overwhelming urge to protect her and our bump to resurface.

A feeling like no other pulsates through my veins. I'll protect our little one. They'll never feel the emptiness, the lack of love and support Emi and I have endured growing up. I squeeze her hand back and stroke over her thumb as our eyes remain locked in silent recognition of our combined feelings.

When I told Emi how disappointed I was about missing the scan, she suggested booking another. I jumped at the chance and suggested we get the nursery ready together. Seeing her smile at my suggestion made my heart swell and excitement bubble through me.

"Mr. and Mrs. Varros." And just like that, my good mood is tampered. My spine bolts straight and my jaw grinds in annoyance at effectively being renamed by Luca, being stripped of myself for the sake of his organization. Yet again something else that is out of my control, and I fucking hate it, but I want my child to have my surname, and according to him, this is the only way. When I told Emi I wasn't happy about it, she spieled her usual comment, "In blood we're bound. In trust we live."

Well, I wasn't born into this fucked-up family of theirs, so I've no idea why they continue spouting their little motto to me. When she said it was an honor that Luca allowed me to share their surname, I lost my shit.

A fucking honor?

The man is a known psychopath who intends on railroading not only my life but my child's too.

I stand, tugging Emi to her feet. I refuse to look at her, even though I know she's as innocent a pawn as me. I can't help but take my feelings out on her; she's my only outlet for the rage bubbling inside me.

The nurse scans my body with interest, and the hold I have on Emi's hand tightens as I draw her into my side without thinking. The disrespectful nurse ignores Emi entirely. "Mr. Varros, so pleased to meet you. If you'd like to follow me." She holds her arm out toward the corridor, but I remain standing in shock. My feet refuse to move as I glare at her in contempt. Her eyes flick over my face, looking for a sign of what the problem might be. "I'll help you out, shall I? My wife is the one having the baby. If you weren't so busy eye-fucking me, you'd realize it." I wave my free hand toward Emi's protruding stomach, then when I glance up at her face, I notice her eyes have widened at my words, but I'm on a roll. "Have some fucking respect and apologize to my wife."

The nurse's mouth drops open, then closes before she opens her mouth to speak again, only for nothing to come out.

I hold up my hand to stop her when she tries again. "I'll save us both the time. Before we go any further, get me a different nurse." She jolts at my words before her cheeks flush, and she gives me a small nod of understanding without eye contact before she scurries off down the corridor.

Emi leans into me, her voice a whisper. "Was that really necessary?"

I glance down at her, her black orbs staring back at me, waiting for a reply. They practically sparkle in amusement, making my lip quirk at the side, and she doesn't miss the action as her face breaks out into the most beautiful smile, making me glean with pride. "Thank you." She stands on her tiptoes, and I lower my lips to meet hers. My free hand wraps into her hair, holding her tighter, pulling her closer as my tongue sweeps into her mouth, devouring every low whimper and swallowing it down, savoring it. *Fuck, she's incredible.*

"Shaw." She pulls back, breathing heavily, her face flushed and her eyes full of need. I stare at her as she trails her tongue over her bottom lip, as though savoring my taste, causing my cock to twitch at the thought.

All thoughts of Luca dissipated by a simple kiss.

"Mr. and Mrs. Varros, apologies. If you'd like to follow

me, please." We trail behind a doctor in his mid to late fifties and into a small room with a bed and chair.

"I really must apologize about my colleague. I can assure you she will be dealt with." The doctor's gaze shifts between Emi's and mine.

I give him a firm nod but can't help but comment further. "Good. She was unprofessional and damn right disrespectful to my wife. In fact, she's a walking lawsuit waiting to happen. Unassuming happy families are coming in here, and that tramp is potentially about to destroy them and your business." I cross my arms and stare the doctor down, causing him to swallow deeply.

"I understand your concerns, sir."

"I suggest you terminate her contract with immediate effect." *That'll show the little wench.*

"Shaw!" Emi gasps beside me, making my eyes dart down to hers.

"What? She was eye-fucking me." I shrug, my tone almost childlike.

Emi scoots her ass onto the bed, and I suck in a sharp breath as she raises her t-shirt above her bump.

I spin around on my heels to face the doctor. "And you're not sticking anything in my wife's pussy." My tone is stern and laced in threat.

He flushes and wipes his brow before walking over to use the hand sanitizer.

"You're making him nervous, stop it," Emi snaps in my direction. I grunt back at her noncommittally, because the thought of anyone but me touching my woman makes my chest feel like it's caving in. It makes me feral.

Lowering my ass into the seat beside Emi's bed, I take her hand in mine as the doctor rubs the gel on her stomach with a small device. Anxiety rushes through me when Emi winces. She narrows her eyes, as though realizing a change in my demeanor. "It's okay," she soothes. "It's cold, that's all."

I nod at her, dumbstruck when a whooshing noise fills the room. My eyes flick from the doctor to the doors, then around the room, unsure of what's happening.

Emi giggles, pulling her lip between her teeth. "Shaw, it's the baby's heartbeat."

I scan her face, and she tilts her head toward the screen beside her, so I lean forward in my chair to see a perfect image of our baby. It's not a blob like you see on scan photos online. No, this is just like it was advertised. You can see all the baby's features, and when the doctor presses a button on the screen, the angle changes and we can see the baby's toes. "Fuck, bump has toes."

My pulse races and my heart skips a beat when bump's hand stretches out, showing fingers. My whole world is right here. I'm right where I belong. Emotion clogs my throat, making my words come out gravely. "Fingers too," I tack on in awe.

Emi's laugh fills the air, and I can't help but laugh with her as I once again entwine our fingers and swallow away my unshed tears.

This has to be the best day of my entire life.

This week with Emi has been incredible. We've reached a turning point in our relationship, and when we went for the scan, I got to see my future on a small screen with my wife's hand in mine.

The feeling was indescribable. Pride, along with a fierce need to protect them, made my body tense, my heart swell, and my mind determined.

Emi hasn't mentioned Lizzie again, and I'm grateful for that. The last thing I want to do is unload my previous shitty relationship on my wife. Not when she's the only thing that matters to me now.

At one point during my relationship with Lizzie, I thought I was falling in love with her—I even told her so. But now I can look back and realize I was in love with the idea of a relationship but not willing to take the next step. I know now it could never have been love because with Emi, I'm all in, and without a shadow of a doubt, I want her and our babies, forever. I love her with everything I have, and what I don't have, I'll create for us.

I still can't believe I'm going to be a dad when I never considered that for my future at all. I knew Lizzie wanted children eventually, and it's one of the reasons we broke up. I also knew her behavior was not acceptable, so there was no way in hell I'd want to father a child with her. There's no doubt in my mind she'd use the child as a weapon against me, and that's something I wasn't willing to let happen. Ever. Being on the receiving end of that behavior as a child, I know the damage it can cause. The thought alone would tear my heart out, so I vowed never to let our relationship develop further, and her erratic behavior made it easy to follow through.

I tug on my joggers and make my way downstairs. Emi insisted the staff leave early tonight because my best friends have accepted an invitation by her to come over for dinner. I walk into the kitchen and, not for the first time, she takes my breath away. She rushes around flustered, unaware I'm watching her, taking her in.

I walk over to her and grip her shoulders and turn her around. "Red, you need to calm down."

Her black orbs sparkle, and she licks her lips. "I want them to like me."

I startle at her words. Never in a million years has Lizzie wanted my friends to like her. She saw them as an inconvenience, that they took me away from my time with her. She was rude to them, and in return, they were rude to her, so I kept our relationships as separate as possible, vowing never to bring the two relationships together again, until now.

Until her.

She leans up on her tiptoes and kisses the corner of my mouth. "You said Reed is a fussy eater, right?"

I smirk because the fact that she's made a mental note of all the snippets I've given her about my best friends is incredible and a show of how amazing she is.

But calling Reed fussy is a fucking understatement. Reed was brought up with a silver spoon so far wedged into his ass he's unable to shit without it coming out sparkling.

"He'll be fine, baby." The fact she's worried about Reed makes my heart swell, and I swear I fall for her even more.

The security intercom buzzes, and I reach out to the wall and press the button. "Sir, your guests have arrived."

"Thank you, send them up."

I kiss Emi's forehead and gift her with a reassuring smile, take her hand in mine, and head toward the front door.

Opening the door, Tate pushes past and annoyingly

ignores me and throws his arms around Emi. "Come here, beautiful." My body tenses with an insane jealousy I'm not used to feeling. I tug her from him and place my hand firmly on bump. On both of them. "Keep your fucking hands to yourself."

Tate throws his head back on a chuckle and holds his hands up. "Calm down, I was just saying hello."

My temple pulsates. "Then fucking say hello, Tate. I don't need you to maul her and our baby."

Emi places her hand on my chest, but my glare remains on Tate until her soft lips meet with mine and I relax into her. "Be nice." She smiles playfully.

"Yeah, Shaw. Be nice," Mase mimics, grinning as he holds his hand out toward Emi. I growl and almost want to push it away, but I relent with the reassurance of her soft touch. "I'm Mase. Nice to meet you, Em."

"Her name's fucking Emi, dumbass," I snap back.

Owen pushes past Mase with a bundle of beers in his hands and a nod toward Emi. Other than that, he blanks us both, and I can't say as I'm disappointed. If only my other friends could do the same.

"We have beer, Owen," I say as I turn to follow him, heading toward one of the numerous living rooms.

EMI

Shaw stalks after Owen, and I turn to watch Mase and Tate shove one another like schoolboys while making their way toward the living room. I can't help but smile in their direction.

A throat clears from behind me. "I'm Reed. Good to finally meet you." I turn to face the voice and find myself awestruck at his handsome face. He has thick dark hair, reminding me of my Italian ancestors, green eyes, and broad shoulders. His sharp jawline gives him an edge, making him ideal for a modeling agency. He's the only one wearing dress pants and a shirt, whereas the other guys opted for jeans and t-shirts. Reed stands stoically still, making no effort to disguise his perusal of me. "You're not his usual type."

I swallow back the emotion at the shock of hearing those words. They cut far deeper than I could have ever imagined. My heart thumps at knowing I'm not what Shaw prefers.

He tilts his head to survey me and takes a step forward,

but I take a step back. Reed clears his throat again. "Apologies, I think you misunderstood me, Emi. What I meant was, you're not his usual type, that's a good thing."

I startle as my mind works over what he's saying. My throat clogs, making it clear I'm emotional. "Why would you say that?"

Reed's lips tip up at the side. "Because the others have all been a bunch of conceited bitches. Materialistic, manipulative, and only after his money."

I raise my chin higher. "How do you know I'm not like that?"

His smile is gorgeous and no doubt makes women drop their panties. "You're standing here covered in flour, have an army of men outside, and the financial backing of the Mafia. It's safe to say you're none of those things."

I stare down at my black t-shirt covered in flour. "My brother would kill me for entertaining guests like this," I huff.

"I won't tell." He winks at me, making me smile at his lightheartedness. "Come on, you best get us fed before Tate orders in, apparently he could eat an army." His lips tip up at the side at his joke. I like Reed a whole lot more than I did a few minutes ago.

"Where the fuck did you learn to cook like this?" Tate moans around another slice of pizza, rolling his eyes.

"She's Italian. All Italians can cook, dipshit." Mase clips the back of Tate's head with his palm.

"Pretty fucking sure that's not true, am I right?" Owen laughs toward me.

I point my pizza in his direction. "You're absolutely right." The idea that any of my family actually know how to cook is absurd. I smile to myself, imagining Luca having to serve his own breakfast.

Shaw kisses the top of my head again as I rest lazily against his chest. He's been doing it all night, and it hasn't gone unnoticed by the others.

"How far along are you now?" Mase asks. He's the quiet one of the group; he seems lost in his own head a lot of the time, and I can't help but sense his unhappiness. He's the fairest-haired of them all but equally as handsome. All of the guys have bodies sculptured by the gods, and Mase is no exception. In fact, when he leans forward, his shirt stretches over his chest.

A sharp pinch on my thigh has me darting my eyes toward Shaw's. His blue eyes have darkened and his jaw tics . . . he's jealous. The thought makes my heart flutter like a schoolgirl. I push back against his cock and trail a hand over his thigh, making him tense below me, then I entwine our hands and, as if on cue, his body relaxes into mine with the reassurance.

"She's seven months and three days," Shaw replies.

"Do you know what you're having?" Tate asks, taking a swig of a beer.

"No, we want a surprise." I smile triumphantly at the fact I have a say in the matter.

"How's things going with Luca?" Owen asks with his eyes latched onto Shaw.

My throat dries at the mention of my brother, knowing the obvious tension around Shaw and Luca.

Shaw drinks from the bottle of water. "Things are going fine. We have an event with him next week to celebrate the wedding."

"Nice. A Mafia event." Tate grins mockingly, making Owen kick his leg.

"What the fuck, man? I nearly dropped my pizza," he moans back, shooting daggers in his direction.

Owen bends his pizza slice in half and crams it all in his mouth, and my eyes widen in shock at how easily he can make it all fit. Not for the first time, I consider how much he looks like a Viking with his broad shoulders, blond hair and rugged good looks. "Owen, you deal with the security side of the business, right? So how exactly do you know my brother?"

He grabs another slice from the coffee table. "Yeah." Folding it in half, he pushes it into his mouth again.

"Jesus. You're eating those like they're chips." Mase stares at him in disbelief, his mouth dropped open in disgust.

Owen grins, showing the pizza hanging from his mouth.

"Fucking disgusting," Shaw grumbles in my ear, making me laugh.

"I know a guy on your brother's security team. So, I met him before." I nod at Owen's basic explanation. In the Mafia world, I wouldn't have even dared to ask the question, and I sure as hell wouldn't have received an answer.

"How's Thirsty Thursday going?" Mase smirks, aiming his question toward Tate.

Shaw freezes behind me, and the hairs on the back of my neck stand at his reaction.

"What's Thirsty Thursday?" I ask.

Tate drops his beer to the floor before cussing and using a dozen napkins to mop up the mess.

I tilt my head up to Shaw's face. His eyes have

narrowed on Mase, and he grinds his jaw so loud I can hear his teeth.

"What's Thirsty Thursday?" I repeat.

"Yeah, Shaw. Care to explain?" Mase crosses his arms over his chest and raises his eyebrows in jest.

Reed sits back in the only armchair in the room with a calculating smile on his face, as if enjoying the exchange.

Shaw clears his throat. "It's a dare that dipshit over there got us all doing." He throws his arm out toward Tate.

"Yeah, well, I'm the fucking winner." Tate smiles while brushing down his jeans.

"What did you have to do?"

Shaw drops his head back on the couch with a loud groan. "Come on, baby."

I bite on my lip to stifle a laugh. I've grown up around men my entire life, so I know the antics they get up to.

I turn toward Mase, the one who appears the most levelheaded. "Mase, what did you have to do?"

He looks like a deer caught in the headlights at my question. "I didn't do anything." Mase holds his hands up in surrender.

"Nah, Mase didn't do anything. Any-fucking-thing," Tate jokes, earning him a glare from Owen.

"Wait. What's going on, Shaw?" I turn back toward Shaw, who is now pinching the bridge of his nose and staring up at the ceiling.

"Fine. Fucking fine." He stares back down at me, and his Adam's apple bobs. "We had a dumb bet that we had to receive a blowjob every Thursday, and the winner was the one to maintain it the longest. Hence the nickname 'Thirsty Thursday.'"

"I'm the winner!" Tate declares while tensing his biceps

and kissing them, earning a chorus of groans and cusses from the others.

Shaw bends his head and kisses my neck, whispering, "I'm sorry you had to hear that."

"You can make it up to me later." I push my ass back against his cock, making him chuckle.

"Mase, were you the first to tap out or something?" I ask innocently.

Mase chokes on his beer, and I can't help but laugh at his reaction.

"Something like that." His jaw tics, and I realize I've stumbled upon something of a sore point.

"Mase doesn't get any sexual activities. Ever," Owen declares nonchalantly. "He's practically a born-again virgin."

I raise my eyebrows, shocked; I mean, the man is gorgeous and sculptured and well . . . gorgeous.

"His wife doesn't want to have sex with him," Tate announces, picking up another slice of pizza while my mouth drops open at his lack of tact.

Watching Mase not react to those words makes me wonder how many times the guys have said something about it. Clearly, he's unperturbed and used to it.

I pull at the label on my water bottle, unsure of what to say. "I'm sorry about that, Mase. Maybe therapy would help?" I shrug, not wanting to overstep the line.

Mase exhales loudly. "A divorce would be nice."

"You can't divorce her because she won't have sex!" My heart races with panic for the poor woman.

"Baby, shh . . . there's so much shit going on over there." Shaw strokes his hand up and down my arm.

"You should just order one of those women from Indulgence. They're like mail-order brides without the wedding," Reed throws in.

Mase shakes his head. "Nah, I at least want to be legally separated first."

Tate leans forward and takes another slice of pizza, making me wonder where he puts it all. He aims the slice at Mase. "Then once you are separated, order multiple at once. You've a lot of years to make up for."

Did Tate just suggest Mase hasn't had sex in years? Wow, that's unheard of. In the Mafia, a man would take another woman to please him, and that's assuming he was a good enough man to not just take it anyway.

"Is the tomato sauce organic too?" Reed breaks my trail of thought with his random question.

I glance over at him pushing his pizza around his plate with a fork. "Yes. It was all organic produce."

Tate rolls his eyes.

"And the cheese. Where did you say it was from?"

"It was from a dairy farm my brother's staff use."

"Mm," he muses, unconvinced at the authenticity of my pizza.

"Jesus. What the fuck's it matter? Just eat it," Owen snaps in his direction while bending another slice of pizza and shoving it in his mouth.

"It matters because my fitness consultant has me on a strict diet to maintain my health and physique."

"Just do a few more weights in the morning. That's what I do." Tate shrugs between mouthfuls.

"Reed, if you don't want the pizza, you don't have to eat it," I tell him when he grimaces down at the plate.

"It's fucking delicious." Tate grabs the pizza from his

plate and literally throws a slice toward Owen, who catches it as though it's an everyday occurrence.

Shaw bends down and speaks in a low voice. "It's a regular occurrence, Tate throwing Owen food." I nod in acknowledgment at his words and smile in their direction.

"Thank you for tonight, baby. It's been incredible." His words make me beam with pride.

I tilt my head back, and his soft lips meet mine.

Tonight has gone perfectly, and I never want it to end.

I never want a day without Shaw in my life.

TWENTY-TWO

EMI

Shaw's legs bounce, and he holds my hand as they rest on his thigh. The journey to my brother's should only be another half hour, but it feels like a lifetime.

Luca sent over my usual stylist this morning, and I've been pruned and poked at and once again look like the perfect Mafia princess.

My royal-blue dress fits me elegantly and showcases my bump, which makes me nervous about how exposed I am. But Luca is making a statement tonight, and the point is that there's no backing down from the decision that was made. It will be clear I'm pregnant with my husband's child, leaving for no alternative to the agreement with Ravlek.

I move my hand from Shaw's, and he's so lost in his head he doesn't realize it. I bite into my lip in consideration, fully aware I now probably have lipstick on my teeth.

Making the decision to help relax him, I glide my hand over his pants and down toward his cock.

Shaw's eyes snap toward mine, filled with heat. His breath quickens as I stroke over him and then I move lower to toy with his balls. He opens his legs farther and relaxes his body while resting his arm along the back of the car seat.

I'm thankful we're in the back of one of the secure SUVs because there's a privacy screen between us and the driver. It's only now that I wonder if this is the reason for that screen.

I snap open his pants, causing Shaw to hiss between his teeth. I delight in the fact that his chest heaves and his mouth drops open when my hand pushes into his boxers and wraps around his smooth cock. It's hard and wetness drips from the tip. I struggle to maneuver my hand around him, so Shaw pulls down his zipper and pulls his cock free.

I pump him quickly. "Such a good girl," he praises while toying with my hair.

I lift my dress, allowing me to kneel onto the seat beside him. My tongue connects with the tip of his cock, making Shaw curse and ball his hands into fists. I flick it over the slit and moan when the saltiness of his pre-cum hits my tastebuds.

"Fuck. Lick my slit clean, baby." His hips rise, forcing me to take more in my mouth. I push down, allowing him to hit the back of my throat. "Fuck, yes." His hand finds my hair and tangles with the pins holding it up.

"Jesus. Keep sucking, baby."

"Mm," I groan around his cock and caress his balls, giving them a tug that makes his ass lift off the seat.

"Fuck." He holds my head tighter, then begins to fuck my face. "Fuck yes."

"Mm." I gargle around his thickness.

His voice is full of grit. "Fucking greedy for it. So greedy for my cum." *Thrust.*

The pinch of my hair causes me to moan. "Mm." *Thrust.*

"Take it all." *Thrust.* "Like that." *Thrust.* "Just like." *Thrust.* "Fucking." *Thrust.* "That." His body becomes still as his cock swells and his cum floods my mouth. I swallow it down; there's so much of it I choke, but he holds my head firmly in place, giving me no option but to accept it all.

I slowly withdraw his cock from my mouth, trailing my tongue over his length to clear up any excess cum. His hand loosens in my hair, and I melt against him when he strokes it, then down my cheek and over my jawline. "Such a good girl, sucking away my stress."

"Did it help?"

He tucks himself in while my expectant eyes hold his gaze, and his eyes soften. "Of course." He flicks my bottom lip with his thumb. "These lips were made for sucking."

I smirk back at him. "I thought they were for kissing?"

"That too, come here." He hoists me onto his lap and wraps his arms around me before dipping his head to nuzzle behind my ear and then he peppers kisses along my jawline to my lips. When Shaw's soft lips meet mine, a chill runs through me and goose bumps cover my skin. He holds me tighter and pushes his tongue delicately past my lips, as though asking permission to enter my mouth. Such a contrast as to how he fucked my face only moments ago.

I move my hands around his neck, and a moan catches in the back of my throat. When Shaw drags his hand up and around my neck to hold me in place, I whimper at his strong possession. His hand cradles my face while his action speaks a thousand words, mine.

Our tongues mingle, like we have all the time in the world. A lifetime.

It's delicate and sensual, seductive and tantalizing. It's absolutely perfect. This feeling gathering inside is momentous; he's quite literally taking my breath away.

We pull away from one another, completely breathless. Our foreheads meet, and our eyes remain locked, a force between us so strong, so confounding, my heart flutters and my breath catches. I want to tell him how I feel, that I've fallen in love with him and that, besides our baby, he's the best thing to ever happen to me.

I open my mouth. "I—"

A knock comes from the door, making us startle at the same time, and my heart leaps into my throat. I giggle away the moment when I realize we were so enthralled with one another we hadn't realized the car had come to a standstill.

We've arrived.

TWENTY-THREE

SHAW

If I thought my house was ridiculous, then this one takes the crown. Why the hell you need a house as big as this is beyond comprehension. I turn my head toward Emi and roll my eyes, making her giggle at my silent words. She agrees with me, I can see it in those sparkling orbs of hers.

A butler approaches and draws out his hand. "This way, please." I try my best to ignore the men standing guard every few feet as though there's going to be some sort of attack any minute.

The ballroom is alive with every Mafia family from the East Coast, apparently one from the West too.

There are senators and other people of power I wouldn't put in the same room as the Mafia, but I'm coming to realize everyone plays a part in allowing this organization to continue in some way or another, even law enforcement.

Albeit in a peaceful way, according to Owen.

He's here tonight as part of STORM Security, and the dick gave my wife a thorough once-over as we walked in. I'll punch him in the balls for that when I next see him.

She looks absolutely incredible, and I don't miss every man's head turning at my wife's beauty, nor them locking eyes on our bump. Even the women glower in her direction, and I'm convinced it's from jealousy. You'd have to be a moron not to realize she outshines anyone in this ludicrous mansion Luca calls a home.

She holds herself with confidence and poise. Her luscious tits fill the top of her dress and a perfect bump is on full display for the world to see, making me want to beat my chest with pride. I put that there. Mine.

Our hands are clutched together as one. We make our way across the ballroom toward Luca, who is engrossed in a conversation with a man looking equally as menacing. Emi's hand tightens in mine, and her body coils tight. I glance down at her in question, but she gives me a small head shake and I look away, acting unperturbed at her sudden change in demeanor, but inside I'm hyperaware of her anxieties.

As we move closer to Luca, he stands from his chair to greet us. "Luca," I greet, lifting my chin, then I hold my hand out to meet his. The firm squeeze on mine is meant to be threatening; I read it in the unspoken words oozing from his eyes. "Act in love. Put on a show of solidarity." I give him a sharp, meaningful nod, and he releases my hand, allowing me to step back as he moves on to Emi.

He gifts her with a kiss to both cheeks. "Good to see you, Emi. You look . . ." His eyes trail down my wife, and if I'm not mistaken, he grimaces. ". . . big."

Emi's cheeks pinken, causing every muscle in my body to coil with rage. I grind my teeth, stepping forward to correct my brother-in-law's ill manners when Emi places a hand on my chest to stop me from moving closer.

Luca chuckles darkly and moves his head closer to mine, his voice low and dark. "Wow, stronzo. You actually look like you care." He raises an eyebrow at me, and I ball my hand into a tight fist.

Emi huffs loudly. "Luca. Stop toying with him."

Luca grins at his sister. Even his fucking smile looks sinister.

The man who Luca was in a heated discussion with stands, and I don't miss everyone around him standing to attention as he does. The tense atmosphere cuts through the air with his presence, and I take him in. His Italian features are evident. He looks in his mid to late thirties. "Lorenzo," he offers, making me realize this is her family Don.

Emi's eyes implore mine, and I realize she's waiting for me to offer my hand. I casually hold out my hand in greeting, and he glares at it with disgust before flicking his dark eyes back up to my face.

Just when I think he's not going to shake my hand, he slides it in. His eyes are laser-focused on my face as if seeing straight through me, into every thought, every action and assessing it, picking apart my thoughts, and drawing his own conclusions. I swallow away an uneasy ball of anxiousness knotting in my throat and glare right back at him, causing his lips to twitch in mockery.

"Congratulations." The word slides from his lips with a calculated ease, and I glance around the room to see everyone watching us, making me realize this is the Mafia

Don's way of showing his acceptance of our relationship. Acceptance into the organization.

"Thank you for your support," I reply and nod my head in acknowledgment of his approval. He drops my hand and walks away, but I don't miss the menacing edge to Luca's glare directed at Lorenzo's back.

A throat clears behind Emi, and we turn to face a man staring at her with such intensity I push her behind me as a natural reaction to protect her. Her body flinches against mine when she moves to stand beside me. He's tall, around six foot five with broad shoulders, a shaved head, and small scars on his face as though he's been in a knife fight. I dread to think what his opponent might look like.

Emi clears her throat. "Shaw, this is Ravlek." I recognize the name from my discussions with Owen. He's the notorious Ravlek, the Russian Emi was promised to.

"You look well." His eyes lock on to my wife's protruding stomach, and he licks his lips with a sleazy look of envy.

I grind my teeth at his blatant disregard for me being present. He's practically eye-fucking my very pregnant wife. Rage boils inside me, and my chest heaves in temper at his complete disrespect.

I step forward, past giving a shit who this asshole could possibly be. I lower my voice. "Carry on eye-fucking my wife and I'll take your fucking eyes out," I grit out.

Luca appears at my side. "Ravlek. You were warned not to cause trouble." Luca clicks his fingers and several men appear from nowhere, surrounding the man who holds his hands up in surrender, but his glare toward Emi remains, and the calculation behind his eyes sends a wave of unease through my body. A tremor passes through Emi, making my patience snap with how uncomfortable she is in his presence. I fly toward him but am held back by three of Luca's men as I struggle against their hold.

Ravlek backs away. "I'll be seeing you, Princess." He smirks, the words sounding more of a threat than a promise.

Their hands release me, and I spin to face Luca. "I want him fucking dead!"

Luca chuckles darkly. "Then you'd best follow me."

My eyes latch on to Emi's as she strokes over her stomach protectively.

I drop my head beside her ear. "I don't want to leave you here."

"It's fine. I'll go grab a drink from the bar." She points at the bar, and I survey the room. "I have my brother's men watching my every move, Shaw." She huffs, making me take in the room once again, and this time, seeing the guards mingling within the guests makes my shoulders relax with the knowledge. After all, she was brought up in this world.

I duck my head and place a gentle kiss on her cheek. "I won't be long." My heart hammers painfully, making me draw my eyebrows in confusion at my reaction to leaving her, and judging by the look in Emi's eyes, she senses a change too.

"Maxim is here too," she reassures me, as if sensing my anxiety.

I turn my head slightly to see Maxim watching us, and he gives me a firm nod, as if understanding my apprehension.

Pulling away from Emi, I turn and walk away, following Luca and his men as he leads me out of the ballroom, down a corridor, and into what I can only assume is his office. His men stand at the door as I follow him inside.

"Close the door," he barks, and my jaw grinds at his sniping commands.

Luca sits behind a large wooden desk and lifts his feet onto it, crossing his legs at his ankles. He withdraws a pen knife from his pocket and flicks it open, back and forth, back and forth.

I stay standing, my hands balling into fists as I try to tamper down the raging storm inside me. "Sit." He points his knife at the chair opposite the desk.

My feet stay planted to the ground, ignoring his command. I'm done being bossed around by this prick. Mafia or no Mafia.

Luca's jaw grinds, and his eyes sharpen before he opens his jacket, revealing a handgun. The insinuation is there. It's in his eyes, in his movement.

I swallow past the lump lodged in my throat, and my ass finds the chair, his sinister eyes never leaving mine.

"You put on a good show out there, stronzo." He points his knife toward the door.

I grind my teeth, seething with rage at his insult.

"I'm impressed. When I invited Ravlek here tonight, it was to make it clear to him and everyone else that Emi belongs to you now."

My shoulders bunch tight and fury runs through my veins at his implication. Ravlek is Emi's ex-fiancé. "You invited him here to parade her in front of him?" I shake my head with an unamused laugh before staring back at him with rage. "You're twisted."

"Si." He smirks back at me and leans forward. "What is the saying?" He glances around the room before his eyes lock back on to mine in such a calculated way. I'm convinced he knows what he wanted to say all along. "Two birds, one stone?"

I breathe through my nose, desperately trying to tamper the raging inferno inside me at the way he controls each and every aspect of my life. "Meaning?"

"Meaning, you showed the world you're in love with my sister." He points his knife at me. "Your wife. At the same time, it showed Ravlek and everyone else that he no longer has any rights toward her."

I seethe inside at his words. The way he talks about Emi as though she's a possession, a pawn in his games. Our child too. I bite the inside of my cheek, stopping myself from telling him what a sick piece of shit he is while I replay his words. *"You're in love with my sister."* My heart jumps, and not for the first time, I question my feelings for Emi. But when Ravlek's face flashes before me, my anger returns tenfold. "He looked like he wanted to kill her."

Luca throws his head back on a twisted laugh, then settles his gaze back on me. "He's into some twisted shit."

Disgust roils my stomach. "Meaning?"

"Meaning, what he does with his woman, he does with his woman." He shrugs.

This asshole was going to sell off his sister to some scumbag that would treat her like shit? I stare it him, making him chuckle at my reaction.

I'll never understand this lifestyle, and I never want to.

"Your ex made a scene at your office." He raises an eyebrow at me in question, and I swallow with the intensity behind it.

"She's been dealt with."

"Do I need to kill her?"

My eyes bulge in horror. "No, you don't need to fucking kill her. I told you it's been dealt with."

"I won't have my sister upset, stronzo. Having your ex lurking around devalues your relationship and our reputation."

He talks with no feelings at all, making me wonder how him and Emi can possibly be related in the first place. Where she's soft, gentle, and compliant, he's devoid of all emotion, a powerhouse of hate and vengeance.

"She won't be a problem," I reiterate.

He regards me for a moment before sighing. "Very well. But the next time, she won't be so lucky."

I make a mental note to speak with Owen, to make sure Lizzie is not able to cause us any more issues. I refuse to have her death on my conscience. Not with my mother's always playing in the back of my mind.

Dropping his feet, he leans forward in his chair and steeples his hands together on the desk. "Now, about STORM Enterprises."

TWENTY-FOUR

EMI

I gaze around the room once again. Luca's team has done impeccable, as always. There are white drapes lining the walls and ceiling, candles adorn the glass tables, and the band from my sweet sixteenth play lively music, giving it a party vibe as opposed to a formal event.

I've plastered on my perfected smile and accepted a "congratulations" from so many people my cheeks ache from smiling. I scoff at the thought, and Maxim looks at me in question. I take in my brother; he's handsome and strong. His short, cropped hair isn't as dark as ours and his skin is fairer.

Growing up, Maxim always had issues with looking the odd one out in our family. He said people never took him seriously because he wasn't blood. But the softness in Maxim's eyes gives him a different edge to my brother's fiery ones; they give him compassion, whereas Luca puts the fear of God in people. Maxim gives people relief and comfort, and Papi says sometimes that can drive a message home just as much as being fierce. That's why they work so well together; he's the calm in Luca's storm.

"You deserve to be in love." The words fall from my mouth before I can think to stop them, and I cover my mouth with my hand.

Maxim scans my face and jolts at my words, and when our eyes lock, I see a tirade of hurt behind them before he glances away.

"You've been in love?" It's a rhetorical question, judging by his reaction.

"Mm," he muses, taking another drink of his whiskey.

"What happened?" I stare at my brother as he watches the guests dance.

"The organization." My stomach sinks for Maxim. He's in love with someone and they have a role to play too, to marry another, no doubt.

Emotion gathers in my throat. "I'm sorry."

He turns his head. "You have nothing to be sorry for, Princessa. You did good. You got out." He glances down at my stomach, and my hand finds bump. *Does Maxim think I did this on purpose?*

My lips move to explain otherwise when I notice Aldo, one of Luca's soldiers, tip his head toward the door. I gasp at seeing him again.

There was once a time when all I could think about was Aldo and his messy brown hair. I'd run my fingers through it as his lips devoured mine with stolen kisses. My heart would hammer, and my legs would wobble each time we'd sneak off to meet. I knew I was on the verge of giving Aldo my virginity, and I knew if Luca ever found out about him, he'd kill him. It was one of the reasons I decided to do what I did at the casino that night. I wanted the control, to be able to decide who took my virginity. At the very least, I wanted to be attracted to them.

"Maxim, I just need to use the restroom. I'll be back shortly." Maxim stares into space as I turn and walk toward the door. Glancing back over my shoulder, I notice the longing behind his gaze as he watches a couple dance. It can only be described as heartbreak, and as much as I hate to see him like this and I'm desperate to know more, I need to speak to Aldo.

I owe him that at least.

SHAW

I take another deep breath, splash water over my face, and rest my hands on the edges of the sink, staring up into the mirror, wondering how the hell I could have fucked up my life so epically.

To not only lose all control over my own life but to have little to none over my wife's and child's too is unfathomable. I mean, I even have to live on someone else's property with their furnishings and staff when I'm quite capable of purchasing and running my own home. Every fucking move is dictated by Luca Varros, and I couldn't detest him more if I tried.

I take a deep breath and steel my spine, reminding myself that Emi and the baby need me in all of this chaos. They rely on me and are just as innocent, being used as Luca's pawns. Just like me.

I throw open the door, determined to get this ridiculous parade of power over with so I can get my family back home. As I stride down the corridor, I hear hushed voices, and a familiar giggle makes the hairs on my neck rise.

I slow my step and stay in the shadows as Emi talks to some guy who has her cornered with his hands above her head.

Rage bubbles inside me, forcing me forward, but when I realize she's making no attempt to move and gifts him with a smile, I'm almost brought to my knees as my step falters. My heart free falls from my chest and I gasp for breath, flicking my gaze away from theirs to control my emotions. I lick my suddenly dry lips and turn my head back, trying to listen in on their obvious private conversation.

"Please don't do this. You said you didn't want to hurt me. This is hurting me." The guy talks so low I have to strain to listen.

"Aldo, I'm sorry." A tear trickles down her face, and I can see me gently wiping it away, but I wince, not allowing myself to consider doing it. Not when she's ripping my heart out. She doesn't deserve my kindness, my loyalty.

I've sacrificed my life to protect her, and this is the thanks I get? Her sneaking away with a lover while at our wedding celebration? Rage floods my veins, and without another thought, I stride from the shadows and crash my fist into the guy's jaw.

He stumbles back, holding his jaw in shock as I move toward him again with purpose.

"Shaw, please stop it." But I ignore her pleas and grab the punk by his collar and smash him into the wall face-first, causing blood to splatter onto the pristine paintwork.

Emi gasps, the sound only enraging me more at her

concern for him. "Fuck, man. It's not what—" I punch him again, in his gut this time. I've had enough of this fucking family. Another punch to his stomach. My chest heaves in fury at another man touching my woman and her embracing it.

"Shaw, please." She grasps my arm and tugs at me, but I ignore her and launch myself forward again. "Shaw. I'm begging you." My knuckles split when I punch his face with such force a loud crack can be heard, and he falls to the floor.

I spin to face her, and taking in her reaction only enrages me more as tears streak her face for him.

Grabbing her hand, I march us up the corridor I just came from, and as Luca's office comes into view, I can't help the burst of excitement that flows through me when I consider my options.

It's time I showed Emi and Luca what control looks like.

EMI

I've never seen Shaw so angry. Not even when he found out I was pregnant.

He practically throws me into Luca's office, and I stumble to stay upright. He slams the door closed and turns to lock it while my eyes take in the empty room with relief.

Shaw tugs his bowtie from his shirt, throwing it to the floor. "Who the fuck is he?" He glares at me.

I'm so shocked by the evening's events I can't speak. The husband standing before me right now is unrecognizable.

His once-perfect white shirt is splattered in blood, his fists are tight, and his knuckles are bleeding. Those blue eyes are wild and full of hate, and his hair is disheveled.

"I asked you a fucking question. Now talk!" he yells, making me jump.

"His . . . his name is Aldo."

Shaw takes a step closer to me, making me step back. "I

didn't ask his fucking name, Emi. I want to know who he is to you."

I squeeze my eyes closed at the pain of who Aldo was to me. What do I tell him? I once thought he was my everything? That I was a silly girl with a crush, craving for some affection, so I risked our lives in order to get it.

"I liked him."

"You liked him?" he mocks with a raised eyebrow.

His Adam's apple bobs as hurt mars his handsome features.

"Do you love him?" His voice is low with a hint of vulnerability behind it, and he glances away as though he's so hurt he's unable to look at me.

I gasp. "No. Of course not." I shake my head.

His eyes snap back to mine. "Was he the guy you kissed?"

I bite my lip and nod. "Yes."

He flinches and makes a choking noise. "Have you let him touch you? Touch your pussy?"

"No. I swear I haven't." I take a step forward so he can see the truth behind my eyes, but it's him who steps back this time.

"On your fucking knees." He unbuckles his belt as I move to my knees, but I'm willing to do anything to reassure him.

He tugs down his zipper and takes out his hard cock, fisting it roughly in the process. "Those tears belong to me. Do you understand me? You only cry for me!" he bellows, making me flinch again.

"And I will make you cry, Emi. I'm going to shove my cock so far down your fucking throat you'll forget anything other than my taste. I'll fucking consume every morsel of you, like you do me."

My heart jumps at his confession, but the hate in his eyes makes me realize this is nothing more than a power trip, control. This isn't feelings toward me, this is possession. I belong to him; this is no different from the Mafia. A lump of hurt gathers in my throat, but I have no time to swallow it down because Shaw grips the back of my head with such force I whimper as he shoves his thick cock to the back of my throat with a slam of his hips, making his groin hit my face.

"Fuck." He exhales loudly before thrusting back out, then repeating the motion. "Fuck." He bends his head and spits in my face, his eyes filling with lust at his action.

My tongue tries to move, but his thick cock is wedged inside with complete control of my mouth, making me aware I'm nothing more than a hole for him to fuck. "Have you any idea how much I hate you right now?" My heart sinks, and I whimper at his words as he continues to thrust with aggression inside my mouth. "I hate you so fucking much." *Thrust.* "You ruined my fucking life." Tears spill down my face, and I feel like my body is going to give way at his devastating words, but the grip on my head holds me upright as he continues to use me.

"Fuck. It's a good thing my wife is a hot fuck. I'm going to use your fucking holes like you use me, Emi." *Thrust.* I splutter and try to gasp for air, but he's relentless with his movements. I close my eyes to block out the hate oozing from his eyes. "Destroy you like you destroy me." *Thrust.*

"Tug my fucking balls and make me cum, Princess," he spits out spitefully, and his jibe about me being a princess makes me whimper in hurt. But I do as he asks and move my hand to his balls, rolling them gently, a contrast to his powerful movements.

"Fuck." I open my eyes to him throwing his head back and squeezing his eyes shut. "Fuck, I hate you." His cruel words slice through my heart as his cock pumps into my mouth brutally. Shaw's hips stutter with the force of his orgasm, but his grip on my head tightens, making me want to cry out in pain, but nothing can hurt me as much as the words that sliced through me, leaving me broken. I swallow down his warm cum.

When he comes down from his orgasm, I glance away from him, unable to meet his eyes, not wanting to give him an ounce of the hurt behind mine. He pulls out of my mouth, and I quickly turn my head away. He bends down, takes my face in his hands, and flicks his tongue over his spittle, gathering it back into his mouth.

"You've no idea how much I fucking hate you."

I push him back, forcing a mocking laugh from him, and I realize maybe I didn't know Shaw Grant at all.

Maybe I hate him too.

TWENTY-FIVE

SHAW

After pulling myself together, I told Emi to convince Luca she needed to go home and rest. I stare out the car window, ignoring my wife and the anger radiating from her and the devastation we caused to our relationship tonight.

The car pulls to a stop outside our home—correction, Luca's home—and I can't find it within me to get out and go inside and pretend everything is fine when it couldn't be further from the truth.

I can sense her looking at me for direction, but I refuse to face her. I refuse to see the devastating look on her face, and instead, like the coward Luca delights in me being, I stare through the window. "Get out of the fucking car, Emi." My voice is deep and stern.

Out of the corner of my eye, she jolts and sucks in a sharp breath, but, still, I refuse to turn and face her.

"I'm sorry, Shaw." Her voice wavers but she does as I

instruct, like the good Mafia princess, and that just makes me hate her all the more. She slides out of the car, shutting the door behind her.

Clearing my throat, I turn toward the driver. "Take me to Club 11."

I knock back another shot, then motion for another. Reed eyes me, and I loathe him for it. "I'm just fucking saying you didn't even ask the girl what the deal was before you flew off the handle."

I scoff, ignoring his attempt at thinking diplomatically. Always the voice of reason. I grind my teeth in annoyance, not giving a shit about his sense of reasoning.

"He has a point. I mean, did you even hear any of their conversation before you saw red?" Tate throws out while eyeing the dancer in front of him. I grimace at the waitress wearing the little G-string; she's nothing like my wife, and I couldn't be more grateful for it. Glancing at Tate, he's curling his lip in disgust at the waitress. Interesting. If only my life wasn't a shit show, I'd have time to analyze my friend's unusual behavior further.

"She's good for you, Shaw. Don't fuck this up by being a jealous prick. Besides, you don't have a choice," Mase adds while taking a swig of his beer.

I want to roll my eyes at his words, but the truth is, even if I did have a choice, Emi is who I want to be with.

Two of the dancers come over to the table; one sits her ass on Reed's lap while the other makes her way toward me. The sway of her hips would normally entice me, but there's no way in hell I want her anywhere near me. I hold up my hand to stop her, showing her my wedding finger. "This is a wedding ring, sweetheart. Happily fucking married." I glare in her direction.

Reed throws his head back as though what I said is the funniest thing he's ever heard, and I guess he's right, considering I just called a meeting based on how pissed off with my marriage I am. Still, I'm not about to walk out on Emi and our baby.

"Married men still like their cocks getting sucked," she pouts.

I grab another shot and knock it back. My shoulders broaden. "You're right, they do. By their hot-as-fuck wives." My mind can't help but wander back to earlier, seeing Emi on her knees for me. I'll never need another woman again.

The dancer stares down at me like I have two heads. I push my thumb in Tate's direction. "He, on the other hand, is not married."

I don't miss Tate tense at my words, so I turn toward him to ask him, but before I get a chance to question him, the dancer drops down in my lap and throws her arm around my neck, pushing her tits into my chest.

My whole body revolts at her touch, and her cheap perfume invades my nostrils, making me want to vomit.

My feet find the floor as I push back on my chair like I've been burned, and without holding onto the dancer, the whole table winces at the sound of her ass hitting the wood.

"I said no." I drag a hand through my hair, exhaling loudly. "Jesus. No means no."

The dancer rolls onto all fours and crawls toward Tate, practically salivating at the mouth, she licks her lips as I watch on in horror. Tate scoots his chair back so quick he topples it over when he stands to his feet, then leaps out of the dancer's way as if determined not to be touched by her.

"I'm out. I'm not about to get eaten a-fucking-live by that." He points at the woman on the floor rising onto her knees where she once again locks eyes with me while she opens the loose ribbon holding her halter top in place.

"Yeah, me too." I follow Tate while Mase throws money at the table and heads our way, leaving Reed with the two dancers, not looking the least bit concerned.

In fact, he looks like he's enjoying every minute, and not too long ago, I would have too.

But now? Now I have a family.

Now I have everything I ever wanted. I just need to make it work.

EMI

I can sense his gaze on me as I roll onto my back. As tired as my body is, my mind hasn't allowed me to sleep, replaying every hurtful word he said to me.

"Do you still hate me?" I ask the question so low I'm unsure if he heard me, but the sharp intake of his breath lets me know he did.

"Let me apologize to you." His voice is husky as he tugs the sheet from my sleepy body, exposing my sleep shorts and camisole top that's ridden up over bump. "Fuck. I'll never get enough of you pregnant, Emi." His cool hands trail over my legs up toward my shorts. I brush the hair from my eyes and sit up on my elbows to watch him.

Taking in Shaw's disheveled state, a pang of guilt hits me that I caused that. When he lets out a sharp intake of breath after smelling my sex, I smell the alcohol oozing from him, and the thought makes me slightly uncomfortable. He rises on his haunches, and when I see lipstick on his shirt, my body freezes, and I scoot up to take a closer look. His shirt reeks of a woman, making my stomach roll in a wave of sickness. "You smell of cheap perfume, Shaw," I grit out.

His eyebrows shoot up. "There was a dancer. Nothing happened." I hold my hand up for him to stop talking and close my eyes to hide the hurt building behind them, determined not to expose my weakness to him. *Never cry, Emilia.*

"In blood we're bound. In trust we live," I mumble.

I snap my eyes open with a newfound strength. Shaw stares at me, pissed, and I choke on thin air at his audacity. "I told you, nothing happened." His eyes implore mine.

"You need a shower." I dart my eyes toward the bathroom, and Shaw sighs before stalking toward the bathroom, slamming the door behind him.

It feels like an eternity before the shower turns off and Shaw comes back into the bedroom with a towel around his waist.

I nibble at my fingernail and turn to face him. "I don't want you to hate me, Shaw. But I refuse for you to treat me that way."

His eyes soften. "I could never fucking hate you." He crawls on the bed and brushes my hair from my eyes. "I shouldn't have said those things, Emi. I'm sorry." My eyes meet his, and the regret in them is unmistakable.

My chest rises in emotion. "I can't bear the thought of you hating me." My eyes pool with tears, but I refuse to let them fall.

He brushes his trembling finger over my cheek. "Shh, please don't." His warmth spreads through me, and I turn into his touch, forever seeking his warmth and protection.

"Let me show you how sorry I am, baby." His lips meet

mine, coaxing my mouth open. "Let me make love to you." My heart skips a beat at his words, wishing they meant the real thing. That he isn't just going to fuck me slowly and call it making love, but actual love. If it was the real thing, I'd happily let him make love to me. But it's not, and I can't bear his tenderness.

I whimper as he works his way down my body. He pushes my t-shirt over my head and latches onto my nipple. Sucking it into his mouth, he flicks his tongue over the peak, making me squirm beneath him. "Mm, so responsive. I can't wait for you to feed our baby from these." He squeezes my tits, and my pussy melts with wetness.

My fingers find his hair and I hold him close to me as he sucks my nipple hard, and my body tenses with a mixture of pain and pleasure. "Oh god, Shaw. Don't stop, please don't stop." He sucks harder, then flicks his tongue over the swollen nub before moving to the next nipple. "Fuck, I'm going to suck these when they're full of your milk." He rocks his hard cock against my thigh, thrusting against the towel for friction.

He's trying to control himself, to give me what he thinks I want. But not like this, I refuse to accept it. So instead, I tell him what he needs to hear.

"Shaw. I want you to fuck me. Please, I need you to fuck me so hard."

His mouth pops off my breast, and I sink against the pillow. "Remind me who I belong to, Shaw." I know I'm poking the bear when his eyes flare with a combination of searing heat and rage. He stands, throwing the towel from his waist onto the floor before he takes hold of my ankles and drags me down the bed, spreads my legs wide, then he thrusts inside me so hard I wince at the intrusion. "Don't fucking complain when you've been testing me, Emi." *Slam.* "I tried to be soft." *Slam.* "Gentle." *Slam.* "And you push me to fuck you hard like this, so you can fucking take it." *Slam.* I moan with each thrust, my body wound so tight it's going to explode any second. He grinds his hips, hitting the perfect spot as my pussy clenches around him, earning a low growl from his chest that makes my heart soar in delight.

Wetness pools between us, and the slam of the bed against the wall is a testament to the powerhouse between my legs. His chiseled body is taut, his eyes focused on the bounce of my tits, so I push them together and strum my nipples with my thumbs, reveling in the torturous expression of pleasure on his face.

"Fuck, I want to keep you pregnant." His words cause me to let out an involuntary moan. It's not the first time he's said the words to me, and the thought that he wants another child with me makes me want him all the more. Makes me want us.

"Shaw, please suck my nipple."

His mouth drops open and his heavy eyes flick up to mine in awe. He ducks his head and takes my nipple into his mouth, and groaning against the tender flesh, he sucks like a man possessed while his hips drive into me wildly. I dig my nails into his ass and meet him thrust for thrust. "Oh god, Shaw."

He growls, and a sting of pain hits my tit before his tongue caresses the spot. My pussy convulses around him, gripping him as my back arches off the bed. The head of his cock swells and he lets out a low groan as I scream his name. "Shhhhaw."

He slows down while my pussy contracts around him, milking him for every drop of cum.

Shaw slides out of me and is careful to move onto his back but wastes no time in tugging me onto his chest.

His hand finds my hair, and he plays with it as I throw a leg over his body while his other hand holds onto bump.

"I meant it, you know."

I lift my head to meet his gaze. "I'm sorry for what I said. I was mad at the circumstances, and I never touched the dancer."

I nod my head and rest it back against his chest.

If he was a Mafia man, he'd never admit his fault and he sure as hell wouldn't have apologized for it.

"I can't bear the thoughts of you in love with him," he admits, making my heart constrict with guilt.

"I wasn't in love with him. I told you that."

He sighs. "I know what you said."

I lift my head once again. "You don't believe me?"

Shaw shakes his head and swallows harshly. "I want you to want me—" His Adam's apple bobs. "Not just need me."

I nod in understanding. He's as vulnerable as I am in all of this. But the difference is, I've never had a relationship. He has and he's been in love.

"I'm worried too." I meet his eyes, determined to let him see past the bravado I've been taught to portray. "You've had relationships, Shaw. Lizzie." I bite into my lip at the mention of her name, and his body freezes below me, giving me all the confirmation I need about his feelings toward her.

"I told your brother you don't have to worry about her." He glares at me.

I laugh softly, the bitterness evident. "Don't you see? I'm not worried about her. I'm worried about you."

He stares back at me in confusion, so I rest my head back on his chest and ignore the silence between us.

Instead, I concentrate on the steady beat of his heart and the soft gliding of his hand searching out bump's movement.

I close my eyes and wish I'd let him make love to me after all.

TWENTY-SIX

SHAW

I barely slept a wink last night, her words replaying in my mind on permanent repeat. *"Don't you see? I'm not worried about her. I'm worried about you."*

She thinks I'm in love with Lizzie. I can see it in her eyes, sense it in her unasked questions, but why the hell won't I allow myself to give her the answer she seeks. Why the fuck can't I tell her I've fallen in love with her?

Thoughts of my mom come rushing back, and I wince.

Bump was active all night, as though reminding me why I am here in the first place. Like I could ever forget the most beautiful woman I've ever laid eyes on. Emi is lying on her side, and I scoot down the bed to move my lips toward her protruding stomach. I place a gentle kiss where I'm convinced bump can hear me. "I'm going to surprise your mommy today. You have to be good."

My eyes latch onto her pussy lips, and my finger glides through her wetness. The thought of my cum still inside her makes my cock jump with excitement. My finger dips farther around to her hole, and sure enough, she's still wet. I push a finger inside, making her moan in her sleep and arch her back, and all I can think about is the need to sink into her wet heat once again.

I ignore my swaying cock as I get up from the bed and move around to the other side so I'm now lying behind her.

Rubbing the head of my cock along her wet pussy, she moans in her sleep, and my cock leaks with pre-cum. I trail kisses down her neck and hold onto bump as I use my free hand to guide my cock into her hole with ease.

"You like me fucking you in your sleep, baby?"

She pushes against me, earning a low chuckle as I bury my cock to the hilt. Her warmth spreads around me, and my balls throb with need.

"Lift up, baby, let me wrap my arm around you."

Her lazy body complies, but she doesn't open her eyes as I lick down her neck and push in and out of her. With one arm on her bump and the other playing with her tits, I have no choice but to move quicker, the excitement of fucking my girl becoming too much. "Fuck, baby. I marked you so good. Open your eyes and see." I stare over her shoulder at the huge hickey on her tit from last night. If I had my choice, it would be on her neck, but I'm pretty sure her brother wouldn't think twice about popping an extra hole in my head.

Her eyes flutter open, and she smiles lazily as she pushes her ass into me. "Be a good girl and play with your clit for me."

One of her arms bands around the back of my head as I pepper kisses along the column of her neck, and when her nails dig into my scalp, I slam into her harder. Her fingers are toying with her clit. "Do you like seeing my mark on you?" I groan against her as her ass continues to press against my hips, her perfect pussy squeezing me as though determined to keep me inside, and I revel at the thought.

"Yes. I love seeing your mark on me."

I nip at her neck and chuckle when she sucks in a panicked breath. "Shaw." She moans in warning, making me want to spank her ass, and I have no choice but to comply.

Her fingers brush over where we're joined, and she whimpers. "That's right, Red. That's me fucking you, filling you with my cum. Feeding it to my hungry girl." Her fingers work faster with each word spilling from my filthy mouth.

"Reminding you this pussy is mine. Not that bastard's." I slam inside her harder. "A real fucking man to please my girl's pussy." I squeeze her tits hard, and they spill out of my hands. I fucking love it, and my cock does too. Emi throws her head back against my chest, and I stare at her as she comes hard around my cock, milking it to the point I have no choice but to give in. "Fuck." I wanted it to last longer this morning; I wanted a fucking eternity. I take her lips in mine and hold her close to me as I flood her pussy, making our juices gush between us.

Our breaths are labored when we finally pull apart.

"I'm taking you out today." Her eyebrows shoot up, and she maneuvers herself so she's facing me. My poor cock weeps as it slides out of her warmth.

"Where?" Her eyes search mine, and I try to tamper down her unasked question: if I asked Luca's permission.

"Over to Tate's parents'. For dinner." Emi's eyes soften

as she considers what this means. Tate's parents are the closest thing I have to a family of my own, before her and bump.

Effectively, I'm taking her to meet the parents.

Finally.

EMI

Mr. and Mrs. Kavannah are not what I imagined. They're refined and have social standing not dissimilar to my own upbringing. No wonder Luca was okay with me coming here. Mrs. Kavannah explained that they became an extended family to Tate's friends over the years, and Tate rolled his eyes as though he's heard the story a thousand times.

Owen, Mase, and Tate have joined us for dinner, along with Tate's younger brother, Dex. He's eighteen although he looks older; he'd easily pass for twenty-one.

Shaw's hand tightened in mine when I greeted Dex, and he tugged me beneath his chin, making Dex laugh and slap him on the back at his ridiculous actions.

"Each year, Steph and Mark hold a dinner to raise funds for foster families and their kids to attend college. Then during the summer, they open their home to some foster children for them to have a break from their foster family," Shaw explains as we eat dinner.

I glance around the dining room and out into the

garden. There's a pool, beautifully manicured lawns, tennis courts, and a treehouse.

I imagine to some foster children this must truly be heaven. "It's incredible," I tell Steph, who smiles broadly at mine and Shaw's joined hands.

"How old are the children you have staying with you?" I'm already wondering out loud; I can't help it.

Tate chokes on his water, earning a grin from Owen, who has pretty much been silent for the duration of dinner.

"Anywhere from four to eighteen," Steph replies with a wistful smile.

Tate glowers and I glance around the table, wondering what the cause might be, when the front door opens and Steph darts toward the entrance.

Tate shovels food in his mouth, so I look to Owen, but when he hears the voice of another woman, his spine straightens on alert. I glance at Shaw, who has squeezed his eyes closed, as if asking for mercy, making me chuckle.

"Mom, it's fine. Jeez, stop fussing."

"Here we fucking go," Dex grumbles, and my eyes flick around the table in question.

In strolls a gorgeous young woman, who looks a similar age to me.

She has olive skin and the most unusual green eyes I've ever seen. Her hair falls in loose waves over her shoulders, and her red lips look natural and only add to her beauty.

"Laya, this is Emi. Shaw's wife. Emi, this is my daughter, Laya." I stand and hold out my hand to Laya, and she gifts me with a warm smile, the beauty behind it making me blush.

"I'm sorry. I didn't know you were married, Shaw." She raises a playful eyebrow, as though scolding him.

I sit back down, and Shaw places a now familiar arm over my shoulder, toying with the strands of my hair.

"You wouldn't fucking know. You're never home," Owen grunts as he stares straight ahead, refusing to even look in Laya's direction.

Laya's jaw tics, but she masks it quickly and glances away from Owen. "Well, I'm here now and I have news."

Dex sits with a grin that Shaw would describe as shit-eating.

"What news? Is everything okay?" Mark's eyes trail over Laya protectively.

A smile breaks out on her face, and she sticks her hand out. "I'm married."

The table is quiet as they all stare at her outstretched hand, apart from Owen, who still hasn't so much as looked at Laya. Instead, he lifts another fork full of green beans into his mouth.

"And there's more." She bites into her bottom lip with glee.

Tate stares at her wide-eyed while Dex stretches his arms out over the backs of the chairs, as if enjoying the show.

"I'm pregnant!"

"Holy shit," Shaw mutters.

"What the fuck, Laya?" Tate explodes while Owen's chair slams back onto the floor while he strides outside, slamming the door behind him.

"You want to make an exit, Red?" Shaw kisses my shoulder, sending a tremor through my body.

I give him a nod, and he motions toward the door at Mase, who looks as lost as I feel right now.

We head out of the Kavannahs', and I can't help but feel a little relief that there's problems in each home, no matter how well put together they are.

"You think Owen will be okay?" Shaw asks Mase as he heads toward his car.

Mase chuckles. "Not if Tate realizes. He needs to rein in his feelings, the time for showing them was back then." Mase eyes Shaw knowingly, and Shaw sighs, making me wrap my arms around him to comfort him.

Mase glances back at the house and breathes out. "I'll wait around for him."

Shaw gives him a sharp nod, then bends and kisses the top of my head. "Come on, let's get you home."

His words cocoon me in warmth and protection, making me wish for the impossible. I glance straight into Shaw's bright-blue eyes staring back at me, making my heart flutter and making me wonder if it's the inevitable after all.

TWENTY-SEVEN

EMI

It's been a week since we went to dinner at the Kavannahs', and I didn't ask Shaw about Owen and Laya. It's clear whatever they had was in the past and not something that needed trudging up. Apart from whatever was going off between them, it appears Tate was blissfully unaware, and I didn't want to risk anything to do with Tate or his family getting hurt by discussing old feelings. Let sleeping dogs lie.

Shaw hands me another onesie and I fold it, placing it in the drawers he built only an hour ago. He insisted on building them, though I haven't told him I know Luca will send over his men to check the crib out to make sure it's secure enough. Shaw spent way too long scratching his head at all the screws, so I humored him and told him he did a fantastic job, knowing my brother will make sure they're secure enough.

"What the hell are these?" Shaw holds up the nipple

pads, and I have to place a hand over my mouth when I make a grunting noise through laughing at his scrunched-up nose.

"They're nipple pads." I grab them from him and swat at him.

He pulls me into his lap, my bump huge now at thirty-two weeks. "I don't need my woman to have nipple pads. Not when I have these pads." He holds up his thumbs.

"You're such a dumbass." I smile into him as he kisses me tenderly, his smile breaking the kiss.

His phone rings on the floor beside us, making our eyes dart down toward it. Shaw lets out a groan of annoyance when the word *Gatehouse* dances along the screen. No doubt thinking it's my brother. But I know without a shadow of a doubt that Luca would walk straight into the house; he certainly wouldn't be announced at the gatehouse.

Shaw presses the answer button. "Yeah."

"Sir. I'm sorry to bother you, but we have a Miss Elizabeth Wright here. She's in distress. Should I call Mr. Varros to deal with her?"

Shaw's body freezes below me, no doubt realizing if my brother finds out Lizzie has called upon the house, he'd order her to be killed.

I move to climb off Shaw's lap, but he holds me there with panic in his eyes.

"Sir?"

I swallow back the lump in my throat, cursing myself as I say the words, but I do it for him. "Let her up. Shaw will deal with her."

Relief floods not just his face but his body too as he relaxes below me. This time, when I climb from him, he doesn't stop me, and that lack of reassurance hurts more than ever.

"I'll give you both some privacy. But she's not a guest, Shaw." I give him a pointed look. I refuse to have another woman in my home. He can be amicable in the foyer.

He jumps to his feet, brushing a hand through his hair. "I'll get rid of her, Emi. I'll be quick, I promise. You won't regret it." He throws the door open, leaving me standing in the baby's nursery, his words ringing out that I won't regret it, but truth be told, I already do.

SHAW

I practically throw myself down the stairs, relief and anger warring within me. If Emi hadn't taken pity on Lizzie, there's no doubt in my mind she'd be dead. My wife is caring and compassionate, something else I love about her.

But still unable to tell her.

The door to the house opens, and I stare in shock at the woman before me. She's not manicured as I know her, she's not put together, she's destroyed, and panic and guilt flood me. "Jesus, Lizzie. Are you okay?"

Her eyes meet mine and they're broken. We might not have had the best of relationships, but I don't deny I had feelings of some sort toward her, and seeing her like this is like a knife through my heart and another stark reminder of my mom.

"I'm not okay." She shakes her head, her hair covering her face, making me wonder if someone hurt her. *Was it Luca?* My spine straightens. *If he broke our promise, I'll kill him my fucking self.*

I tuck her hair behind her ear and use my fingers to lift

her chin and face me. Her face is clear of makeup, something I never remember seeing before now. It gives her a softer look, but at the same time, the makeup enhances her better features. She needs it as a mask, whereas Emi is completely natural and beautiful without all the crap.

"What happened?" I keep my voice low. I don't trust the staff that work here; after all, they are Luca's, and I refuse to give the asshole reason to shoot Lizzie.

"I'm pregnant." She moves her coat aside, revealing a small bump, and I feel like my whole world is crashing down on me. The air is sucked from my lungs, my legs shake with a combination of shock and fear, and my heart shatters into a thousand pieces, because how the hell am I meant to handle this?

I stare at her in utter disbelief, numb as my mind swirls so fast I can't think straight.

When her cold hand rests on top of mine, I realize we're touching the bump of our baby, and I force my eyes closed, willing it not to be real.

This is bad. So fucking bad.

I jump back as though electrocuted; the only bump I'm used to feeling is my wife's. I scrub an uncomfortable hand through my hair.

"I'm scared, Shaw."

I stare back at the woman in front of me, then down at her bump. "I've nowhere to go." Her eyes dart around the mansion, and panic builds up inside me. *Does she think she can stay here? Fuck no.*

"You can't stay here, Liz." Her bottom lip trembles, and I lower my head to reassure her. "It's not fucking safe."

I pull out my phone and call Owen, knowing without having to even ask that the line will be secure.

"Owen. I need help."

"What the fuck is it?" He groans, and I imagine him rolling over. Either he drank himself to sleep or he has a woman in bed with him. Either way, he's using it as a distraction for the real issue, Laya.

"Lizzie."

"Fuck."

"I need a secure place."

"Okay. I'll text you an address." I nod like an idiot, even though he can't see me.

My eyes latch onto her bump, onto my baby. "And security. I need security too."

"Gotcha."

The line goes dead, and I close my eyes for a brief moment. When I open them, it's with a steely determination to get Liz and my child to safety, then get back to Emi as quick as I can.

I have some explaining to do, and I don't even know where to fucking start.

EMI

I watch from the landing, staying in the shadow of the doorway as her hand clasps over his. He closes his eyes, and I'm overcome with emotion as my hand tightens on the metal railing. I want to scream; I want to cry and yell. I want him to want me.

My body sags to the floor as he makes arrangements to find somewhere for the woman he loves. Her eyes light up when he tells her he has a place for them, and I close my eyes at the expression of relief on his face. My world is disappearing through the front door, but then he stops at the doorway and his body freezes. I expect him to look up, for his eyes to search for mine, but instead, he continues out the door without a second glance in my direction.

He's gone.

My stomach rolls, forcing me to my feet as I rush to the bathroom, overcome with dread and disappointment. I heave the contents of dinner into the toilet and whimper at the pain in my chest.

I'm becoming everything I never wanted to be.

I'll be the perfect Mafia wife who bears the heir while my husband's heart longs for his mistress. He'll play happy families with me when he needs to while his joy will be for his real love.

I sit on the bathroom floor and ponder where it all went wrong.

Maybe I should have let my brother deal with her. But then Shaw's child would be dead too, and as much as I despise Lizzie, I could never hurt an unborn baby.

Would he expect me to welcome it into the family the way some Mafia men do with their bastard children? No, Luca would never allow that. It would show disrespect.

A wave of panic rushes through me when I think of my brother and him hearing about this. He won't accept it. I know he won't. I jump to my feet and pace; a tremor works through me at the thought of Shaw getting hurt.

There's not a doubt in my mind my husband would die for his child. And there's no doubt in my mind my brother would kill for mine.

I close my eyes, but all I see is Shaw and Lizzie and their hands clasped together on their baby.

The way they should have always been.

TWENTY-EIGHT

SHAW

"The place is secure, right?" I question Owen for the thousandth time as I glance around the apartment.

He quirks a brow at me, his jaw locking tight, pissed at me for asking again, but I can't have my child at risk, and right now, keeping distance between Luca and Lizzie is the only thing I can do.

"What the hell are you going to do, man?" Owen scan's my face, side-eyeing me with concern lacing his tone.

When he volunteered his apartment, he didn't know Lizzie was pregnant with my baby, and now the stakes just got higher.

I fidget from foot to foot and drag my hand through my hair. Panic and frustration don't feel significant enough to describe how I'm feeling. "I don't know. I went from being an on-off boyfriend to being a married father of two within a matter of a few fucking months," I grit out.

"I'd be more concerned about how the fuck you're

going to keep Luca on your side. Not to mention your wife. She's going to want to cut off your balls."

I grimace at the thought of telling Emi. She's going to be heartbroken, but if I tell her how I feel about her, then surely things can be different. She needs to know I'm not with her just for the baby, I want her too. I love her. My heart hammers at the thought of losing my wife when we only just really found one another again.

I want to be around bump when they're born, watch them grow. Help with night feedings. I want it all. I want my family. My shoulders sag and a deep pain pierces through my chest, causing my throat to clog. I drop my head forward to disguise the tears welling in my eyes at how helpless I feel right now.

Owen grips my shoulder and gives it a reassuring squeeze.

"Shaw, can you stay the night? I don't want to be alone." My body freezes with the sound of her voice. *Did she always sound so whiny?*

Our eyes snap to Liz, who cradles her bump, and I force my eyes away into the disapproving stare of Owen. *Jesus, I need to catch a break.*

"You'll be catching something if you don't start wrapping the little fucker up." Owen nods toward my dick, and I realize I said my thoughts out loud.

"Very fucking funny. I always wrap it, smartass." I startle at my own words. "Before my wife," I clarify, earning a chuckle from Owen.

He slaps me on the back as he heads toward the door, making panic overcome me at the thought of leaving me with this mess. I quickly follow him. "Wait, where the fuck are you going?"

He scans my face before coming up blank. "I have other places to stay." He shrugs.

I move closer to him and lower my voice so Lizzie can't overhear me. "Don't fucking leave me here with her." I tilt my head toward her.

Owen bites his lip to stifle a laugh, and I've never wanted to punch him as much as I do right now. My eyes drill into his with desperation. Owen's face relaxes, and a look of sympathy flashes in his eyes before he spins on his heels and sighs. "Liz, you need to put your big girl pants on. Shaw here has a knocked-up wife to go home to," he spits, shocking me at his abrupt tone and language. My nose scrunches up in disgust. It really shouldn't surprise me. No wonder Laya had problems communicating with him.

"I'm his girlfriend and the mother of his baby." She puts her hands on her hips and raises her chin. *Here we fucking go.* I pinch the bridge of my nose.

"Newsflash, sweetheart, ex-girlfriend. His wife and kid come first. Your kid, second, then you . . ." he winces, ". . . somewhere. I'm not sure where. Point bein', darlin', your feelings don't matter. Shaw, we leaving?" He stares at me pointedly, giving me a blatant option to stay with the psycho ex or leave with him.

I snatch up my car keys, fumbling to push past Owen. "I'll drop by tomorrow to discuss." I point my finger in the direction of the bump as Liz stares at me open-mouthed.

I've never left a property so quickly in my entire life. Not even when I got caught fucking my piano teacher and her husband, a kickboxing champion, burst through the door. Nope, my heart is racing so fast I'm concerned I'm about to have a heart attack.

"Really wouldn't want to be you right now," Owen jokes as we head toward our cars.

"Very fucking funny."

"Although the whole pregnancy thing appears a little more inviting lately." His gaze and voice wander, making me realize I wasn't meant to hear the comment, so instead, I thank him and get in my car, wondering how the hell I'm going to explain things to Emi and where the hell we go from here.

TWENTY-NINE

EMI

I pace the bedroom, chewing on my fingernail. It's a wonder I haven't worn the carpet down. Shaw has been gone for what feels like hours, and every time I think about what I'm about to do, a wave of nausea rolls through me.

Bump gives out a small kick, as though reminding me of the repercussions of my forthcoming actions. I swallow thickly, my throat tightening, and the overwhelming thoughts of dread, coupled with my heart breaking, is enough for me to rush toward the toilet, heaving mercilessly into the bowl yet again.

Tears fall from my eyes as I imagine Shaw embracing Lizzie with their child, followed by a flash of fear striking through me when I consider Luca's reaction to the latest news. I know my brother will stop at nothing to make sure I'm not hurt and the organization's reputation is not in tatters. His potential actions already haunt me, filling me with dread and despair, causing fear to swirl through me to the point of pain.

There's only one way to dispel any further heartache.

I need a new truth. One that may well hurt me but will protect the ones I love above all else. Because the thought of Shaw being hurt is almost too much to bear. I can't allow that. I won't allow it.

I rush back into the bedroom and into my closet to rummage through my bags. I locate the burner phone I have, the one that holds the only name that can help me through all of this.

The only other man I have ever considered a lover: Aldo.

I'll share the truth and set us both free.

SHAW

The house feels emptier than ever when I return, and I want nothing more than to climb into bed and pull Emi into my arms, embracing her and our baby. But I know that's not how this is going to go down. I know it's going to be a tough topic, one we need to figure out as a married couple.

I climb the stairs one by one, my feet weighed down with guilt at each step. *How the hell do I tell her this?*

I take a deep breath and steel myself before pushing down the door handle and stepping inside our bedroom.

Her red-rimmed eyes find mine instantly, and my heart stutters at the sight of her. She's sitting on the bed but stands to her feet as I step closer.

Emi holds out her hand to stop me coming any closer, and I swear my heart plummets at that action alone.

"Emi, listen."

She shakes her head, causing her hair to fall around her like a curtain. "I have something to tell you." She sniffles, making my chest constrict with a need to comfort her.

My eyes narrow.

Emi raises her chin high and tightens her shoulders back, as though preparing for a fight, the Mafia princess mask back in full force. Annoyance at those actions makes me clench my jaw. *How quickly she can become the person she isn't.*

My gaze scans over her, looking for a reason for her sudden change in demeanor. Her chest heaves and her hands have a slight tremble to them. "Emi?" I question with a raised brow.

She takes a deep breath. "The baby isn't yours."

I choke on relief, a small smile gracing my face, because truth be told, I was kind of thinking this myself too. My next move was going to be a DNA test before we cause any unnecessary drama with Luca.

"I was wondering the same thing. I'm going to get tested tomorrow, Emi. I swear it." I step forward, but she takes a step back.

"That's not what I meant, Shaw." Her eyes drill into mine, causing the hairs on the back of my neck to stand with the insinuation. But confusion must cloud my face because she continues without me having to prompt her. "This baby." She taps on bump. "This baby is not yours."

My throat closes up and my mind is blank, unable to process what she's saying. Unwilling to process it.

My chest tightens, making it difficult for me to breathe. "E-Emi?" I gaze into her eyes for her to tell me I'm mistaken on what I thought she said. She doesn't, she stares back at me with confidence and determination.

"The baby's not yours, Shaw. I'm sorry."

I drop my head as I play over her words. *"The baby's not yours, Shaw. I'm sorry."*

Anger boils inside me. *Is she fucking serious? Not mine?*

My hands turn to fists as I snap my eyes back toward hers, making her suck in a sharp gasp at my reaction. "Not mine?" I grit out.

Her lip quivers, giving away the only sign of emotion. "I'm sorry."

"Sorry?" My voice raises so loud she jumps. The veins in my temple pulsate, every fiber of my being coiled tight with rage. "Sorry?" I repeat with a venomous tone. "Who the fuck's the father?" I step toward her, making her back hit the wall until she's boxed in beneath me. "Who the fuck is the father?"

She's turned my whole world upside down again, and I hate her for it.

I stepped up. I became the man I wanted to be. The husband and father I wanted to be for her and our bump. My entire world was turned on an axis for her, and this is how she repays me?

"Answer the fucking question!" Spittle flies from my mouth. I slam my fist into the wall behind her, making her startle.

She's taking everything away from me that I care about. My eyes close with emotion, but I'm unwilling to let the tears spill over. Not when I deserve answers. Opening my eyes once again, I stare into the blackened orbs of the woman I've fallen in love with. The crook, the cheat, the con artist.

"Aldo. Aldo's the baby's father." Her words slice into my heart, the agony of her betrayal too much to bear as I stumble backward. Uncontrollable tears spill from my eyes at the thought of another man touching her, fathering my baby. The one I talk to every morning, the one whose clothes I folded into drawers earlier today. The one I love.

"We couldn't be together. He's a soldier."

The fuzziness in my head finds it hard to concentrate on what she's saying.

"He wouldn't have been good enough." She wrings her hands in front of herself before settling them on bump, and I want nothing more than to rip her hands away, tear her away from her baby like she has done to me.

The silence stretches between us, both of us uncertain of what move to make. So many things unsaid, yet nothing being spoken at all.

My happiness was just an illusion after all.

I drag my palms down my face to wipe away the wetness. Taking a deep breath, I raise my head, and Emi takes a step toward a luggage bag I'd not noticed before now.

"You're free now, Shaw." Her eyes shine back at me, those orbs penetrating into my soul and forcing me to take a sharp intake of breath as they seize my capacity to breathe naturally.

Jesus, she's so beautiful it hurts.

"I really am sorry, Shaw. I hope you find your happiness." She picks up the bag and walks out the door, taking my heart with her.

She's wrong, though. I'm not free. I'll be forever imprisoned to a life of misery without her and our bump.

They were my everything.

They were my happiness.

THIRTY

SHAW

I slam my glass down on the table and hold my hand up for another. The waitress wastes no time in dumping another scotch in front of me. I don't miss the critical glance of the guys around the table, but I scoff at them and tip the drink back, determined to wash away the misery.

When Emi walked out the door, taking my child with her, I felt like my heart was going to combust.

Uncontrollable sobs fell from me as I dropped to the floor.

When my eyes met with Mase's standing in the doorway, I couldn't help but feel a combination of relief and hate for Emi. She knew I'd need someone to help me pick up the pieces and she chose wisely, with Mase being the better option of my friends. I loathe her for how well she knows me, and I grinded my teeth at the thoughtful gesture behind her action.

Sitting up to tell Mase she's left me and I'm not going to be a daddy after all, made me hiccup on my words. But like the good friend he is, he pulled me into an embrace while I sobbed into his shoulder.

Today's a new day and one I intend to drown in alcohol instead of tears. Emilia Varros does not deserve a second thought of mine, not after the shit she's pulled.

"Maybe you've had enough to drink." Reed raises his eyebrows and tilts his head.

"Maybe you should mind your fucking business," I snipe back, refusing to look at him.

"Have you spoken to Lizzie? That woman has upset my housekeeper, and she hasn't been there twenty-four hours yet." I can feel Owen's gaze drilling into the side of my head, but again, I refuse to acknowledge my friend. Instead, I opt to raise my hand for another drink.

"I think there's more to it." Mase's comment makes my spine straighten and my nostrils flare, but I refuse to acknowledge him, or his words, choosing to throw back another drink and exhale the burn in my throat. I slam the glass on the table.

"Me too," Reed throws in, making my head spin in his direction.

Reed glares back at me, unwavering, before speaking again with confidence. "There's more to it." He holds my gaze, refusing to back down.

"She fucked her brother's soldier. They spawned a kid. She freaked out and pinned it on me. The billionaire. The better option." I grimace, and even as I say the words, I almost give in to disbelieving them.

"Do you love her?" Tate asks.

I roll my head to face him but refuse to give him an

answer. "If you love her, it doesn't matter whose kid it is. You'll love the baby like your own." He shrugs, but his words hit deep. There's no doubt in my mind that I love bump. I ball my hands into fists at the suggestion that I don't love my baby; it couldn't be further from the truth. They're mine, I want to scream, but the realization that they are in fact not mine makes me slump back in my chair and hang my head in devastation.

"Shaw, man. Why don't you go speak to her? Get some answers. This is all out of character for Emi." Owen squeezes my shoulder.

"Maybe she was pissed at you for fathering another baby with your ex?" Mase leans across the table and delivers a sharp slap to the back of Tate's head for his comment.

Reed shuffles forward. "You have to admit, he has a point. Why now? Why'd she choose now to deliver this information?"

I sit forward and mull over his words. "Right? She's probably lashing out; you know what women are like." Tate waves his hand around like an idiot.

But something in my friends' words hit me, making me also question, why now?

"She thought she was doing you a favor." Mase stares at me, and I scan his face for an explanation. "You said she said that you're free?"

I nod at his words, a sickening realization taking place in the pit of my stomach. She thinks she's setting me free? She couldn't be further from the truth.

Owen lifts his chin in my direction. "You need answers, man. Something isn't right. She must know about the baby and thinks she's doing you a favor." Sickness rolls through me at the thought of her thinking that. I'll never be free without her and bump.

And for the first time since meeting Luca, I'm determined to get him on board with how I feel too. I need him to know that I love his sister and our baby.

She's my wife to love and care for, and bump will be mine. Blood or no blood.

"In blood we're bound. In trust we live," I mumble the words with a new sense of purpose, believing every one of them.

THIRTY-ONE

SHAW

Owen pulls up outside of Luca's mansion. It's weird how quickly you can become accustomed to the security surrounding you. When you see it on a daily basis, it almost doesn't exist anymore. No wonder Emi is so nonchalant about it. My heart tugs just at the mere thought of her.

I refuse to let her go. I don't care that the baby might not be mine. I want them, both of them.

I swallow past the lump in my throat as I survey the thick, heavy wooden doors leading to Luca's home. No doubt he's in there waiting for me after security alerted him to my presence.

My leg bounces. This is going to be a shit show, I can feel it.

"Are you sure you're sober enough for this?" Owen's disapproving gaze snaps toward mine as he passes me another bottle of water.

I glare back at him. "Of course. I want my fucking wife back, and he's going to give her to me." I open the bottle and chug the water, hoping to get a level head as soon as possible.

Owen sighs and scrubs a hand over his cropped hair. "Just don't go getting us killed."

I scoff. "I'll try not to. But I'm not leaving there without them."

Owen's stoic face softens. "I've got you, brother. Let's go."

We open the car doors in unison. Before my foot touches the first step, the doors to the property open by one of Luca's security team, allowing us to step inside.

"I want to speak to Luca!" I snap.

"Mr. Varros's time is valuable. He won't have long to spare you." I share a glance with Owen and roll my eyes while he stifles a smile.

Our shoes click on the marble floor as we follow him toward another doorway. Giggles can be heard on the other side of the door, and when the security guy knocks, the door is pulled open by a blonde buttoning up her blouse.

My eyes once again flick over toward Owen's, and we share our thoughts silently. *Mr. Varros's time is valuable.*

The blonde pushes past us, but I don't give her a second glance. Instead, I walk around the security guy and straight into Luca's office. He's zipping up his pants, and my nose turns up at the sex fermenting the air.

"I want my fucking wife back," I demand with anger radiating from me.

"Jesus," Owen grumbles behind me, exhaling loudly. I

spare him a quick glance, and he's pinching the bridge of his nose and staring up at the ceiling. *What did he think I was going to do? Ask him politely? Screw that, they're mine.*

Luca's spine straightens and he turns to face me, his eyes so cold and deadly, making me second-guess my approach. *Maybe I should have been more polite after all?* I push out my chest with determination, not wanting him to see any apprehension I'm suddenly feeling.

His eyes search my face in an icy standoff, the silence so cold the blood in my veins pumps slower, on the verge of freezing and forcing my body to still at his bitter reaction to me.

"What the fuck are you talking about?" His words are dark and calculated, and his eyes never leave my face, as though he's looking for a sign of deception.

I fidget from foot to foot as a sudden burst of heat surges into my chest at his response. My eyes narrow back on him in equal confusion.

But he doesn't give me the chance to question his reaction. "I'll ask you again, stronzo. What the fuck are you talking about?" His voice is low and controlled.

My pulse races in trepidation. *What the fuck is going on?* "Emi." My words come out low and confused, even to my own ears, but I can't seem to grasp what's happening. *How can he not know what's happening?*

Owen steps forward. "Luca. Emi and Shaw had a disagreement, she left their home yesterday."

Luca's face transforms into some sort of deranged savage. His face reddens, his veins protrude, and his eyes bulge. "What fucking disagreement? And why the fuck don't I know about my sister leaving the property?" he bellows at me while I stand there stoically still, trying to grasp onto the fact that Emi isn't here. And Luca doesn't know where the hell she is.

Luca storms back to his desk and lowers his hand beneath it. I can only imagine he's pushing a button to alert security of assistance. Sickness swirls in my stomach at the thought.

"Answer my fucking questions!" I jump when he screams across the room at me before moving so fast I don't know what's happening. He has me pushed against the wall with his hand wrapped around my throat like a coiled viper. He presses on my pulse points, making my vision blur, the warning evident.

Owen steps forward to intervene, but the office door bursts open with Maxim and another guy I've never met rushing inside.

"What the fuck's happening?" The guy I don't know speaks to Luca, but it's Owen who answers.

"We came to speak to Emi. But she's not here."

"Where the fuck is she, then?" Maxim asks. I dart my eyes over to his. His panicked expression makes my blood curdle. He taps away on his phone, ignoring my situation.

"I'm going to fucking slaughter you, strozno." Luca presses harder, and I swear I can feel the veins behind my eyes popping as my breathing becomes a struggle.

"Brother, let him speak." My vision blurs as I witness the other guy put his hand on Luca's shoulder. Muffled voices are spoken as I drop to the floor, gasping for breath while chaos ensues around me.

I grasp at my throat as I try to steady my breathing, the desperation to fill my lungs with air.

As my breathing regulates, I stumble to my feet. "You fucking psychopath. You nearly killed me!" I spit out through labored breaths with equal hatred.

Luca flies toward me once again, but Owen and the other guy step in his path, blocking him from touching me.

"Her tracker is switched off," Maxim declares, and all eyes swivel in his direction. Panic rushes through me, making my legs unsteady once again.

"Tell us exactly what happened," the guy cuts in, his eyes flicking from Owen to me.

"Emi told me the baby isn't mine." Luca jolts at my words. "She said it's Aldo's." His expression is blank, so I fill in the gaps for him. "Your soldier, Aldo." I wave my hand in Luca's direction. The look of pure shock marring his face should make me want to throw my head back and laugh in glee, if it wasn't for the fact my girl had betrayed me.

"She wouldn't do that," the guy responds.

A pang of guilt cuts into my chest at the thought of the information I'm withholding regarding Lizzie, but I don't have a death wish. Not when I want my wife back.

"I don't care whose baby it is. I want my wife back and my fucking child!" I boom in their direction, and the room falls silent once again.

"You don't care?" Luca's lip curls at the corner menacingly.

I lift my chin. "No, Luca. I don't fucking care. I love your sister, and I'm pretty damn sure she loves me too. If the baby isn't biologically mine, then so be it. But I will be the best father and husband I can be. I just need to tell her that."

Luca's face transforms with pride, and his shoulders slacken as though a weight has been lifted. He gives me a sharp nod; a sense of unwavering approval pours from him.

The guy I've not seen until now steps forward, offering his hand. "I'm Enzo Varros. Luca's right-hand man." I shake his hand as his face gives way to a small smile, as though pleased to meet me.

"We need to find Aldo." Maxim taps away frantically while Luca moves behind his desk to pick up his phone.

Damn right we need to find Aldo, and when we do, I'm taking back what's mine.

I'll happily let Luca Varros deal with that sly fucker. If he thinks he can steal my family right from under me, he has another thing coming.

Luca slumps into his chair. He holds his head in his hands and tugs at his hair as he unravels before us. "I can't lose another sister."

Sympathy builds inside me for the man I so easily hate.

"I have eyes on Aldo, he's at Ravlek's compound." Maxim's eyes cut to Luca's, and he squeezes his eyes closed before snapping them open with a fierce determination.

My chest tightens at the knowledge of Emi and the baby in Ravlek's presence. The guy looked like he wanted to eat her alive, and not in a good way. Nausea rolls through me.

"You don't think he'll hurt them, right?" I ask Luca.

His throat bobs, and I don't miss the glimmer of sympathy and despair behind his eyes.

"He'll hurt her. He'll hurt them both," he replies

emptily as a tsunami of terror washes over me, forcing my lungs to deflate with crippling agony.

"They're mine," I choke out through fractured breaths as I keel over, struggling to control the panic bubbling inside me.

"We'll get them back, brother." Owen's hand clasps onto my shoulder in support while, surprisingly, Luca's hand finds my other shoulder, giving it a reassuring squeeze.

"They're both yours," Luca states. My gaze lifts to meet his. The familiarity behind those black orbs no longer appears so cold. They feel safe.

They feel like home.

Like Emi. And I've just had the seal of approval from her brother.

I raise my head with a newfound vigor, giving Luca a meaningful nod. "Hand me a weapon."

His eyebrows shoot up in surprise, his lip tips up into a brief smile, and he strides toward a bookcase that slides open when he moves a book, unveiling an arsenal of weapons.

"I'll have a Subnose thirty-eight." I point toward the top shelf, and Maxim chuckles, my knowledge taking him by surprise.

"You surprise me, Shaw." Luca turns and holds out the loaded gun. "I wonder if you will continue to prove yourself?" he muses to no one in particular.

I snatch the weapon from him. "I want my family back, *stronzo*," I snipe back, making them all chuckle lowly. The noise sounds ominous among the tense silence.

"In blood we're bound, in trust we live," Enzo says to Luca.

"Si. In blood we're bound. In trust we live."

Maxim repeats the words, "In blood we're bound. In trust we live."

Owen gives a sharp nod.

And when all eyes settle on me, I load the magazine in the handgun before turning my eyes on them. "Abso-fucking-lutley. Let's get my family back."

THIRTY-TWO

EMI

When Aldo first showed up at the house, it was easy to leave. Knowing security knew and trusted him so well, we were able to formulate a plan that he was trailing me on my brother's command.

We had a brief encounter with Franco, my personal guard, but Aldo somehow had a voice note from Luca giving him strict instruction for him to bring me to his mansion. Franco eyed us skeptically before his body eased and he nodded for us to leave.

My body melted against the car seat with the built-up tension coiling inside me so tight it was a relief to finally break out.

Aldo rested his hand on my knee, and where it would have in the past been a comfort, it now felt like a thousand insects creeping over my bare skin. I pushed his hand away in discomfort, only for guilt to edge in when hurt flashed behind his eyes.

"I'm sorry." My broken voice longed to fix the pain I had created in so many people, but deep down, I knew it was an impossible feat.

"I understand. I'll protect you, Emi." He lifted my hand and dropped a gentle kiss onto my fingers, making me resist the urge to slap his cheek.

Jesus, what have I done?

My eyes flare open on a panicked breath, realizing I fell asleep.

"Hey, relax. We're almost there." Aldo smiles coolly toward me, but the hairs on the back of my neck rise as I glance out of the window to unfamiliar terrain.

"Aldo. Where exactly are we going?" His nostrils flare at my question, making my throat go dry with unease.

"I told you I'd look after you, Emi." He glances my way, then continues on. "Care for you. You didn't have to go and get knocked up by someone else. You should have just trusted me, ya know?" Spittle leaves his mouth as his voice becomes higher on each word.

Blood pumps through my veins faster as he puts his foot to the pedal, making us lunge forward and the seat belt tighten across bump. My hand goes there protectively. Aldo side-eyes the movement, and I don't miss the flare of his nostrils at my motherly instinct.

Surely, he wouldn't hurt me and bump. My breath hitches at the thought.

"Aldo. Can you slow down? You're scaring me."

Aldo takes his eyes off the road to scan me over, giving me a small nod, and I breathe out a sigh of relief when he eases off the gas. "My uncle, he's going to help us."

We approach what can only be described as a concrete fortress, and again, a wave of nausea assaults me. This is bad, really bad. Large wrought iron gates open, and two men with machine guns wave Aldo on. Whoever Aldo's uncle is, he's important, judging by the vast building and the security surrounding it.

My lips move, but I struggle to compute the words. My hands fidget, and I try again. "Aldo, who is your uncle?"

We park outside the larger building, and I peer out of the window and wonder if this is in fact someone's home. "Does your uncle live here?"

Aldo scoffs. "He operates from here."

"Operates?" I scan Aldo's face, my brows furrowed.

"He's in the business. Come on." Aldo steps out of the car and the door slams with a thud, making me jump.

My head screams at me to lock the car, to get away, that I'm in danger, but as I scan the car for the keys, I know there's no escaping. I know I'm going to have to play along with Aldo's plan at whatever cost, until I find a way out. I was stupid thinking I could evade the constraints of my brother in hope for freedom. In doing so, I feel like I'm walking into the lion's den.

A knock on my window startles me, and Aldo's face fills the glass with a sweet smile. There's no doubt in my mind that Aldo would ever put me in harm's way, but to what lengths he'll go to keep me is what has sickness rolling in my stomach. He's hiding something, and I think I'm about to find out exactly what that something is.

I plaster on the perfected smile and mask my apprehension. Opening the car door, I slip my hand into Aldo's and fight the urge to pull away. Ignoring the fear bubbling inside me, I raise my chin and straighten my shoulders back, feigning a confidence I no longer feel. Perfecting the perfect Mafia princess mask.

However, my brother didn't help raise your typical princess. Hell no, he helped raise a fighter, and that's exactly what I'm about to become.

Ice fills my bloodstream when I realize the men surrounding the foyer are speaking in Russian. They eye me like fresh meat, like a prize has been won, and like the fool I am, I've walked straight into the home of my enemy, delivering them their win.

My hand tightens in Aldo's as my heart rate skyrockets in silent terror. I glance up at Aldo, and his eyes bore into mine; a look of longing and protectiveness pool in his. "I won't let them hurt you. We just need my uncle's help getting out of the country, then we'll be together." My breathing stammers at the thought of leaving the country, leaving my family, leaving Shaw, and not for the first time, regret pumps through me as I fight back tears and continue with this charade. "You just need to do what I ask you to, okay?" His eyes implore mine.

I search his face for sign of deceit but find none. I only hope my instincts aren't betraying me when I give him a subtle nod of confidence.

"Just do as I say and everything will be okay." He clears his throat to distract the fact there's a tremble to his voice, but I didn't miss it. Not in the least, and that only solidifies the severity of our predicament.

Aldo tugs me along the corridor, past the winding staircase to the last door where a man stands guard. There's a sick gleam in his eyes as his gaze travels over my body, making me shudder and huddle into Aldo's side.

Aldo's hand tightens in mine, his body tense. "Take your eyes off her," he spits, and the man stares back at him, raising his chin with a smug grin. Aldo steps forward and pushes his chest against the man's, but I tug him back into me, too terrified at what might happen. "You're a traitor." The man clears his throat, then spits down at Aldo's shoes.

Aldo smirks back at the man, then looks down at me with pride. "Doesn't look like it from where I'm standing."

The statement is obvious. I'm proof that Aldo isn't a traitor. I'm what? A pawn?

I bristle at the insinuation, and Aldo recognizes the motion, so he bends down to my ear. "Trust me." He squeezes my clammy hand as reassurance, but all I feel is a sickening sense of dread, and when the man finally opens the door and Ravlek's menacing eyes lock onto mine, I feel like I'm going to pass out. My head swirls and my legs sway.

I'm not just in danger.

I'm in hell.

THIRTY-THREE

LUCA

I've never felt so enraged. Yet a strange sense of calm is allowing me to think clearly, strategically.

After discussing an action plan with Enzo and Maxim, we have a plan in place. One that Owen and a team of his men are assisting us with. I'm confident we can get Emi out of the compound safely. I just hope she's managed to evade trauma. I hope I've taught my little sister enough to know when to fight and when to let her passive instincts kick in. She needs to protect herself and the baby however she deems necessary.

Aldo, how I entrusted him with my home and my sister, only for him to not only disrespect me and the organization but to be a traitor will be punishable on the greatest of levels.

Knowing I've had a viper in my nest, one I've trained as one of my own men for years, is almost too much to bear. I want to kill all my men to set an example, but that's clearly not an option, as my Don, Lorenzo, is already looking for an excuse to end me.

No, I need to step careful when I have him back in my control. I will make an example out of him, and if one hair on my sister's head is harmed, I will keep him alive to make every day a tortuous, sad existence.

"It seems he has ties with Ravlek. He's the boy's maternal uncle." Enzo, my right-hand man, taps away on his tablet. The information was gathered by another one of our Mafia allies. Oscar O'Connell is a known genius, there's nothing that man cannot do with technology. I ignore the fact that the favor we put in to gather the intel will be used when we least expect it because my sister is worth everything to me, even selling my soul to another family.

"I want them dead. I want my fucking wife and baby back, and I want them dead," Shaw bleats from opposite me. The man is becoming more unhinged by the second. His leg bounces, and not for the first time, I wonder if the guy needs some sort of therapy for his lack of control over his own body. I roll my eyes and stare out the window of the chopper. Still, with how he has stepped up for Emi and the baby, his loyalty is confirmation I made the right decision in allowing them to marry.

"ETA?" I question without turning to face Enzo.

"Ten minutes."

I give a subtle nod and drag my finger over my lower lip just as my phone pings against my chest pocket.

Pulling my phone from my jacket, I glance down at the screen and find my body locking up tight and my teeth grinding at the name on the screen.

"Luca?" Enzo questions.

I raise my eyebrow in his direction, and he moves to sit beside me as I open the message.

My body tenses at the sight before me, a photo of my sister so soul-destroying I cannot control the agonizing roar that tears from my chest as I throw the phone across the seat, desperate to release the burning sensation on my hand. The image of my sister scarring so deep it's like Eleanor's brutal death all over again.

Shaw moves toward the phone, but I nod for Enzo to retrieve it in a panic. No man should see his woman like that. No man should see someone they love in that position.

I will have my vengeance.

In blood we're bound. In trust we live.

THIRTY-FOUR

EMI

My feet dig into the marbled floor, but Aldo braces a hand around my waist and purposefully moves me closer into the room where Ravlek stares at me with menacing contempt.

His eyes latch onto bump, and the overpowering wave of revulsion coupled with protectiveness encompasses me. My hand finds bump as I cling to the only thing that truly matters right now.

Aldo chuckles as he drags a hand over his head. "Can we get this out of the way?"

The door closes behind us, and the sound of the latch engaging feels ominous. Terror creeps up my spine, but I refuse to show any sign of vulnerability, apart from the one currently cradling my unborn child.

"Welcome, Emilia." His words are thick with a patronizing tone. I stare back at him, glued to the spot, both unwilling to greet him and scared to. I need to figure out what exactly he wants from me before I commit to how I play this. Because there's no doubt in my mind Ravlek wants something from me. "Cat got your tongue, yes?" He grins with delight, clearly enjoying my vulnerability.

I give him what he wants. "Ravlek, a pleasure as always." I smile in his direction, polite as always, as to not rile the beast standing before me.

Aldo's hand tightens on mine, giving away his nervousness, and suddenly, I don't feel as confident in his presence.

"My nephew took what was mine, yes?" His seedy eyes roam over my body, making me cling tighter to Aldo as I digest his words, and when his gaze settles on bump, I realize he's also under the impression the baby is Aldo's. Aldo gives my hand an encouraging squeeze.

My throat goes dry, and I struggle to swallow as I try and think of a comeback. *Does he also think Aldo took my virginity?* I cringe at the notion.

"They're mine." Aldo stands taller and pushes out his chest. Right now, my heart aches for the man prepared to step up to his notoriously brutal uncle to help me.

Ravlek's hand travels behind my neck and tangles in my hair, causing me to wince as he tugs my head back sharply for him to stare down into my eyes. Cruelty oozes from his. "You were meant to be mine." He draws his free hand between my legs and squeezes me. "This cunt was meant to be mine."

I close my eyes as tears threaten to spill over, but I refuse to allow them. Aldo's body covers my back. "I won't allow you to hurt her, Ravlek." My eyes flare open on his voice.

Ravlek chuckles, glaring back at him sadistically. "Allow?"

He trembles behind me, and I know he feels just as out of his element as I do.

Aldo clears his throat. "You said you wouldn't hurt her and my baby." I ignore the pang in my chest at him referring to the baby as his.

"I told you she was a whore!" My eyes flick toward the voice, only now realizing we're not alone in the room. I startle when Lizzie steps forward from the corner of the room. She eyes me like I'm prey, a cruel, taunting smile plays on her lips, and I realize I've been played.

We've been played, because as my eyes trail down her body, I realize there's no sign of the baby bump that was there yesterday. Anguish flows through me at the repercussions at what I've done. I turn my panicked face to Aldo, who looks down at me with a hint of guilt in his longing eyes.

"She wanted to be with Shaw. I approached her and she was more than willing to help." The words slide from his lips with a small smile, as though proud that he managed to orchestrate it all.

"Get on your knees." Ravlek clicks his fingers, and I react with a jump.

"Ravlek," Aldo warns.

Ravlek presses his fingers tighter on my neck, the pain causing me to flinch and whimper. "Now."

He pushes me to the floor, and I kneel but refuse to cower. I jut out my chin and clench my teeth at his satisfied smile. Biting back the need to insult him, tears pool in my eyes as his thick hands unbuckle his belt. My eyes dart to Aldo's but he stares ahead at the wall, as though blocking out what's about to happen to me. My lip trembles. "Aldo?" But he ignores me.

My body shudders, and when Ravlek's thick fingers dig into my chin, I finally allow the first tear to fall. "Open, Princess."

His thick cock leaks from the tip, and sickness churns in my stomach, threatening to expel the meager contents on the floor. I tremble against his hand, making him chuckle with glee.

Feeling bump kick against me gives me the reminder to do what I need to do in order to survive, to protect us both.

My instincts kick in and I open my mouth to accept him while I close my eyes and tune out the disgusting grunting noise surrounding me. All but the click of the cell phone, no doubt evidence of my betrayal, becomes background noise as my mind shuts down and my mouth accepts his disgusting thick cock.

THIRTY-FIVE

SHAW

"How much fucking longer?" I snap.

Owen glares at me in warning, and I glare straight back, uncaring.

Luca and his men are ignoring me, acting like I'm an annoying tic. But I refuse to shut up and be locked out of this mission. It's my wife and baby they're discussing.

Maxim throws a bulletproof vest in my direction, and I'm thankful to have something to do other than sitting in a chopper wondering what the hell was on Luca's cell phone that made him shake violently and his face pale.

Owen gave me a warning look, and this time, I chose to adhere to it. Not wanting to make what is clearly a tense situation worse.

"ETA: two minutes," Enzo declares as the men gather their weapons. Luca tucks two small knives into his socks and nods toward the open case of blades, offering for me to do the same.

I've no clue how to handle them, but I'm not missing out on taking them.

"North and south points of the compound are covered," Maxim confirms as the chopper lowers.

"East covered," Enzo confirms into his earpiece, earning him a nod of approval from Luca.

"We're west, in case you were wondering." Luca stares at me, and I'm unsure of whether he's joking or if he really sees me as being that dumb.

"Funny," I quip back, earning a tug of his lips, not quite a smile, and I know his comment was meant as a joke.

"Stay behind me. We're going straight to his office as soon as team one has cleared the area." I nod, thankful he's allowing me the privilege of rescuing Emi and bump.

The chopper lowers, and my heart rate picks up with the adrenaline pumping through my veins at the prospect of getting my girl to safety.

"Now!" Maxim's voice booms through the whirring of the rotor blades as we jump from the chopper doors one by one.

Keeping our bodies lowered, we rush toward the gates as Owen and his team use rocket launchers to blast through the solid concrete walls, allowing us a quick entrance into the compound.

It's like something out of a movie as shrapnel and smoke fill the air. "Keep moving forward," Luca throws over his shoulder. I ignore the gunfire both in front and behind me, praying that Luca's team is clearing the area as we run into it.

Shouts and screams are blurred as my only focus is getting to Emi, and quickly, because there is no doubt that

Ravlek is fully aware we've breached his perimeter walls and entered his carefully structured compound.

Luca reassured me he knows exactly where Emi will be held. How, I'm not sure, but all I can do is have faith in him and his experience and hope that his knowledge prevails.

We move toward either side of the property doors, and Luca gives a thumbs-up as a whiz sounds through the air before blasting the doors to smithereens. My eyes widen in shock before I mentally shake myself and follow Luca through the haze and into the foyer of the building. Men race down the spiral staircase, and me and Luca take aim at them, taking them all down with controlled ease.

A mountain of a man steps out in front of Luca, his yellow teeth gleaming in delight as he tenses his fists. Luca wastes no time in rushing toward him with a loud growl that takes them both to the ground. But before I have a chance to intervene, I'm knocked sideways and stumble into the wall. My gun skitters across the marble floor, and the man grabs me from behind and pulls my head back, the glimmer of his blade in his clenched fist reflecting on the window, making blood surge through my body and my muscles strain tight. I relax my body and use all my strength to bend at my knees and throw him over my shoulders, causing him to slam to the floor with a thud, a move I'd perfected in boarding school, thanks to Owen who insisted on keeping us all sparring with one another over the years, and I couldn't be more thankful than I am right now.

I catch my breath as the sly fucker makes a grab at my feet, but I anticipate the move and step back, remembering the blades hidden in my sock. I step forward and place my foot on the side of his face while retrieving one. I tug a blade from my sock, and during his thrashing around to gain the upper hand, I slam it into the side of his throat so hard my hand becomes flush with his sticky flesh. I pull it back out and ignore the garbled noise and push back the notion of potentially killing a man for the first time and keep my mind on my target.

Moving quickly, I locate my handgun and turn around to take in Luca now on his feet but in a chokehold. Clearly, the other guy has the upper hand as Luca's eyes bulge under the same realization. I fire off two shots; one hits the guy in the shoulder and the other directly into his forehead. He drops to the floor with a thump, allowing Luca time to catch his breath and relocate his weapon.

He gives me a sharp nod before tipping his head toward a corridor. With blood pumping furiously through my veins, I follow him down the corridor, able to take cover behind two pillars when a shoot-out breaks out between us and two other men.

"Step out." Luca side-eyes me, and I stare back at him as though he's crazy.

"No. You step out." I fire off another shot, knowing my ammunition is running low.

"Step the fuck out. I'll cover you." He wants to use me as bait? No chance.

I tilt my head toward the corridor. "You do it."

His eyes seethe with venom, and he points toward the corridor. "Stronzo, step the fuck out there for my sister."

Of course he had to pull the sister card, didn't he? I sigh, knowing yet again I'll have to prove myself to him. *Will I ever stop having to prove myself? Will he ever accept me?*

"Fine." I exhale, then step out with my hands in the air,

giving both men a chance to step away from the pillars and into the firing line. Luca pops off two rounds, and the men fall to the floor.

My body relaxes as blood pools around them.

"ETA: one minute," Luca speaks into his earpiece, and my stomach somersaults at the thought of what's to come.

A step closer to Emi.

Hang on, Red, I'm coming for you.

THIRTY-SIX

EMI

Fear like no other creeps up my spine as I choke around Ravlek's cock. The tight grip on my throat is so punishing the pain is immense, and it takes all my control to remember to breathe. I whimper in discomfort, but even that sound is lodged in my throat.

"Ravlek, you're hurting her. You've had your fun. You got your evidence, now leave her alone," Aldo begs from beside me, but Ravlek pushes harder into my mouth, making my knees shake. He holds me in place with his meaty palm at the back of my head. I peek through tear-soaked lashes to find Ravlek biting his lower lip. His eyes ooze with a combination of possession and hate, and a sob leaves my mouth along with saliva at the prospect of this going much further than a blowjob.

From the corner of my eye, I see Aldo move forward, only for two of Ravlek's men to hold him back. He fights against them, causing Ravlek's body to lock tight. His fingers disentangle from my hair, causing me to flinch as his cock slips from my mouth, giving me much-needed relief as I suck in sharp, desperate breaths. But it's short-lived when he pulls a gun from behind his back; my heart seizes with terror, only for him to aim past me and release a bullet into Aldo's forehead.

I drop my head on a wail, sobs catching in my throat at the severity of this stupid plan turning so wrong, so deadly. Sickness rolls in my stomach and panic grips my throat.

"Princess, you have a job to finish." I raise my head at his cold, detached voice to see him jacking his cock, unfazed by the fact he just stuck a bullet in his nephew's head.

I try to gather my thoughts as tears fall down my face and my body shakes involuntarily. "Please."

He grins down at me and trails the knuckles of his fingers down my cheek, almost lovingly, but his eyes hold a cruel detachment that allows me the insight that he will show no mercy; he's enjoying my fear.

A loud boom rocks the property and penetrates the room, causing pictures to fall from the wall.

"Take her to the cellar," he instructs one of his men who tugs me to my feet. "Get them to get the baby out at whatever cost." His words send fear so violently through me my legs give way, forcing the man to lift me into his arms.

I beg for Luca to rescue me. I beg for his help. When I've spent my entire life begging for freedom, I wish for nothing more than the comfort of his protection.

Him and Shaw.

SHAW

We stand beside Ravlek's office door. Luca counts down on his fingers. When he reaches zero, a team of men will shatter the windows to his office and gain entry, allowing us to enter and retrieve Emi.

I watch with bated breath as his fingers move: five, four, three—my heart beats faster—two, one. On cue, the glass shatters and Luca kicks open the door. We move low, and I fire at the first man that steps in front of me.

A rope transcends through the window and into the room as planned. I scan the large office space that doubles as a library, only for my eyes to widen in shock at Lizzie standing with a gun aimed in my direction. I feel a sharp stab of hurt in my chest as her eyes seethe with abhorrent distaste. I swallow at her deception, emotion lodging in my throat.

Did she really despise Emi so deeply that she put her and the baby in danger? My gaze tracks down her body, and the clear absence of a baby bump makes me jolt with awareness at just how deep her betrayal runs.

The usual unhinged glimmer flickers in her eyes. "Drop the weapon, Shaw." My eyes don't leave hers as I release the gun, sending it to the floor.

My mind doesn't register what's happening quick enough, but she falters and drops her weapon, followed by a pool of blood seeping from a knife wound in her shoulder as she lets out a garbled shriek.

I dart my eyes around the room, taking in the man standing at the window, his piercing blue eyes drilling into my own. His lips tip up in a smirk, and he spits out a toothpick onto the floor. "Luca went down there." He tilts his head toward a doorway, and I don't hesitate in moving forward with my unknown accomplice on my heels as we descend the stone stairway.

A gut-wrenching scream stills my movement and sends a wave of nausea through my body. My accomplice retrieves a variety of knives from inside his jacket as I turn to face him. A maniacal expression coats his face in delight at what's to come, whereas the thought sickens me.

He licks his lips. "I'll go first, slice some fuckers up. You get your woman."

I scan his body, hoping for a sign that he knows what he's doing. I have none.

Another scream puts my feet in motion, pushing past the grumblings of the satanic knife guy and into the dark, cold cellar.

My mind takes a moment to comprehend what I see, and the image almost brings me to my knees. My girl is bleeding from between her legs on a makeshift hospital bed, where a man stands at the bottom, tying her feet to the metal bars.

Luca is tied to a chair, thrashing about, trying to loosen

the restraints. When he notices me, Ravlek's head darts up from beside Luca, followed by a sharp sting in my shoulder as I launch myself in his direction and ignore the repeated sounds of his gun firing at me.

I throw myself at Ravlek, catching him off guard with my determination to reach him. We fall to the floor, where I pummel his face time and time again, and I revel in the crunching of his bones. Each punch sends a searing agony up my arm and through my shoulder, but I ignore it and fight on until his body falls lax below me.

"Shaw," Emi sobs, and her broken voice makes me stumble to my feet, ignoring the maniac slicing up the man who was tying my girl down. "Shaw, the baby." My lips find hers as I untie her bound hands from the rail. "Please, the baby." Her body tenses below me. "Can you see anything?" Her eyes implore mine, and I steel myself, moving between her bloodied thighs, and I lift the hem of her dress.

Shit. "There's a head, Emi." My eyes bug out at the sight.

"I'm scared." Her whimper breaks my heart because I'm scared too.

I take her hand in mine. "Me too, Red. But we got this." I stare into her eyes, knowing I have no choice; I have to do this. I should have done it a long time ago, and I'll not allow another minute to go by without her knowing how I feel.

"I love you, Red. You and bump, you're mine. Blood or no blood. You're mine. You both are." Her eyes shimmer with the endearment, and they seep the love I feel for her and our baby. And then her fingers graze over my hand, sending tingles over my body.

"They gave me an injection. I can't feel the baby at all." Her lip quivers on her words.

"Fuck, it was probably one of those epidural things. They numb your body so you can't feel shit. She probably doesn't even know when to push," the knife guy asserts as he frees Luca.

"I'm scared, Shaw."

"Shh, it's okay, Red," I soothe, trying to ease her anxiety and sound confident when I sure as hell don't feel it.

"Get me a medical team in here, now!" Luca screams into his earpiece.

THIRTY-SEVEN

SHAW

The last thirty minutes have been the hardest of my entire life. I watched as an influx of men flooded the cellar and took Ravlek captive, followed by a medical team working tirelessly to regulate Emi's body while figuring out what exactly the bastards have given her.

Luca stands stoically still beside the head of Emi's bed, watching over her like a pit bull, his unwavering stare of promised death now becoming second nature to me, and I'm finding I can easily ignore him.

Emi whimpers as the doctor works between her legs, causing Luca to growl in boiling rage.

"It's okay, Red." I stroke her hand. "It won't be long, and we'll have your baby in your arms."

"Ours." I stare at her blankly. "The baby is ours, Shaw." She squeezes her eyes closed before opening them with renewed vigor. "I lied. I wanted you to be happy, to keep you safe. I pushed you away, and I lied." Tears streak down her face. "I'm so sorry." She pauses and my heart stutters with desperation to hear her words. "Please forgive me. I thought I was setting you free." My pulse races with elation. "I love you, Shaw."

My head falls into the crook of her neck. "Jesus, Red," I say as tears spill from my eyes. *I'm going to be a daddy after all.* Yet, deep down inside, I could feel it all along. I didn't care if the baby had my blood or not, the connection was always there. The love for them was always at the forefront of my mind. If only I could have shown it beforehand, none of this would have happened.

"There's nothing to forgive, Red." I raise my head, and her lips tremble as I gently take her lips in mine.

A throat clears. "Do you fucking mind? Can you push the fucking baby out, Emi. I have people to kill, or did you forget about that?"

I roll my eyes at his groaning, causing Emi to stifle a low giggle.

"Okay, Emilia. One more big push and the little one will be out."

Emi gives the doctor a nod, and I pull my shoulders back and allow her to squeeze the blood from my hand as she pushes, forcing out a scream so loud I think she burst my eardrums. "Ahhhh."

A squawking wail fills the air, making my heart soar with pride. The doctor moves quickly, wrapping the little one in a blanket that seems to have appeared from nowhere.

The doctor hands me the baby, and I stare down into eyes the exact shade as my own, a bright blue.

"Is it a boy?" Luca snaps, not giving the baby a second glance.

The doctor's shoulders slump. "A girl."

I smile down at my little bundle, a little girl.

"Fan-fucking-tastic," he grumbles. "Congratulations," he throws out like it's nothing. Like I'm not holding the most precious gift in the entire world. "I'm off to torture people."

My head snaps in his direction. "Luca?"

He turns his black orbs on me. "Keep them alive." He stares back at me before nodding in understanding.

When my wife and baby are settled back in our home, I intend on dealing with them both.

I place our little girl in Emi's arms and marvel in the love seeping through her. We did this, we created the perfect little family, and I couldn't be happier.

Scrap that, I want more.

"What are you thinking?"

My gaze meets with Emi's. "More. I want more." I nod at the baby who doesn't have a name yet.

"More?" Her eyes widen, making her look so damn cute I grin.

"Yeah, more." I pepper kisses over her face. "What shall we call her?"

Emi swallows, and I know what's coming before she utters the words. "Can we call her Eleanor?"

I smile at how well I know my girl. "Of course."

We sit marveling at our baby girl in a comfortable silence as the doctors tend to Emi.

"When you said more. How many more?"

Our eyes meet. "A lot more."

Something tells me there will never be enough little Emi's.

THIRTY-EIGHT

SHAW

I lift my chin at the guard on the door, and he opens it, allowing access to what I can only describe as a torture chamber.

"Oh, thank god, Shaw. Shaw, help me!" Her shrieks fill my ears and filter into my bloodstream, but I don't feel an ounce of guilt as I take in a tear-streaked, piss-soaked Lizzie. I've spent too much of my time and life trying to forgive her behavior, trying to interpret it differently to what it actually was. She's a bitch. An evil, conniving, manipulative bitch, and I hate her for it and the trauma she's put us through.

"He cut me. He cut me with a knife. He's mad!" I glance over my shoulder at the guy that surged through the window like a dark avenger. He flips a knife in his hand before turning it over and holding it out, handle toward me.

All I know of him is his name is Finn, he's from another

Mafia family, and he has a tendency to play with knives, earning him the moniker of his expertise Finn-finishing.

I take the knife from him and lift Lizzie's chin.

I'm not the same person I was before all of this, and she sure as hell was never the person I thought she was.

When Luca filled me in on what the image on his cell phone was that sent him in a tailspin, I can understand why he never told me. It would have broken me when he needed me to be as focused as possible. It also occurred to me that a small part of him was protecting me from the pain, and I thank him for that.

He gives me a subtle nod from across the room, and I ignore the look I've come to realize Lizzie uses to tug at my heartstrings, the one she knows will get what she wants with ease.

As my face changes to register the acknowledgment of her expression, transforming my own into a cunning smirk, panic flickers across her face.

"You manipulated. You lied. Then you tried to trap me while setting my wife up with a man you knew would harm her. You stood by and watched him assault her." My stomach churns at the thought. "Then you allowed him to violate her, you allowed them to force my baby's labor at the risk of harming them both!" I scream into the room but don't miss the departure of Finn., no doubt feeling assured of my actions.

"Please have mercy," she wails.

"The only mercy you'll have is a quick death, Lizzie." I surge the knife into the side of her neck, and her gargles fill the air before I turn my attention to Ravlek.

He's strapped to a chair with his face so disfigured I'm not even sure it's him. His flesh hangs from his naked body. His limbs are disjointed and burn marks mar his flesh. I glance up at Luca, repulsed by the sight before me. He smiles at me with what seems like delight, making me grimace so hard my balls shrivel up to hide from his wrath.

Ravlek snivels before me, and the sound grates on my nerves. *Did he take pity on my wife when he violated her?*

I ball my hand into a fist and smash it against his face, the force of the blow making his head drop back.

"I wanted him conscious when I had him!" I spit back at Luca, who picks at the blood under his fingernails.

He shrugs. "You should have said."

I grind my teeth, but the anger subsides slightly when Ravlek's head rolls forward, allowing me to deliver another blow.

"Would you like to drag it out for a long period of time? We can fix him up so that you can toy with him."

I glance down at the piece of shit. His battered body is useless; every breath of air he breathes becomes contaminated. I don't want him part of the same world as my family for another second.

I shake my head and opt for the knife. It seems only fitting he dies with the same blade dripping with the blood of the traitorous bitch. I tug his head back and slice into his jugular, painting myself in his blood. Copper fills my nostrils, and I can't find it in myself to care. I drop the knife to the floor; the clang fills the room as his spluttering comes to an end. A life that once existed is now extinguished. All his evil gone from the world.

Luca steps forward, slapping me on my back with a broad smile. "You did good, brother."

"In blood we're bound. In trust we live." I say the

familiar words low but loud enough for Luca to hear while I slice into the palm of my hand so it's clear where I stand in the family.

Inside with them.

"In blood we're bound. In trust we live," he repeats, squeezing my shoulder with a comforting acceptance.

A hint of pride winds through my body at his words, and I exhale, feeling a weight lifted from my body.

"We're moving into our own property, Luca." His hand tenses on my shoulder in response, and he takes a step back to analyze me. "Your security will be appreciated, but we need to create our own home."

He tilts his head and eyes me up and down before he appears to relent and gives me a firm nod of consent. "Very well."

I turn toward the door, feeling a rush of triumph.

"Oh, and Shaw?" I turn to face him, only for him to raise his gun and fire off a bullet, the familiar searing pain of heat explodes through the muscles of my shoulder, hitting the bone. "Fuck!"

"That's for taking my sister in my office, *stronzo*," he spits, making me choke in disbelief.

He really is fucking deranged.

THIRTY-NINE

SHAW

I step into the bedroom and take in my girls.

When we brought them back from the compound, Luca had yet another medical team waiting on hand to check them over.

I helped Emi into the bath and proceeded to climb in myself, fully clothed, while I cradled her to my chest. Her sobs made guilt rack in my body at the thought of Lizzie working with Ravlek to bring us down.

Emi spoke about how they were under the assumption the baby was Aldo's and that was probably the only reason why she was still alive. I held her tighter at that knowledge, the fear of losing them unbearable. I kissed the top of her head and gently washed away the grime. When I reached the marks around her neck, I swear I felt my veins explode with rage. Her solemn eyes met mine, and I did the only thing I could—I rested my forehead against hers. "I love you so much. You're everything I never knew I needed. I'll protect you forever, Red."

A lone tear slipped from her eye, and I kissed it away from her cheek, refusing to allow any more tears to fall. "You and Eleanor are my everything. You own me, Emi." I took her hands and placed them over my beating heart. "In blood we're bound. In trust we live."

Her eyes shimmered with pride at my acceptance of her life, our life. "Thank you."

She moans in the bed, breaking me from my thoughts, and I rush toward her, tugging off my t-shirt and joggers that I changed into after showering at Luca's house.

Climbing into the bed, I tug her toward me and sink against the mattress when her warm body curls into mine and her fingers find my hair as she lazily toys with it.

"Is he gone?"

My heart beats rapidly below her. *Will she think any less of me for doing what I've done?*

"Yes, baby. They're gone. They both are."

Her body stills as she processes my words before she places a tender kiss on my chest.

"Thank you."

I nod against her.

"I love you, Shaw." I smile into her hair, embracing her scent just as Eleanor stirs in the crib beside us, making us turn to face her.

She suckles her tiny fist into her mouth, and I chuckle watching her. Emi winces as she sits up in bed, and I move to hand her Eleanor, delighting in the soft cooing noise she makes. I place a gentle kiss on her head and hand her over to her mama.

"I love you both." I smile at Emi, already plotting when we can add to the family.

EPILOGUE

SHAW

Watching my wife breastfeed has got to be the most rewarding display of affection I've ever seen. So much so, my cock pays attention every damn time her tit comes out.

Sure, it could have something to do with the fact that on the doctor's orders I've had zero action whatsoever for the past six weeks, but watching her feed Eleanor is like an aphrodisiac for wanting more little ones.

"Can you take her into the nursery?" Emi lifts her head as she tucks her breast back into her top.

I clear my throat and push off the doorframe, adjusting my cock to a more comfortable position as I walk to my wife and daughter. Emi hands me Eleanor, and I smile down at my perfect little girl sleeping so contently.

After placing her in her crib in the adjoining nursery, I waste no time in dropping my clothes to the floor.

"Fuck. I've been counting down the days for this."

My eyes travel up my wife, from her pink-painted toes all the way up her silky-smooth legs to her silk sleep shorts, over her soft curves, and up toward those luscious tits. Mine. Every inch of her. She smiles at me. "I was actually planning on sleeping." She feigns a yawn and stretches her arms above her head.

I grab onto her ankles and tug her down the bed toward me. "Yeah, well, I'm tired of waiting for your pussy." She giggles, the sound hitting me in the balls.

I tug on my cock to ease the ache. "Fuck, this is going to be quick, then I'll take my time." I lick my lips as my gaze travels over the most beautiful woman I have ever set eyes on.

She holds my heart so tightly it threatens to explode.

My cock leaks sticky pre-cum as I pump it up and down while Emi discards her clothes. Her heavy tits bounce, and she nibbles on her lip when my cock jumps at the sight.

"They'll probably leak, Shaw." Her words come out low with a hint of vulnerability to them, and I hate it.

I crawl over her bare body, using my arms to cage her in. "Then I guess you best let me have a taste, huh?"

Her eyebrows shoot up in surprise, but I don't miss the flush of her cheeks, the way she swallows deeply and squirms below me, no doubt trying to rub away the ache between her legs. "Lift one up and feed me your nipple, Red." Her breath hitches, and I delight in it.

She complies, lifting her heavy breast and darkened nipple to my waiting lips, and my mouth waters at finally getting to taste my girl. I've waited. Boy, have I fucking waited to have her completely. I wasn't lying when I said

I've been counting down the days. Truth be told, I had a countdown on my phone, guaranteeing the exact hour I could have my girl raw again.

Her soft breast fills my face, and my eyes roll to the back of my head with the taste of her warm milk leaking onto my tongue. She holds her tit and gasps as more milk leaks into my mouth, making me groan with need as I suck harder. I use a hand to guide my dripping cock into her waiting pussy and tentatively push inside her warm heat while her legs wrap around me.

Her pussy molds around my cock, and the reminder I'm the only man that has ever been here sends a surge of arousal flowing through my veins. She arches her back into me with each controlled inch I push inside.

I withdraw and slam back inside. Again and again.

I groan against her, relishing the taste of her milk on my tongue and the whimpers of pleasure escaping her lips. Our moans and pants become music to my ears. *Fuck, I've missed this.*

With my solid cock already threatening to burst, I withdraw my lips and already miss her taste.

"Fuck, Red. I'm going to come soon." My hips move quicker. "I'm sorry." I withdraw and thrust back inside her. "Fuck, I'm sorry." I chant as my lips find her nipple again, her milk filling my mouth sends me over the edge as I grind my hips against her, the friction rubbing her clit and sending her pussy into spasm as my balls draw up, and I work my hips at a furious rate.

"Oh. Oh god, Shaw. Yes. Yes. Yessss," she screams as her thrusts meet mine.

My cock explodes, pumping my hot cum into her bare

pussy. "Fuck, that's it." I gargle around her tit. "Take it all."

My cock is finally spent as my hips come to a standstill, and I drop to my arms, hovering over her once again.

I scoop my hands under her head and roll us so she's on top of me, my cock not leaving her warmth once.

Emi pushes up to stare down at me. Her flushed cheeks and sweaty hairline make her look like a goddess riding me. I smirk at my analogy.

"I want you to fill me with your cum, Shaw." My eyes fill with lust watching her ride me, grinding her hips on me.

My cock stiffens to full mast again, desperate to fill her needy hole. "Fuck, baby, yes."

I trail my hand up her body and to her throat, gently holding her there, and her pupils blacken.

When she first told me how Ravlek hurt her, I never thought she'd allow me to hold her like this again, but she was determined to not let him own that part of her.

"In blood we're bound. In trust we live, Red."

Her lips part, allowing me to graze my thumb over her slick bottom lip, and when her tongue darts out to suck me in, I lose control, surging up into her hard.

Her words fill my ears and seek comfort in my veins, reminding me of how far we've come.

"In blood we're bound. In trust we live, Blue."

THE END

Do you want to read more of Shaw and Emi. Along with a sneak peek into Luca and Tate's stories?

Sign up to my newsletter here for a bonus epilogue.

TATE Book 2 in STORM ENTERPRISES is available for preorder here.

Luca's story will be told in Veiled In Hate and is available to preorder here.

ALSO BY BJ ALPHA

Secrets and Lies Series

CAL Book 1

CON Book 2

FINN Book 3

BREN Book 4

OSCAR Book 5

CON'S WEDDING NOVELLA

The Brutal Duet

Hidden In Brutal Devotion

Love In Brutal Devotion

The Born Series

Born Reckless

ABOUT BJ ALPHA

BJ Alpha lives in the UK with her hubby, two teenage sons and three fur babies.

She loves to write and read about hot, alpha males and feisty females.

Follow me on my social media pages:

Facebook: BJ Alpha

My readers group: BJ's Reckless Readers

Instagram: BJ Alpha

ACKNOWLEDGMENTS

**Tee the lady that started it all for me.
Thank you, thank you, thank you!**

I must start with where it all began, TL Swan. When I started reading your books, I never realized I was in a place I needed pulling out of. Your stories brought me back to myself.

With your constant support and the network created as 'Cygnet Inkers' I was able to create something I never realized was possible, I genuinely thought I'd had my day. You made me realize tomorrow is just the beginning.

To Kate, our brains are entwined making you the perfect soul sister.

Emma H, thank you for all your continual support.
Tash, thank you my lovely for cheering me on.

Swan Squad
A special thank you to our girls;
Bren, Sharon H, Patricia, Caroline, Claire, Anita, Sue and Mary-Anne who constantly support me.

Beta Readers

Thank you to my Beta Readers for all your help. Your advice and support is much appreciated as always.
Libby, Jaclyn, Kate, Savannah and Tash.

ARC Team
To my ARC readers thank you.
I have such an incredible team, I couldn't do it without you.
All your message, shares, graphics and reviews are amazing, thank you.

To my world.
My boys, you make me want to be the best version of me.
And remember you can be anything as long as you're happy.

To my hubby, the J in my BJ.
Love you trillions.

Printed in Great Britain
by Amazon